"For goodness' sake. Just this one time, all right?"

Amagi was exasperated, but she was secretly happy in her new dress too.

FUKA

"I'm Riho Satsuki—the *true* successor of the Way of the Flash."

RIHO

She enjoyed more than just piloting her custom-made mobile knight. She was enjoying killing people.

BFC-X201CS

ERICIUS Λ

CONTENTS

I'M THE EVIL LORD OF AN INTERGALACTIC EMPIRE

NOVEL

6

WRITTEN BY

YOMU MISHIMA

ILLUSTRATED BY

NADARE TAKAMINE

Airship

Seven Seas Entertainment

ORE WA SEIKAN KOKKA NO AKUTOKU RYOUSHU! Vol. 6
©2022 Yomu Mishima
First published in Japan in 2022 by OVERLAP Inc., Ltd., Tokyo.
English translation rights arranged with OVERLAP Inc., Ltd., Tokyo.

Seven Seas press and purchase enquiries can be sent to
Marketing Manager Lianne Sentar at press@gomanga.com.
Information regarding the distribution and purchase of
digital editions is available from Digital Manager CK Russell
at digital@gomanga.com.

Follow Seven Seas Entertainment online at
sevenseasentertainment.com.

TRANSLATION: Amy Osteraas
ADAPTATION: Jeffrey Thomas
COVER DESIGN: H. Qi
INTERIOR LAYOUT & DESIGN: Clay Gardner
COPY EDITOR: Dayna Abel
PROOFREADER: Catherine Langford
LIGHT NOVEL EDITOR: T. Burke
PREPRESS TECHNICIAN: Melanie Ujimori, Jules Valera
MANAGING EDITOR: Alyssa Scavetta
EDITOR-IN-CHIEF: Julie Davis
ASSOCIATE PUBLISHER: Adam Arnold
PUBLISHER: Jason DeAngelis

ISBN: 979-8-88843-124-5
Printed in Canada
First Printing: January 2024
10 9 8 7 6 5 4 3 2 1

Prologue

IN THE ALGRAND EMPIRE, there existed a planet without time zones.

The Capital Planet of this intergalactic empire was entirely encased in a metal shell that blocked the sun's light. That would make it uninhabitable for humans, of course, so the inside of the metal shell emitted light to make up for it. The planet also had a climate that was managed to be comfortable for the planet's residents. The weather was completely under human control, which meant forecasts were accurate for as far as a year in the future. Furthermore, the entire planet operated under a unified time system, which meant no matter where on the globe you were, morning always arrived at the same time. The controlled weather varied throughout the planet, but the time was the same no matter where you were. The only reason I found this situation unnatural was because I, Liam Sera Banfield, had reincarnated here from another world.

The illustrious luxury hotel where I resided on the Capital Planet was a high-rise building with a number of surprisingly spacious balconies available for use as you made your way to the top floor. Since population density on the Capital Planet was high, real estate was very pricey. Buildings stood close to one another, so it was a mark of extravagant wealth to have any sort of yard or garden on the ground. Even this long-established hotel couldn't afford much ground space, so it used the space around its upper floors to provide its guests with some greenery instead.

I reserved one of those sky-high gardens a little before dawn so I could train in the Way of the Flash sword style with my new apprentice, Ellen Tyler. While I practiced my moves, she stood beside me swinging a wooden sword in much the same way. I was performing basic training, demonstrating my form for her and explaining things as I went along.

"The Way of the Flash has only one technique. Everything else is just standard movements."

"Yes, Master!"

Sweat dripped from Ellen as she vigorously swung her wooden sword. She had the appearance of a six- or seven-year-old girl, but her actual age might have been closer to fifteen or sixteen. In this world where people lived long lives, there was hardly an appreciable difference in a single year's worth of aging. Adulthood began at fifty, and people only tended to start paying attention to age once they hit that point.

As she practiced, Ellen's face scrunched into an earnest frown. This small girl with short red hair possessed a good amount of energy. I chose her as my student when I returned to my own domain, but I knew I wouldn't be back there for some time, so I brought her with me when I left. She was still just a kid, a girl who should have been having fun without a care in the world, but now she was living with me away from her mother.

My vertical practice swings gave way to horizontal ones, and Ellen hurried to copy me. Her movements were still clumsy despite her efforts.

"Pay attention to the way your whole body moves. If you focus too much on one area, you'll neglect the rest."

"Y-yes, Master."

Maybe I favored her just because she was my first student, but she sure was cute when she called me "Master" so respectfully.

"C'mon, keep going."

"Yes, sir!"

If she had proved to have no talent, I'd have regretted my decision, but she was absorbing all the things I taught her at a steady rate. I felt pretty good about it. If there was a problem with our arrangement, it was just on my end. Master Yasushi had told me to train three students of my own at the very least, that being a rule of the Way of the Flash so the style wouldn't die out. I understood the logic behind my master's order, so I intended to carry it out, but the problem was my own abilities.

Could I truly call myself a master of the Way of the Flash? Lately, that question wouldn't leave my head, and it was all because of the technique Master Yasushi showed me when I was a child. Just like Ellen, I was entranced by the Flash—a strike that was impossibly fast—when I first saw it. Of course, it was less that I actually saw it and more like I only saw the *result* of it. The strike Master Yasushi showed me that day was so incredibly swift that I didn't even notice him draw his blade from its sheath. To me, it was as if the logs he aimed at simply snapped in half on their own while he just stood there. *That* was Master Yasushi's Flash.

Ellen, on the other hand, had seen the moment I drew my blade when I showed her my amateurish version of the Flash move. Masters of the Way of the Flash demonstrated the Flash to their students as their first lesson.

Of course, it wasn't actually something anyone should be able to see, so it was more like explaining the concept of the technique, but Ellen had completely seen through my Flash nonetheless.

Ellen had special vision—not enhanced through use of an education capsule, but apparently an inborn ability. Occasionally, people were born with such special abilities in this world. These were not replicable with science or magic, so they couldn't be developed in an education capsule no matter how much time someone spent in one. Many of these individuals went generally unnoticed by the world. I heard a lot of them were born as commoners and went their whole lives without even knowing they'd received these gifts simply due to their lot in life. When they were blessed by circumstance as Ellen was, however, they had an opportunity to distinguish themselves. Such blessed individuals often went on to accomplish amazing things.

In House Banfield, the oft-rampaging Christiana Leta Rosebreia and Marie Sera Marian were good examples of that. Chengsi Sera Tohrei might've been another one. The same went for Kukuri, who commanded my more unsavory forces. It wasn't uncommon for such unique individuals to be gathered under a family with the rank of count in the massive intergalactic nation known as the

Algrand Empire. Yet, all this talent still wasn't enough for me. If I wanted to be an evil lord capable of real savagery, I needed even *more* talent on my payroll. One more, at least... So, right now, I just wanted one more underling I could really count on.

If all went well, Ellen would eventually become a talented knight herself. Watching Ellen continue her practice swings, I muttered, "I could just wait for her to get to that point on her own, but that wouldn't be very fun..."

While I toiled, showing Ellen how to execute her practice swings, dawn gradually broke and was announced by a simulated rising sun projected on the inside of the metal sphere that encased the planet. As I turned my face toward the man-made sun, a figure in classic maid attire arrived on the balcony with us.

My maid, Amagi, held a basket in one hand. A knight followed behind her—my personal guard, Claus Sera Mont. He was an experienced knight, and this showed in his face. In other words, he looked a little old, but that was proof of his many experiences in life. Claus was valued by House Banfield for his ability to make calm, rational decisions. He also stood out just for being a *man* in the upper ranks of my knights, which was otherwise dominated by fierce women. Claus was guarding the door to the balcony while Ellen and I practiced out here.

Amagi approached me and announced the end of our training session. "Master, it is almost time for the next item on your schedule. Please consider your morning training concluded."

I sighed and glanced at Ellen. I wished I could have devoted more time to training my student, but unfortunately, I was a busy guy.

I ceased my practice moves, and Ellen already looked a little sad. Now that I could no longer supervise her, she'd be stuck doing the training I assigned her on her own for the rest of the day. I would have liked to leave a guard with her, but I didn't want unrelated people seeing how practitioners of the Way of the Flash trained. As a result, Ellen would remain alone. I felt sorry for her, but there wasn't much I could do about it.

"That's enough training for now, Ellen. Let's have breakfast."

"Yes, sir..."

Amagi handed us towels and drinks, so we wiped off our sweat and rehydrated.

Claus watched on in silence. He never tried to suck up to me to get on my good side like Tia and Marie did, and that pissed me off sometimes, but there was something to be said for a knight who did his job properly. It would be way too much trouble if all my knights were as erratic as

Tia and Marie. Claus was cool, collected, and knew how to get the job done, which made him one of my more useful knights. Nothing about him struck me as particularly exceptional, but he *had* been recommended to me by Amagi. Plus, the fact that he had that Chengsi woman under him and was able to make use of her without issue did seem rather extraordinary. Maybe he was the sort to exhibit his strength in a group rather than on his own?

"Getting used to the job, Claus?" I asked him.

He responded in his usual expressionless way. "Sir!"

"Good. Keep it up."

"Of course."

Our conversation was over instantly, just like that. There were all sorts of things I wouldn't have minded talking to Tia and Marie about, but they always overreacted when I said anything to them, and it wore me out. Claus was laconic in comparison, but maybe that was better than the alternative.

I headed inside from the balcony with Amagi and Ellen trailing me, and Claus walking a bit behind them.

Amagi started informing me of my schedule before we sat down to breakfast. "Master, you have a meeting with the new members of your faction today."

"Yeah... I've got a bunch of new friends now that I've kicked Linus's ass."

"But some nobles are acting suspiciously as well, so please keep your guard up," she urged.

Not long ago, Linus, the second prince in line to become the next emperor, had picked a fight with me. The end result was that I'd destroyed him. I'm sure no one had expected the second prince to drop out of the running quite so soon. Now, a bunch of nobles were cozying up to the third prince, Cleo Noah Albareto, whom I supported. Of course, a lot of these nobles were just in it to come out on top in the end, but what we had to be the most careful of were enemies who only pretended to be allies to get close to us.

In other words, people like me—villains.

"Things are getting interesting," I mused aloud.

Amagi looked exasperated to see me enjoying myself when she had just advised me to be careful. Since she was a lifelike robot, that didn't show in her expression, but I could tell what she was feeling. In fact, her next words stung me a bit.

"I do not think you should be enjoying the situation."

"Nothing I can do about that," I said. "This is a political battle where villains compete to see who comes out on top. Whoever does will be the biggest villain in the Empire. A fitting position for me, don't you think?"

The biggest villain in the Empire—a worthy goal for

an evil lord like me. I was supporting the third prince, Cleo, who no one thought would ever become emperor, and I was planning to install him for my own gains. If that wasn't evil, then I didn't know what was.

I'm gonna win this and become the biggest bad guy in the Empire!

"Justice" was quite a handy word. No one would choose to be scorned for being "evil" instead of being lauded for being "just." It was useful that people fell in line whenever you started talking about justice as well. Even if they didn't know if what they were doing was truly proper, if they convinced themselves something was just, people felt like they were on the right side. I found it disgusting and hypocritical, but still, I didn't hesitate in the least to use the word myself.

"Justice is on our side!" I cried out. "Cheers!"

"Cheers!"

We were holding a welcome party in the hotel's banquet hall for the Imperial nobles who had just recently joined our faction. The scale of the event was rather large for a simple welcome party, but anything you did in an intergalactic empire was excessive.

My speech to welcome the latest group of nobles joining Prince Cleo's faction was full of platitudes. *Good grief. Fighting for justice? The duty of the nobility? I know it's coming out of my own mouth, but this is more than ridiculous.* Justice wasn't real. After all, I was the one talking about it, and I knew I was only in this for myself.

I was sure no one else here believed in it either—and why was that? Because the whole room was filled with other villains just like me. The hundreds of people in the banquet hall were pure evil on the inside; I was sure of it. I was equally sure they understood my own aims here from the start. I was supporting Prince Cleo because I put my own gains above all else. "Justice" was just a pretense, and all the nobles here had joined my faction because they were also looking out for themselves first and foremost.

With my speech concluded, I headed out onto the floor and began to chat with the attendees. As the organizer of this little event, it was my duty to entertain my guests.

"Enjoying yourself?" I asked a viscount whose territory lay on the outskirts of the Empire. Most of the domains on the outskirts were poor, so this man was the hard-working type. He had a gentle-looking appearance, but I was sure he harbored some ambition on the inside.

He replied with a smile, "Yes, very much so. You are a remarkable one, aren't you, Count Banfield? Not many nobles throw parties this grand on the Capital Planet, you know."

It was only natural that I'd put some money into this shindig. Part of it was to demonstrate that I had wealth to spare, but it was mostly just because throwing lavish parties was what evil lords were expected to do. I had to be a bit humble with my guests, but what I really wanted to do was throw my weight around.

"Well, I do like to show off, so I'm glad you think so."

The viscount nodded, looking impressed. "Showing off for Prince Cleo's sake, I presume? I hear you're offering the prince quite a bit of financial support."

"You could say that."

That support was mainly for my own amusement, but I also considered Prince Cleo to be an investment. After all, if I, as the boss of the faction, arranged grand displays like this, more and more people would be convinced to come join us. Naturally, I planned to get a good return on my investment.

The viscount smiled at me. "Prince Cleo must be greatly reassured by your support, Count Banfield. I may not be able to contribute much, but I'll do whatever I can for the sake of the faction."

"That'll really help. I appreciate you lending us your aid, Viscount."

Nobles like him claimed to want to contribute, but I knew they were only in it to benefit themselves. Most of the people attending the party were lords of their own domains, but I paid for their travel to the Capital Planet and for their lodging expenses myself. Why? Well, who would want to spend money just to come to a party like this, traveling through the vast reaches of space just to listen to that empty speech of mine? If I was the one invited, I never would have come. As the head of this little organization, however, I needed people to attend for the sake of my reputation, so I decided to cover all those expenses.

Of course, money was hardly a concern for me. Thanks to the riches produced from the alchemy box the Guide gifted me, I could afford just about anything. A lavish feast like this was just a drop in the bucket.

Plus, the more I stood out in noble society, the easier it would be for me to accomplish my goals. One goal of this party had been to put on a show that might provoke the faction belonging to the first prince in line: Prince Calvin. If Calvin made a careless move as a result of my provocation, I planned to take full advantage of it.

The situation was more challenging than I hoped, however.

I was able to basically lead Prince Linus to his own self-destruction, but Calvin was a different beast entirely. He wasn't completely unflawed as a crown prince, but he had a large base of support. Another problem was that he was so secure in his position that he likely didn't feel the need to go out of his way to crush our little group. Of course, if we were to betray a weakness of ours, I was sure he would move in to crush us immediately. Calvin Noah Albareto would truly be a troublesome foe, as you might expect considering his position of crown prince. It was actually bothersome that he hadn't made a single move on me in all this time. I was even here on the Capital Planet for long enough to finish my college education.

In fact, the viscount I was talking to brought up my graduation next. "To change the subject... You'll be working as an official soon, won't you, Count Banfield?"

After graduating, nobles were compelled into civil service jobs as part of their extensive training. The idea was that by gaining practical experience, we would deepen our political knowledge and perspectives. Of course, most nobles just fooled around without putting any real effort into their work. It was just a period of fun in the guise of training, but it would be stupid of me to admit that freely.

I put on a serious face and feigned diligence. "Yes. I'll give it my all for the sake of the Empire." The overblown tone I took was a bit of a joke, and I knew if someone was listening to us, they might've thought I was being shameless.

Instead, the viscount looked as serious as I did. "I admire your commitment. I wish my son took things as earnestly as you do."

He was just going along with my joke...right? I couldn't tell by his reaction if he was being sincere, so I didn't know what to say back to him. I mean, I didn't plan on working hard at all. Why should I have to put in any effort for the Empire? Sure, if it were for my own domain, I'd do whatever was required, but there was nothing in this for me.

"So, where will you be working?" the viscount asked.

"Oh, I'll just be pushing papers in some office, I'm sure."

Liam Sera Banfield was a busy man. While attending an Imperial university, he started up a faction in support of Prince Cleo's claim to the throne. As such, he spent all his time at school attending classes and getting his political group up and running. While the rest of his peers enjoyed their college life, Liam alone spent his days being absurdly hard at work.

"Darling's throwing another party today. I really should be attending too, but..." Liam's fiancée, Rosetta Sereh Claudia, was murmuring to herself alone in her room.

Rosetta's quarters at the hotel were on a floor below the penthouse reserved for Liam's personal use. Despite their living so close to one another, however, Rosetta seldom had the opportunity to see her fiancé. One reason was how busy he was, but it was mostly because Liam simply didn't bring Rosetta with him to the parties he threw. Rosetta wanted to support her fiancé, but since he didn't ask for any help from her, there was nothing she could do. Liam's only request of Rosetta was for her to "have fun at school." No doubt he only said this out of concern for her, but Rosetta couldn't help feeling frustrated.

"I can't just enjoy myself while Darling's doing all that work by himself."

A maid noticed Rosetta brooding and became concerned for her. She was Ciel Sera Exner, a young woman who had asked to start her noble training early and was happy to have been appointed as one of Rosetta's maids. She had long silver hair, purple eyes, and an average build for girls her age. The only thing about her that stood out, really, was the simple braid she wore on the right side of her head. It seemed like it might have been a custom of House Exner, since Kurt sported the same braid.

Ciel was as skeptical of Liam as ever. "Is Lord Liam really that busy? Seems like he's having a lot of fun, going to parties every day." It appeared to her that Liam was actually just fooling around, especially since Ciel hadn't attended many parties.

Rosetta sighed and corrected her. "Ciel, not all parties are fun. This is basically work for Darling." It was necessary for Liam to entertain nobles in order to build power for Cleo's faction.

I don't have many good memories of parties myself...and considering the challenging position he's in now, I doubt Darling can enjoy himself either.

In the past, Rosetta was forced to attend certain parties only so she could be ridiculed for others' entertainment. For that reason, her own associations with such events were negative.

Ciel looked apologetic. "That was presumptuous of me. I apologize, Lady Rosetta."

"It's all right. I'd be happy to answer any questions you have. After all, you're training with House Banfield to prepare you for your future in House Exner."

While she was visiting from House Exner, Ciel was in truth no simple maid. She was the daughter of Baron Exner, a sworn friend of Liam's and sister to the baron's heir, Kurt. House Banfield was obligated to treat her especially well, since she wasn't like the children of Liam's vassals who came to train with House Banfield. House Exner might have been of a lesser rank, but Ciel's family was still nobility just like Liam's. That was why she was receiving a somewhat better education than the other children House Banfield looked after, though it was Liam's policy to train all the children in a similar, strict manner. Ciel had the good fortune to receive her training directly from Rosetta, but not so she could be coddled. Rather, it was so that Rosetta could teach her personally and give her a variety of practical experiences.

"Darling works so hard," Rosetta said. "I hope he doesn't push himself too much."

Ciel watched sympathetically as Rosetta resumed fretting.

In Ciel's eyes, Liam just didn't seem like the laudable person everyone else saw him as. To be honest, she considered him her enemy. Why? The reason for this was that he had apparently thrown the heart of her beloved brother into disarray. For that reason alone, Ciel couldn't help but look at Liam with a harsher gaze than everyone else around him.

He's the worst.

Ciel only felt that much more resentful toward Liam when she saw Rosetta worrying about him.

To her, Rosetta's abilities seemed perfectly average. Rosetta wasn't particularly talented, but she wasn't incapable either. On the one hand, Rosetta was a hard worker, which endeared Ciel to her, and Ciel hoped they would share a long-lasting relationship. Personality-wise, Rosetta was basically flawless, and yet she was a fatally bad judge of character when it came to men.

Lady Rosetta is a good person, but she's being deceived.

It was true that Liam was busy every day, but Ciel knew for a fact that he was also enjoying himself at those parties. A few days earlier, she witnessed him talking about a particular event with one of his personal merchants. "I've got more than enough money! Let's throw a lavish event!" Liam had said, plenty excited. It didn't seem one bit like he was throwing these parties only because he was expected to.

Everyone praised Liam to high heaven and called him amazing, but Ciel was the only one who couldn't see it.

After all, he was probably responsible for the fact that her beloved brother may soon turn into her sister...

The very first time Ciel met Liam, she had her doubts about him. Prior to that, whenever she heard rumors about him, she wondered if such a virtuous person could really exist. In order to get closer to him and find out the truth, she requested to have her period of training moved up and applied to be Rosetta's maid. She would now endure this harsh training, all so that she could open her beloved brother's eyes.

You've deceived this kind woman and fooled my brother too. I'll never forgive you, Liam.

Her gentle brother Kurt, whom she always worshipped, had changed after meeting Liam. He had once been so noble and sweet, but now he always changed the topic of conversation to Liam whenever he could. Ciel couldn't forgive Liam for dominating Kurt's thoughts to such an extent.

For her part, Ciel couldn't help hearing everything Liam said as lines from a third-rate villain. His accomplishments *were* impressive, and he *did* live a rather simple life outside of political events. If you looked at the results of his actions, he came across as a perfectly upstanding person, but Ciel just couldn't see it that way. Her instincts screamed at her that there was something wrong about him.

I'll peel off that disguise of his and open everyone's eyes! I have to protect my brother so he doesn't become my sister.

Ciel was determined to expose Liam for who he really was.

In contrast to Ciel's fiery determination, Rosetta wished only to devote herself to her fiancé. She shook her head in an effort to dispel the despondent air that had settled over her. "This won't do," she said, putting on a brave face. "I have to pull myself together all the more since Darling's not here. I have to take charge again today for Darling's sake."

As Rosetta pumped herself up, Ciel manipulated the screen on her bracelet to check her plans for the day. *Let's see... Today's schedule... Huh?*

Looking over it, a question occurred to Ciel. "Do you mind if I ask you something, Lady Rosetta?"

"Yes?"

"Has Miss Eulisia been doing anything besides fooling around lately? She's the only one doing nothing but going shopping or going on vacations. Err...maybe it isn't my place to say, but don't you think maybe she should be doing something else?"

Eulisia Morisille was Liam's adjutant, whom he pulled out of the military just for that purpose. Normally when a noble did that, it was to make the adjutant a mistress or concubine, so Eulisia was being treated well by House Banfield. However, if the mistress or concubine of a powerful noble acted frivolously, that could prove to be a bit of a scandal in itself. As their status was of an unofficial nature, such a person shouldn't stand out quite as much as Eulisia was doing. At the moment, Eulisia wasn't even fulfilling her role of adjutant.

Rosetta's face lost its usual benevolent expression and Ciel let out a gasp of surprise. Rosetta sighed. "Just because Darling is leaving her alone, we can't exactly let Miss Eulisia fool around forever, can we?"

"R-right!"

"Ciel, where might she be right now?"

"In her room. It seems she's usually asleep at this time."

"I see..."

In those days, Eulisia enjoyed residing in that high-class hotel. She fooled around until late every night and often slept in until just before noon. Now retired from the military, she spent every day living it up by Liam's side.

Sleeping without an alarm, she woke at whatever time she pleased.

"Ahhh... I slept good."

With her long blonde hair disheveled and her face still looking sleepy, Eulisia sat up in bed and stretched. She was truly indulging in her happy lifestyle to the fullest degree.

"I don't think I want to do anything today. Guess I'll take a little break from playing."

Just when she was considering going back to sleep, the door to her room suddenly opened.

"H-hey, who's there? Eep!"

Eulisia grabbed the weapon she kept by her pillow. Though she was now living a slothful life, she hadn't completely forgotten all her military training, however rusty her skills might now be. When she saw who entered her room, however, Eulisia's face froze in surprise.

"Ros... Lady Rosetta?"

"Good morning, Miss Eulisia."

Rosetta was smiling, but a group of House Banfield knights stood behind her. They were all women, and all of them were giving Eulisia chilly stares.

"Err... Is there something I can do for you?" Eulisia asked, a strained smile on her face.

"You seem to be enjoying yourself lately," Rosetta said.

"W-well, umm... It's just that Lord Liam won't give me the time of day," Eulisia said, averting her eyes.

Rosetta's tone went harsh. "No excuses! You can't just fool around while Darling is hard at work every day.

I would never tell you not to enjoy yourself at all, but you must consider the timing."

Eulisia indulging in her frivolous lifestyle while House Banfield was so busy was stirring the ire of the family's retainers.

Eulisia shrank under Rosetta's criticism. "I'm sorry... I'll keep that in mind."

"Actually, I think you should go back to the military for retraining."

"Huh?"

"You're supposed to be Darling's military contact, aren't you? You can't just neglect your role. Go retrain yourself!"

"Nooooo!" Eulisia shrieked, but Rosetta's decision was final.

Before even coming here, Rosetta had already received Liam's permission to order Eulisia back to the military. His reaction to her suggestion was nothing more than a disinterested "Sure, whatever."

While Ciel was maneuvering to expose Liam's true nature, his real enemy, the Guide, raged in agony.

"What can I do to defeat Liam? What do I do? What will it take to defeat him?"

No matter how much he considered the question, he just couldn't find an answer. Up until that point the Guide did all manner of things to make Liam miserable, but each and every time Liam unknowingly thwarted his attempts. To make matters worse, as if trying to get back at the Guide, Liam even expressed his gratitude to him.

On top of that, Liam's appreciation now had the thankfulness of his entire domain's population behind it, so it was overwhelmingly difficult for the Guide to endure. Typically, a single person's gratitude was nothing more than a discomfort for him, but with all of Liam's subjects contributing—people numbering in the hundreds of millions—the force of gratitude had become unbearable. A subset of Liam's subjects even worshipped him as if he was a god. The energy of their gratitude sickened the Guide like a physical attack.

"I can't let him get away with this! You're going down, Liam, I swear it!!!"

However, no matter how many times the Guide swore revenge against Liam, it always backfired. He lent his strength to Liam's enemies, but not once had those efforts paid off.

The Guide was reduced to weeping now, having completely lost his confidence. "What am I doing wrong?

Would I succeed if I did the opposite? If I *helped* Liam and made his enemies unhappy? It couldn't be..."

Purposely helping Liam was the last thing the Guide wanted to do. If he did that, he would just end up enduring *more* of Liam's gratitude. He shivered, picturing himself writhing in agony as Liam thanked him once again.

"I'm sick of failing and suffering Liam's gratitude!"

He didn't want to feel this way anymore, but he just couldn't come up with a solution to the problem. After all, he knew that no matter how hard he worked to make Liam unhappy, Liam had gained enough power now that he could deal with whatever the Guide threw at him. Not to mention that the man was personally strong. *Too* strong. So strong, in fact, that the Guide doubted there was anyone in the empire who could beat him.

"How can I take him down? And what the hell is that Way of the Flash, anyway? Damn you, Yasushi—how did a swindler like you manage to create such a monster?"

However, there *were* some similar monsters who might be able to take Liam down. The Guide wanted to find a way to get those secret weapons close to Liam, but at the same time, he was terrified to do so. What could happen if that plot backfired too? The Guide was so completely traumatized by Liam's gratitude that any plan made him nervous.

"S-seriously, what can I do? I...I...!" After agonizing over the matter for a while, he eventually came to a conclusion. "Right. It's the only thing I haven't tried. I'll help Liam by making his *enemies* unhappy. And if that doesn't work, then I'll just have to think of something else! For now, I'll just help Liam out a little bit and see what happens."

Driven into a corner, the Guide made a perfectly preposterous decision.

Crown Prince Calvin, first in line to the throne, looked tired as he addressed his supporting nobles gathered before him.

"How serious is this situation?" he asked.

The reason for his distress lay with the United Kingdom of Oxys. Oxys was an intergalactic nation actually comprised of a group of small, allied nations. Together, the rulers of those nations governed the unified nation as an assembly, and that unified nation was moving to invade the Empire now that their deal with the deceased Prince Linus had fallen through.

"It seems Prince Linus is still causing trouble, even after his death," one of the nobles remarked.

"The United Kingdom is indeed serious," another spoke up. "They're hiding behind the secret agreement they had with Prince Linus."

"They hold a grudge against the Empire, thanks to that deal."

"Now that they're taking control of the unrest within their borders, they'll concentrate all their efforts into getting back at us."

While alive, Prince Linus caused an internal conflict in the United Kingdom of Oxys. He had promised to give Imperial territory to several of the nations that comprised the United Kingdom, and he provided those nations alone with aid. Those actions threw off the Kingdom's power balance and led to an intense internal conflict, resulting in serious damage to the Kingdom.

Linus's death amid all this had changed the situation drastically. The nations he supported quickly lost their bid for greater power, and the United Kingdom was infuriated to learn of the Empire's involvement. All of that led to their planned invasion of the Empire.

The nobles supporting Calvin were nervous. Another of them said, "The present situation is precarious, Your Highness. That Liam fellow is gaining more and more momentum, and according to the spies we've inserted into his ranks, he blames us for escalating the damage caused by the succession dispute. He claims Prince Cleo has justice on his side, and he is gathering additional nobles who agree with him."

"Justice." These assembled nobles felt Liam was just blowing hot air by flaunting that word. The problem was, plenty of people blamed the royals for aggravating the succession conflict and dragging their subjects into it. Such claims were hard to ignore when they came directly from Liam.

Linus had carelessly given Liam the opportunity to exploit his aggression and use it to take him down. These claims of justice were dangerous coming from the man who'd taken a mule like Cleo and turned him into a dark horse. Not to mention the fact that the one spouting this rhetoric was a righteous noble who took a firm stance against piracy. Liam wasn't just some nameless man, but a powerful foe. And chivalrous nobles from the Empire's outskirts were gathering around him—another grave problem in itself.

"If we simply leave him alone, Liam will only gain more fame."

If they just let him be, more and more nobles who were dissatisfied with the Empire would join Cleo's faction, or at least lend them aid. Normally, Calvin would just leave the situation to the military and regain the nobles' support in due time, but he couldn't do that here.

The situation with the United Kingdom was bad as well. They had settled their internal unrest and would attack the Empire in earnest next. If the nations Linus had plotted with didn't make their allegiance known by aiding in this invasion, they would doubtless lose their standings inside the United Kingdom. The other nation was in a complex state of rage and repentance right now, and its momentum couldn't be underestimated. Fending them off would no doubt lead to much damage and many casualties.

Calvin considered his options. "If we assemble a large fleet and dispatch it to suppress the invasion, we'll be shorthanded near the Capital Planet. And Liam wouldn't overlook that opportunity."

The nobles in Calvin's faction wore equally uneasy expressions.

"It was a mistake making an enemy of him," said one.

"But if we lose Imperial territory to invaders," another said, "it will only do more damage to our reputation."

"Circumstances are shifting to be in Prince Cleo's favor. Rather, in Liam's favor. Your Highness, we must take action."

Everyone around Calvin was telling him how unfavorable his current situation was, but there was a reason he'd survived the fierce succession conflict up to this point. He wasn't one to lose his head in the face of a challenge.

"No... We will not take action."

"Your Highness?"

"It's Cleo who will take action here. Let's give the boy a chance to shine."

The nobles in Calvin's faction all began to catch on to what he was implying.

"You intend to have Prince Cleo—no, to have *Liam* suffer those heavy losses?"

Calvin nodded emphatically. "That's right. If he screws up going against the United Kingdom, that will work, of course, but even if he's successful he'll likely lose a vast amount of his fighting force. We'll make sure of it."

What Calvin intended was to join forces with the invading United Kingdom in order to vanquish Liam. All the other nation wanted out of this invasion was to deal the Empire a heavy blow for revenge, but for Calvin, this was a great opportunity to thin the fighting forces of a thorn in his side like Liam. Not to mention that if Liam was forced to send his ships out to war, his activities on the Capital Planet would undoubtedly be slowed.

Calvin already had his eye on the next part of his plan. "Once his forces on the Capital Planet have thinned out, we'll work on thinning the ranks of his supporters as well."

With their new instructions, the nobles all dove into action.

1 Treachery

T HE UNITED KINGDOM of Oxys made its move. When news of this reached the Capital Planet, it sent everyone into a frenzy. The Empire was used to the occasional border skirmish, but a real invasion was an entirely different story. The coming conflict would involve clashes of not just thousands of ships, but millions, and the United Kingdom had already made it clear they were dead serious in their intentions.

"Three million ships?" I asked.

"Y-yes! The United Kingdom has formed a massive fleet centered around the nations that started the internal unrest to atone for their misdeeds. Lord Liam, this is very bad!!!"

In worst-case scenarios, true conflicts between intergalactic nations could go on for hundreds of years.

I sat in my hotel room and casually sipped my coffee. "I see."

"Y-you see? Lord Liam, are you taking this seriously?"

The one who brought me this news was my personal merchant, Thomas Henfrey, who was also serving as my contact in the United Kingdom. It seemed that arrangement was already proving to be useful since he was immediately able to provide me with this intel.

"It's got nothing to do with me," I replied. "This is a job for the military. Right now, I'm nothing more than a civil servant."

A pale-faced Thomas had rushed into my hotel room while I was enjoying a morning beverage before going into work. Right now, he looked at me as if he couldn't believe his ears.

"Th-that may be so, but I don't think the military alone will be able to deal with this! The Empire's nobility will surely be called on to fight."

So they were gonna come to us with "Nobles of the Empire, rise up with us in the face of this crisis!" or something like that? I couldn't say I was too keen on the idea.

"Well, if they call, I'm not answering. I'm still in my training period, and in the military, I'm only in the reserves."

According to Thomas, three million enemies were closing in on us. True, this was a crisis, but the Empire was a vast intergalactic nation. If it wanted to, it could send out twice that number of Imperial Army ships to fight them off, but it was still bound to drag its allies into danger as well.

There would be plenty of nobles like me who'd be content to watch from the sidelines without taking part in the fight themselves. After all, evil lords never got into trouble that they didn't have to. The Empire could likely win the war, but it was still up against three million enemies and therefore bound to suffer serious losses. Could I be confident that *I* wouldn't be affected by those losses?

"We'll limit our involvement and only provide funding and supplies."

"That…may be wise." Thomas calmed down when he heard my reasonable compromise. Did he really think I was actually going to fight in the war myself or something?

As I continued sipping my coffee, I received a communication from Claus on my tablet.

"Lord Liam, I apologize for the interruption, but I have an urgent message for you."

On the screen, Claus looked anxious, and if *Claus* was anxious, then something really serious must be going on.

"What is it?"

If this had been a message from one of my more aggravating subordinates—like Tia or Marie—I would have hung up on them immediately. Of course, those two would probably find a way to get excited about me treating them coldly. I always felt like they were getting the better of me somehow, so I was tired of dealing with them. In that respect, Claus was exactly what I wanted in a subordinate right now.

"We've received a request from the palace. They want us to join the fight in the war with the United Kingdom."

"We refuse. I'm busy."

"The problem is that Prince Cleo's been chosen as the conflict's supreme commander."

"What?!"

In the United Kingdom, there was a noble by the name of Count Pershing who received aid from Liam via Thomas. This connection of Liam's was a count who ruled over a planet, but the king he served was one of those supporting the rebellion. Because of that, Pershing was being forced to participate in the invasion of the Empire as atonement.

Pershing had benefited greatly from Liam's support. From the very beginning, he had never intended to do anything for the United Kingdom's sake...but he didn't intend to do anything for Liam's sake either. Everything he did, he did for himself.

"So you want me to help you lure Liam onto the battlefield?" Pershing said.

It was an Imperial merchant who came to meet Pershing this time, not Thomas. They nodded, grinning. "There are some nobles making a big scene in the Empire right now, you see. They'll be the ones fending off the Kingdom's forces."

When he heard what the Imperial merchant had to say, Pershing realized there were people in the Empire who planned to make use of this war in their own power struggle. "Imperial nobles are pretty scary, hoping the United Kingdom will take out their opposing factions for them."

"In exchange, we'll make sure you always have information on the fleet Prince Cleo commands."

Count Pershing smiled. *That's good,* he thought. *If I have constant updates on the enemy's position, there should be plenty of opportunities for me to make a name for myself in battle.*

This would mean that in addition to the attacks from the United Kingdom, Cleo's fleet would be undermined by his own Imperial allies. The fleet would make the perfect prey on the battlefield, and the Empire wanted this fleet to lose.

Pershing didn't take the deal right away, however. "Of course, Lord Liam has been very kind to me, you know. It's not easy for me to betray his trust."

Count Pershing demanded more compensation, and the Imperial merchant grinned again. "Of course. In the event of your success, we shall provide whatever you desire as a reward. This is just the advance payment."

The merchant offered him a vast sum of cash and a long list of resources. Count Pershing could hardly contain his glee.

It seems you've made too many enemies inside the Empire, Count Banfield. I'm afraid you'll have to give your life for my benefit now.

Prince Cleo's residence in the palace had been in an uproar since the first thing that morning.

"Command a fleet of millions? You haven't even received military education, Cleo!"

Cleo's sister Lysithea couldn't hide her frustration. While she was royalty herself, she had become a knight in order to protect her younger-sister-turned-younger-brother Cleo.

Cleo watched his furious sister serenely. "Calm down, Lysithea. I've learned the basics in an education capsule."

"Education capsules are impressive, I know, but they only install knowledge in you. If you don't make use of it through practical experience, that knowledge is meaningless. If capsules were all it took, then we'd have no need for military schools!"

Education capsules could impart whatever raw knowledge they were programmed with into a person's head, but that person then had to apply the knowledge in the real world to master it.

Cleo turned his head from his exasperated sister, pouting slightly. "I'm sure it'll be Count Banfield commanding the fleet and not me, anyway."

"Count Banfield can only command 100,000 ships at most," Lysithea corrected her brother.

"Huh?"

"His personal ability won't prepare him for commanding a fleet in the millions. Those kinds of numbers can only be mobilized by someone with the requisite rank. Do you think Count Banfield has someone of that rank working for him?"

Even when he went to war with the pirate nobles of House Berkeley, Liam commanded a combined fleet of fewer than 200,000 ships. The count was talented, but this battle would be on a scale he was not capable of handling.

"N-no..."

Lysithea held her head in her hands. "I'm telling you, the count is too inexperienced. Talent isn't the only thing required to command a fleet of millions of ships. Experience is vital. Plus, you'd also need thousands of subordinates to carry out your orders."

And those thousands of people—hundreds of thousands, really—would have to be educated officers themselves. They needed not just soldiers for this operation, but skilled commanders. A mere count had no hope of providing such numbers.

"If we had years to prepare, things would be different, but we don't have the time. We can't win a war with an unorganized army."

Cleo resigned himself to Lysithea's logic. *It seems this is as far as we go, Count Banfield.*

A grand role such as this would normally fall upon the shoulders of the emperor or the crown prince. Success could make a real difference in one's right to ascend to the throne, so this should have been Calvin's moment to shine, and yet he personally recommended Cleo for the position instead.

Tears came to Lysithea's eyes. She knew that what Calvin desired here was to see his brother fail. "This is just awful. If you step down as supreme commander in the middle of the Empire's big crisis, you'll lose the support of all the nobles currently on your side. If you accept the position, we have no chance of victory in the long run."

Even if they successfully repelled the invasion, they would have no way to continue their feud with Calvin's faction afterward due to the damage it would surely do to their forces.

"Calvin truly is a troublesome foe," Cleo muttered.

Lysithea agreed wholeheartedly. "I'd expect nothing less from the man who defended his position as crown prince for so many years. His title's not just for show."

The throne seemed just within reach, but at the same time, much too far away for Cleo to ever attain. This situation caused Cleo to reflect on Liam himself.

Count Banfield isn't omnipotent, but just a young man without much experience in the world. I guess in that way, he's just like me.

When he realized that Liam, a man he previously thought of as practically flawless, actually had weaknesses after all, Cleo felt a little relieved...perhaps even happy, though he didn't understand these feelings himself.

What awaited nobles upon graduating from college was a sort of two-year internship, similar to the two-year military service period they were required to complete after graduating from the military academy. After college, nobles were expected to gain some hands-on experience by serving in a minor government position.

My position was in a building in a remote area far from the palace. To describe it in Japanese terms from my previous life, I was stationed in something like a town hall out in the countryside. It frustrated me that I was pulled from the fast track I should have been on and dumped in some backwater place. Normally, a count like me would be working a cushy palace job, but instead, I was sent to the sticks. I was so far out that they should have prepared a place for me to stay near where I was working, but I was commuting every day from my hotel. On the other hand, cars in this reality were incredible, exceeding the capabilities of small jet planes from my past life. In a quality car, you could easily commute to the other side of the planet if you wanted to.

So anyway, here I was, working in a town hall out in the boonies...and my superior was just infuriating. While

I was at my desk, getting ready to go home, he called out to me with a disgusting grin on his face.

"Saaaaay, Liam. You commute all the way out here from the capital, don't you? I'm sure you have the money, so why don't you rent a place nearby?"

This superior, the thirtieth or something son of a large noble house, was my instructor during my training. Luckily for him, he was born into an important family, but that family was so huge that all he'd amounted to was a small-time backwater bureaucrat. With a bit more skill, I'm sure he could have ended up with a decent position in the palace, so the fact that he was here said volumes about his abilities. He had an overabundance of pride in his meager abilities despite the fact that he never did any work himself, and he spent his time on the clock messing around or playing games. Everyone here seemed to have given up on him, and his superiors never said anything when they saw him fooling around.

Normally I would have ignored him, but today he sent me more work to do right as I was supposed to be leaving.

"Oh, and please finish with these files today. We'll need them tomorrow, after all."

A huge mass of holographic documents opened in the air all around me. I glanced at the clock; I was supposed to be gone in a few minutes. I could tell at a glance that it was too much work for me to finish in that time. He was obviously trying to bully me.

My superior set his hand on my shoulder. "You'll have to do as I say during your training here. I'm not gonna go easy on you just because you're a count."

How dare he speak to me like that? I smacked his hand off my shoulder, grabbed his head, and slammed it onto my desk.

"Ow!"

My superior was bewildered, like his pathetic brain couldn't keep up with my actions. I held him down with one arm and pressed his head into my desk. The wood cracked under the force, but I didn't care; I could afford a replacement.

"Who do you think you are, ordering me around?" I told him. "I'm not listening to a word you say, whether you're my instructor or not."

This was no way for a trainee to speak, but I was a count. No small-town official was going to boss me around.

"H-how dare you speak to your superior that way? I'm reducing your score for this!"

Instructors graded their trainees, but I didn't care how low my score was. I wasn't staying in this job for long, so I didn't care how I was evaluated. Besides, I could easily bury whatever evaluation this peon gave me.

"It's inexcusable that someone like you is even my superior in the first place. Do you understand the position you're in at all?" I asked, pressing down on the man's head even harder. There was a nasty creaking sound beneath him, but I wasn't the one in pain, so I paid it no mind.

For the record, I had nothing against undisciplined superiors. As an evil lord, I was a prime example of one myself. I just couldn't take that there was someone like that above *me*. I knew I was being hypocritical, but I was a villain. I could get away with it.

"Why are you giving me work to do at the end of the day? Aren't you supposed to be a manager? Managing the work is *your* job. The question is, how the hell do you still have work to hand out at a time like this?"

"Nnggh..."

My desk's surface snapped from the force, and my superior's face was driven half into it. I figured he couldn't talk like that.

"This is *your* mistake," I went on. "*You* deal with it."

I let him go and he trembled.

"Y-you bastard! You think you can get away with—"

I didn't think that; I just didn't intend to let *him* get away with this. I pressed down on my incompetent superior's head again and it creaked unpleasantly. Everyone else around us looked on in fear, but I didn't care about that.

"*You* finish the work," I said. "It's your mistake, so that makes sense, doesn't it?"

It was clear I was willing to crush his head outright if he defied me, and I guess he wasn't so stupid that he didn't realize it.

He went quiet, and all the blood drained from his face. "Y-yes, sir," my nominal superior squeaked.

I smiled at him. "You said it needed to be done by tomorrow, so it must be possible. That means *you* can do it, right?"

It was obviously not an amount of work that one person could complete, even if they went at it all night. My superior was trembling. "I-I can't..."

"*You can do it, right?*" I urged. I kicked him, and he rolled away from me across the floor, eventually striking the wall. He remained there, shaking, so I repeated myself again for good measure. "Get it done by tomorrow. You said it could be done, so you'll take responsibility, won't you?"

I walked over to my incompetent superior and peered down at his face. It was covered in tears and snot. I took on a quieter tone, sounding like a supervisor myself. "You better finish it all by tomorrow, without any assistance. I'll squash your head flat if you don't."

"Y-yes, sir."

The end-of-day bell rang, so I tidied up my things and

prepared to leave. Overtime? That was something for people who weren't evil lords. I wouldn't be caught dead doing it myself.

"Be seeing you," I called on my way out. "Hope you get all that done by tomorrow."

My attitude toward my supposed superior was the very height of rudeness, but I was a count. In the Empire, nobility wielded absolute power. A man who couldn't even succeed by using his family's established name had no right to be arrogant with me. I was the real deal, and not just on the inside. I was the only one with real influence in society. Noblesse oblige—the idea of a noble's duty—was simply an illusion.

This incompetent superior of mine was really stressing me out though... Maybe it was time to make some improvements to my workplace.

The next day, I was summoned before the superior of my incompetent superior. He was a blood relative of my immediate superior, meaning he was also a member of that large noble family.

From his tone, my boss' boss clearly looked down on me. "Apparently you did as you liked in the military, but this is a government office. I expect you not to act like those savages in the army."

My trembling, incompetent superior hid behind his boss, and the bastard was giving me a smug look.

Seated on a couch, I ignored the two of them and looked over some holographic documents.

I guess the big boss didn't like my attitude because he started yelling at me. "Do you think everyone will simply bow down to you? My family is part of Prince Calvin's faction! I'm not afraid of you!"

Nobles were beyond help, myself included. When you lived life completely spoiled because of your position, even good people could rot into villains. There were plenty of intelligent nobles though; not all of them were as useless as these two.

Still looking at the documents, I asked the boss, "Do you feel better now that you've chewed me out?"

He didn't answer, so I looked up at him.

He snorted. "You're awfully confident, aren't you? I know you're off to the battlefield soon. I bet you're regretting pissing off Prince Calvin!"

If there was one point I empathized with Calvin about, it was the fact that our factions were so big that we had to expect incompetents like this to be in the ranks. Well, I could always lessen the burden some for the crown prince.

"I admit, I am feeling irritated about that," I said. "By the way, why don't you take a look at these documents? They're evidence of your corruption."

I made the documents larger for them to see, and my two superiors initially showed some surprise, but that quickly gave way to smiles. They weren't even scared about having proof of their corruption thrust before them.

"What of it? This is nothing special. Every—"

"Everyone's doing it? I don't care," I said. "I have material here to remove you, which I intend to do to make myself feel better. I was just lamenting about the state of my workplace, but with you two gone it should be a lot more comfortable around here."

It was proof of just how incompetent they were that I was able to uncover evidence of their misdeeds so easily. There would be no issues getting rid of both of them.

I snapped my fingers, and armed soldiers marched into the room. My two superiors were shocked at the appearance of these hulking soldiers in their powered suits.

"Don't move!" the soldiers shouted at them. "Put your hands behind your head and get down on the floor!"

"Wh-who are you?!"

The soldiers kicked my superior and his superior to the floor and promptly apprehended them. Once they dragged the two useless men away, their commander came to me and saluted.

"Thank you for the tip," he said.

"You work fast." I reported these men's wrongdoings as soon as I discovered them. I was always good at rooting out corruption like this, ever since my early days working with Amagi—and I was good at cleanup too.

"We have a message for you from the prime minister. He says, 'Thanks for the quick work.'"

It was so funny, I burst into laughter. "What, you guys work directly for the prime minister?"

"Yes, sir!"

"I owe that guy. Guess I should thank him too."

Later, I'd have these fast-working soldiers send the prime minister a bribe—a *gift*, rather. I never forgot to reward the people who helped me out.

I was really weirdly unlucky lately though... I got sent off to the boonies with an incompetent boss at a workplace full of corruption, and I was being dragged into a stupid war to boot. Nothing but trouble was coming my way these days.

The war I was being dragged into was between intergalactic nations, so it was going to be on a grand scale. To be honest, it was a lot more than I could handle. Really, what the heck was going on?

2 The Guide's Perfect Plan

THE GUIDE COULDN'T BELIEVE what he'd learned. Liam was *actually* in trouble.

The Guide's hands trembled at the realization, but from joy this time, not fear. He was filled with elation such as he'd never known before.

"Liam's having a hard time?"

That in itself wasn't unusual, but the Guide had never been personally responsible for Liam's troubles before. Up until now, no matter how he used his powers or manipulated circumstances to make Liam miserable, Liam always ended up benefiting from it in some way, so he couldn't stop trembling at his current success.

"I assisted Liam, which made Calvin unhappy...b-but Calvin has made the best of his situation and is causing Liam to suffer instead. So I'm helping Liam, but his troubles are only growing! What's going on?"

He clutched his head as he tried to work out the mechanics of it all, but the Guide just couldn't stop smiling at how things were working out. He was thrilled that his new mode of attack was seeing results. Yes, he was still tormented by the flaming gratitude shots Liam constantly sent his way, but the intense euphoria he felt almost made him forget the pain. This pleasure was all the stronger for the agony he'd suffered up until now.

"It's like *The North Wind and the Sun*! Instead of trying to make Liam unhappy, all I had to do was try and make him happy and it all worked out! Of course! I should have known!"

After all his previous failures, the Guide couldn't see past the excitement of the present situation. He was so overcome with joy that he didn't think deeply about what might have actually transpired.

"Now I know to give Liam as much aid as I possibly can! Ah, it's getting to be so much fun now!"

As the Guide stood there, guffawing, a ghostly dog glared at him sight unseen from the nearby shadows.

As House Banfield's domain gradually expanded, it continued to gain inhabitable planets, but for all this new territory, the domain's overall population was still low. They expanded too rapidly and simply didn't have the numbers to fill the new planets under development. House Banfield needed time to better address this problem, but Liam needed manpower for other things *now*, so he had to find a quicker way to bolster his numbers. That quicker way was immigration.

In this alternate reality, many nomadic peoples wandered through space. It was a common story for a people's home planet to be destroyed, leaving the survivors to travel through space for decades searching for a new planet on which to settle. Some refugees even wandered for thousands of years in search of that new home. To complicate matters, people like that often had their own unique cultures, so it was difficult for other planets to accept them easily. And even if they *were* welcomed, it often took time for the newcomers to integrate into society. For that reason, House Banfield set its sights on intergalactic nations that directly bordered the Empire.

The domestic conflicts Linus had contributed to in both the United Kingdom of Oxys and the Intergalactic Rustwarr Union had caused a flood of refugees to leave those nations, and Liam figured he could boost his territory's population by accepting them. There was one flaw to this plan, however.

House Banfield's domain was relatively peaceful, with good public order. They had recently taken in a large number of immigrants from the United Kingdom and the Rustwarr Union to boost their population, but...

"We won't be ruled by a dictator!"

"The aristocracy is nothing but a dictatorship! Democracy is the only way!"

"Yeah! The Union's way is how it's got to be!"

With his new initiative, Liam succeeded in increasing his domain's population, but in exchange, the immigrants from the Rustwarr Union were already holding protests on several of House Banfield's planets.

On one of those planets, the leader of the local protest group met with someone in a deserted alleyway.

"We have a lot more people now, thanks to you," the protest leader said. "We'll topple the aristocracy—just you wait."

This protest leader was an enthusiastic young man from the Union who hoped to establish democracy within Liam's domain. He preached about the downfall of the aristocracy, trying to sell his fellow immigrants on a democratic system. His name was Alex Rebhorn. With brown hair and blue eyes, Alex looked like a perfectly nice young man, but the Algrand Empire was a nation with a nobility system and Alex was hot-blooded enough to try and campaign for democracy in such a place.

Supporting Alex in his efforts was the person he met with—a spy from Prince Calvin's faction.

"Hey, we just want to help you," said the spy. "We'll destroy the nobility system together."

The spy held out his hand and Alex gripped it firmly. "Of course! We'll start by making this planet a democracy!"

Inside, though, the spy was laughing. *You'll put on a good show for us, won't you? If this weren't Liam's planet, we'd just burn the whole thing down and start over fresh without you troublemakers...but I suppose you don't understand that's how it works in the Empire.*

This young agitator had likely never had his activities suppressed before in the Union. However, it was a whole other situation here in the Empire, where suppression was commonplace. From the spy's perspective, Alex's former freedoms had left him hopelessly naïve.

Make the chaos as big as you can, the spy thought to himself. *Then, when you're done serving your purpose, we'll rid ourselves of you.*

Calvin's faction planned on destroying this politically contaminated planet entirely after they finished dealing with Liam.

The Empire doesn't need democracy.

"THOSE LITTLE SHITS!!!"

"P-please calm down, Master Liam!"

I cleaned up my workplace nicely and returned to my hotel room only to be met with an emergency message from my domain. The person relaying the bad news to me was my butler and personal assistant, Brian.

"What would you like us to do, Master Liam? We didn't expect the immigrants we accepted to stage such large protests..."

"Those idiots from the Union want democracy in my domain, eh?"

"Well, they're used to the political system of their homeland. It will take them time to get used to the Empire's aristocratic ways."

There was no way this group would start organizing for democracy as soon as they landed on one of my planets. Someone was clearly propping them up from behind the scenes. Calvin was the most likely offender, but I didn't have any proof, so I couldn't condemn him publicly.

"Kukuri!"

I called out for my head covert operative, and Kukuri appeared from out of my own shadow. The large man slid out from the darkness on one knee, with his head bowed.

"Here I am."

"There's someone behind this democracy movement. Why haven't you discovered them yet? Did they really organize these protests all on their own?"

For these people to have begun their protests as soon as they had two feet on the ground was just too suspicious. I could understand it if I was mistreating them or something, but I felt I'd prepared pretty well to accommodate them. After all, I wanted to make use of them as human resources right away, so I was sparing no expense and giving as much aid as needed. They were provided for in terms of residences, education, and job training...all so that I could work them to the bone as quickly as possible, of course. Even if they came to my domain penniless, these refugees would be able to have a home and a place to work. Their children would receive free education too. In that kind of environment, why start protesting right away? All because they didn't agree with the political system here?

Yeah, someone really has to be manipulating them. Dammit! Now I regret taking in people from the Union...

"An investigation was launched," Kukuri reported, "but several of House Banfield's people have already gone missing."

The investigators working on this had nothing to do with Kukuri's underground organization.

"What happened?"

Kukuri's men were talented, but there weren't many of them, so they could only cover so much ground on their own. That was why House Banfield also had a public safety organization, much like the one that existed in Japan in my past life. However, if several investigators from *that* organization disappeared, that was a big deal.

"*C-come to think of it, I did get a report about that,*" Brian added hastily, as if he'd just remembered about the missing people.

"Is everyone who works for me an idiot?" I lamented, but Kukuri corrected my assumption.

"I wouldn't say that. They weren't particularly exceptional, but I can't imagine they would be tripped up so easily. Master Liam...I believe there are more people like us operating within your domain."

"Like you?"

"Yes. There are many clans and organizations like ours within the Empire. Even in the age during which we operated, there were more than a hundred such groups. And there was one clan in particular we long feuded with."

Organizations from two thousand years ago, huh...? It wouldn't surprise me if they were still around, but they'd have to be pretty skilled to make it this long. If they could compete with Kukuri and his men, then they were *extremely* capable. If people like that truly were operating within my domain, it could lead to all sorts of trouble.

"So you think they managed to sneak in?"

"We have our hands full protecting you and doing our work on the Capital Planet right now, Master Liam. Unfortunately, only a very small number of us remain to monitor your domain."

It was really exasperating that there was trouble in my own domain when I was already so incredibly busy elsewhere. I'd have to make sure my precious alchemy box, stashed away in my domain, was safe before someone stole it. But where to put it...?

"Would you like to dispatch us to your domain?" Kukuri suggested.

"Well, there's trouble all over the place, but I can't move you around constantly. Just tell the people you have in my domain to maintain their current mission and stay alert."

"Yes, sir." And just like that, Kukuri vanished back into the floor.

I was getting really irritated. Those ungrateful protestors wanted to depose me and establish a democracy?

It made me want to get rid of them right away, but I was so busy that I didn't have time to handle that problem. I had to assume that my enemies were entrenched pretty deeply in my business.

"Once this is all over, I'll execute the whole lot of those troublemakers!" I yelled.

Brian was surprised to hear me say that. *"Y-you can't do that, Master Liam! You must be patient with them!"*

"You want me to simply endure this? Are you an idiot? If you want to know how I really feel, I'd like to return to my domain right this minute and cut the whole lot of them down with my own hands. I only accept subjects who'll obey me, Brian. Any who defy me are no better than garbage."

"M-Master Liam..."

Brian was hanging his head in shock, but why was he surprised? This was how I always was.

My irritation was reaching its peak, and just then, Amagi entered the room, so I cut off the call with Brian. My apprentice Ellen entered behind her, holding my maid's hand. I was in such a bad mood that when I saw the way she hid behind Amagi with her wooden sword, I became even angrier.

"Ellen, what's the meaning of a student of the Way of the Flash hiding behind a maid?"

When Amagi saw how afraid of me Ellen was, she reached out and stroked the girl's hair. The look my maid directed my way was fierce. Of course, her face was as expressionless as always, but her eyes were distinctly narrowed. I knew her well enough to know when she was angry, and she was *really* angry.

Seeing her like that made me flinch. "A-Amagi?"

Amagi stepped forward as if to protect Ellen. "It is disgraceful to take your frustrations out on others, Master."

"I-I'm not! It's just...you know... My subjects are protesting! As a noble, I should use force against them!" I tried excusing my actions by explaining that I was upset about the emergency in my domain, but Amagi remained implacable.

"I have received no reports of these protests. If the matter can be handled with the forces on site, we should simply let them handle it."

"B-but it makes me so angry... I'd like to punish them myself!"

Amagi's eyes narrowed further, into reproachful slits. "There are more important things for you to be doing, Master. Miss Ellen?"

She pushed Ellen forward, and the girl stood before me with head bowed.

"M-Master, you promised to train me, but you haven't seen me in three days."

I gasped when I saw that Ellen was on the verge of tears. I'd been so busy for the last few days that I wasn't able to oversee Ellen's training at all. I figured it was fine since she was only learning the basics at this point, but...what had I done? I couldn't believe I neglected training a successor to the Way of the Flash. How could I ever show my face to Master Yasushi? During my own training, Master Yasushi was always there, watching over me.

Amagi's reproachful glare stabbed into me further. "You brought her here for you to look after, Master."

"Y-yeah."

I *did* say I would raise her as my successor in the Way of the Flash. With Amagi criticizing me like this, I couldn't just run back to my domain and go after those protestors. I didn't have time for it anyway, not with my work at the office and preparing for the war. I was obligated to train Ellen too, but it was stressful that I felt busier than I ever was before.

Amagi's stern tone became a little more consoling. "I understand this is a difficult time for you, Master, but please turn your attention to those around you a little more. I am worried about you."

"Ugh!" It squeezed my heart to hear Amagi say she was worried about me. I sank to my knees.

Ellen ran over to me. "Master! A-are you all right, Master?"

"I-I'm fine, Ellen. Anyway, let's get training. I promised my master I would train my own student, after all."

Ellen cocked her head. "Master's Master?"

"Yeah, Master Yasushi. He's so amazing, he's called a Sword God."

Well, I was the one who designated Master Yasushi as a Sword God, but it was a fitting title for him. *I wonder if Master has heard about that, and if he's happy about it.*

I stood up, determined to bring Ellen to our training ground that instant. "Let's go."

"Yes!"

We went and Amagi followed us.

"By the way, Ellen," I started as we walked, "you're still diligently practicing the basics, right?"

"Y-yes! I'm working really hard!"

Amagi then spoke up, indicating that she'd been watching over Ellen in my place. "While you were absent, Master, I made sure she was practicing properly. Miss Ellen has indeed been working hard."

I was shocked to hear that. "Ellen, you've been alone with Amagi? She hasn't given me any time lately, despite how busy I am!"

"I-I'm sorry," the little girl squeaked out.

Amagi seemed truly appalled when she heard Ellen apologize to me. Anyone else would see the beautiful robot as being expressionless, but I could tell!

"Master, what are you saying to a child?"

"It's happening! It's all going my way!"

From afar, the Guide was able to sense Liam's frustration, and it thrilled him—and actually filled him with power. In the past, every time he did something to curse Liam, something else had interfered and caused the Guide pain instead.

Liam had wanted to increase his domain's population, so the Guide had extended his influence to send him plenty of immigrants. As a result, Liam had obtained more human resources, but the people who'd come from the Union weren't used to the Empire's system of aristocracy and resented it. Furthermore, thanks to the agitation of spies from Calvin's faction, those immigrants were holding protests right in the middle of Liam's domain.

The more the Guide tried to help Liam, the more it hurt him instead. The Guide felt deeply rewarded by these results.

"It was so simple. All I needed to do to bring Liam down was assist him! I've just been doing it wrong this whole time!"

Having realized why he'd failed in all his previous attempts, the Guide vowed to continue helping Liam in the future. He no longer had any doubts about his course of action.

"Liam, let me help you be happy—all so that you might suffer!"

What the Guide said seemed to make no sense, but the contradiction didn't faze him. He had proof now that when he lent Liam his support, things got worse for him.

"I'll help you with everything in my power! I swear, I'll make you happyyy!!!"

In House Banfield's domain, citizens who had been born there watched in confusion as protesters marched through the streets. The demonstrators preached democracy and freedom, but that didn't mean much to the people who had actually lived under the Empire's aristocracy.

"Those people came from a place called the Union, right?" one citizen said to another.

"They sure are full of energy..."

"Is democracy really that great?"

"I hear more and more people are joining them. Lots of young people are getting involved."

Some of the people watching the protest remembered how things had been many years ago. Unlike the younger citizens, they knew how bad things had been before Liam's rule and were therefore appalled by the display.

"Kids these days don't know what it used to be like. They don't know how good we have it now."

"It's been decades since the last protests, right? The last time, it was... Oh yeah! It was when we protested against Lord Liam in favor of the tornado hairstyle!"

"Yeah, right... I remember campaigning for that. Nobody has tornado hair anymore though."

"It was like a festival. I remember people had food stands set up and everything."

"Maybe these people feel like it's a festival too."

"That must be it! I get what they're doing now."

As Liam's subjects continued watching the protest, some youths who had immigrated from the Union approached a group of them.

"Do you all think the aristocracy should continue to exist?" one youth demanded.

The natives exchanged looks.

"Eh? I mean, why not?" a citizen replied.

The youths exploded with anger at the natives who casually accepted the nobility system. "What do you mean, 'why not'? Of course it shouldn't exist!"

The youths passionately raged against the nobility system. "Isn't it wrong for matters like taxes to be decided according to the whims of a single ruler? And for that ruler to be completely untouchable by the law? It's dangerous for one person to have all that power! That's why each person in this nation should have the right to vote, and we should pick our own representatives!"

"R-really?"

An older couple who had been listening reminisced about the past.

"Now that you mention it, things really were bad before the current lord took over," the husband said.

"They were," his wife agreed.

The youths only smiled when they heard this. "I bet they were! But if we carry on with the nobility system here, who knows when things will get that bad again!"

While the youths continued their impassioned speech, some of the younger citizens who were watching the protest came up to the couple and asked them about the past.

"My parents say it was hard when they were kids too. Was it really that bad?"

"It was worse than bad! Everyone has it easy now that Lord Liam is in power, but before him we were all destitute. Most houses didn't even have electricity."

"Oh, yeah... I heard that too."

"Thank goodness Lord Liam became our ruler. Hopefully nothing bad happens and the next lord carries on with Lord Liam's policies. Um, the next lord..."

The couple gasped when they realized something.

"Hey, does Lord Liam have an heir?"

"N-not that I've heard of."

That made the couple nervous, and the young people picked up on it.

"Wait, that's bad?"

"What would happen to us if Lord Liam were to die right now?"

Recalling past examples of such a situation, the older couple explained.

"In situations like that, the Empire will send a ruler or choose someone from the lord's family. F-from the lord's family..."

The couple looked at each other in dread, and the other people around them caught on to what they were thinking. Right now, Liam's only family consisted of his parents and grandparents—none of whom were upstanding nobles by any measure.

A buzz went through the group.

"Lord Liam's engaged to Lady Rosetta, right?"

"But there's no announcement that she's pregnant or anything, is there?"

"And the scary thing is, Lord Liam's the type to charge onto the frontlines of battle himself!"

His people's worries only grew. What would happen if Liam died on the battlefield? House Banfield had no heir right now, so the only ones who could take over for him were his parents, the ones who ruined the domain in the first place. Fearing that the hard times of the past might return, the citizens were suddenly very nervous about their future.

The passionate foreign protestors noticed the sudden change in the crowd's mood. "E-err...have you been listening to us?"

The natives glared at them.

"Can it! We're talking about something important right now!"

"Hey, maybe we should start protesting too," said one of the citizens.

"You're right! We shouldn't entrust our whole future to one person!"

"We should hurry. I'll get some of my buddies involved!"

"Me too!"

"Same here!"

When they noticed the natives talking about joining the protest, the youths preaching democracy walked away happy, believing that their rhetoric had managed to convert more people.

Thereafter, protests on a scale never seen before broke out across House Banfield's domain.

INTERLUDE:
Inspector Eila

EILA SERA BERMAN had gone to the underground of the Imperial Capital Planet, otherwise nicknamed "the trash heap." She strode through the sleazy area in an expensive suit while the residents of the underground cowered before her. In her black pantsuit, Eila looked like a capable working woman, even though an armband identified her as still being in training.

Normally these residents wouldn't give an inspecting official a second glance, but Eila was different. As her intimidating narrowed eyes swept over the vicinity, the residents couldn't meet her gaze.

Following behind Eila was Wallace Noah Albareto. He had long blue hair and also wore a suit, but somehow, he made it look sloppy.

"Eila, wait for me!"

She paid him no mind and continued striding forward briskly. "Walk faster, why don't you?"

Her alert eyes kept a lookout for any illegal goods being sold here. After the two of them had passed by, a pair of brawny local men whispered to each other.

"Are those two officials on patrol?"

"You don't know them? The woman's Berman. She's still in training, but her arrest rate's *way* higher than any of the guys on active duty."

"Sounds pretty crazy."

"They say once she sets her sights on you, there's no escape. What a terrifying woman!"

"I found you."

Deep in an alley in the underground, Eila came across a fortune teller with a grin.

The fortune teller trembled at the chilling smile on Eila's face. The besuited young woman had an air about her that was entirely different from the typical denizens of the underground. Immediately recognizing her as a noble, the fortune teller pulled some jewelry from within the sleeve of her deep blue robe.

"Miss Inspector, thank you for your hard work. This

is just a small token of my appreciation. I would be honored if you would accept it."

The fortune teller held out an ornament crafted from precious metals. The item would fetch a high price if sold, so the fortune teller offered it in the hopes that Eila would pass her by in her inspection.

Eila ignored the ornament, however. Instead, she picked up a small glass bottle of the drugs the fortune teller was selling and analyzed its contents using the bracelet screen on her left arm. The fortune teller grew desperate as she watched Eila silently performing her work.

"Wait, please! One of your fellow inspectors told me that if I paid an agreed-upon sum, you'd pass me by for inspection. Please leave me be!"

Eila still didn't stop her analysis, even when the fortune teller told her that her coworkers would have let her go. Instead, she grew even more determined when she identified the components of the drug the woman was selling.

"So *you're* the one selling these illegal drugs down here. You're a criminal, peddling these substances without permission. I'm taking you in."

"I-I'll pay! I'll give you something worth even more, so please, let me go!"

The fortune teller took a bar of mithril out from her sleeve, but Eila wouldn't budge.

"I'm seizing all the money you've made too. I'm not about to let anyone get away with anything illegal!"

The fortune teller finally gave up, sinking to her knees. She covered her face with her hands and cried. "But I pay my dues every month..."

As Eila made some notes on her bracelet screen, she told the woman coldly, "I'll be investigating that too. You'll get a lighter sentence if you tell us everything, so I hope you're honest."

The fortune teller looked as if she had given up on everything.

When Eila returned to her workplace, her superior ran up to her looking rather nervous.

"I heard you arrested another one, Miss Berman. So every day, you're going into the underground to round up people dealing illegal drugs, are you? Your enthusiasm really impresses me."

"Thank you, sir."

Eila paid her superior no mind, returning to her desk to write up her report. Her superior remained by her side, however, and spoke to Eila while wringing his hands.

"Everyone sees how hard you're working. With all these arrests to your credit, you might even receive a special award from the palace."

"I have no interest in something like that," Eila said as she speedily compiled her report.

Her superior turned instead to Wallace. "I don't think it's good to work too hard, though... You should take a page out of Wallace's book and relax once in a while."

Eila paused and glanced over at Wallace, who was napping with his head down on his desk. That man should have been sent to the boonies with Liam, but for some reason, he ended up at the same place Eila had specifically requested.

She ignored Wallace and went back to her documents. "I think Wallace should work a little harder."

"Y-yes, I suppose you're right." Her superior smiled awkwardly.

Eila finished writing her report, then sat back and sighed. "Is there something you want to tell me, sir?"

With Eila's sharp gaze fixed on him, her superior hesitated. "W-well, it's just that some people think you're going a little too far. It's true that controlling the underground is our duty, but we can't go overboard...

The people who use this job to make a little extra money on the side don't like what you're doing."

Eila cursed at him internally. *Kurt only went astray because you inspectors let so many criminals run free! All of his torment could have been avoided if you people actually did your jobs!*

Eila wasn't working so diligently simply out of a sense of integrity. What she really wanted to crack down on was the sex change drug that was turning her friend Kurt into a woman, if only temporarily. Eila couldn't accept the idea of Kurt becoming a woman, so she was desperate to stop him any way she could. It might look like she was devoted to her job, but everything she did was for her own self-interest.

That fortune teller who sold Kurt the drug doesn't understand anything! Their relationship is so wonderful because they're both boys! If one of them becomes a girl, it's not the same! I can't let her get away with this!!!

Kurt had temporarily become a girl and approached Liam without the Count realizing the truth. When Eila found that out, it upset her so much that she chose this particular office for her training.

I'll clean the underground up good to protect LiaKur, using any means I have to. And the first step will be taking down these dirty officials.

During a break, Eila yanked Wallace outside and forced him into a strategy meeting. "Wallace, I plan on reforming this whole office."

"Why?"

The two sat across from each other at a round table on a café terrace. Eila was drinking coffee while Wallace ate a parfait. When Eila told him she wanted to reform their office, Wallace cocked his head in confusion.

"We're only going to be here for our training. It's stupid to take it so seriously." Wallace took a bite of his parfait.

Eila watched him coldly. "The people who are supposed to be doing inspections can't be taking bribes and letting people go free. We're in charge of the underground, and I'm going to make it squeaky clean. To do that, I have to clean up our office first."

Wallace seemed to understand what she was saying. "You want to get rid of corruption? You're just like Liam, you know? He cleaned up his rural office too. They fired all the nobles there."

It was true: Liam had booted out all the corrupt nobles at his office out in the sticks. He had performed a thorough investigation and saw that everyone involved in the corruption was fired.

Wallace's reaction upon hearing this news had been to sigh. *"Again?"*

"That's just like Liam." Eila nodded her head, impressed, but Wallace felt differently.

"How does it benefit my patron to reform a tiny little region so far from the Capital Planet? Liam is just too serious."

Eila asked, "So what happened there, exactly?"

"Well, all the corrupt officials are gone, and the whole region's grateful to Liam. The prime minister himself is happy."

Even in his training period, Liam was doing a fantastic job cleaning up the backwater region where he was assigned.

Wallace continued, "Though...I hear the HR people who suddenly had to send new workers there resent Liam for it."

Simply firing the corrupt officials wasn't the end of things. New personnel had to be brought there so things could get back to normal. For the time being, Liam was using people from House Banfield to get the work done.

"What's the issue in rooting out corruption?" Eila said. "I think we should take the opportunity to do the same thing."

"What do you mean, 'the opportunity'? Liam's busy

enough right now! What is he doing giving himself extra work at a time like this?"

As Wallace picked at his parfait, Eila told him, "I want you to help me out, Wallace. You're a former prince, so you have to have *some* contacts in the palace, don't you?"

"I don't like the way you said that."

"Can you get in touch with Prince Cleo?"

"It'd be hard for me. I could probably contact his sister Lysithea, but..." Wallace trailed off and grimaced. "You're not serious, are you?"

Eila smiled. "Let's get started doing a little cleanup of our own."

"Whaaat?!"

A few weeks later, soldiers were dispatched to the underground to make mass arrests.

"Don't let any of them get away!"

Leading the soldiers in her severe black suit, Eila made sure that every single person dealing in illegal goods was arrested. In the process, she arrested anyone else breaking the law in the underground as well.

One of the civilians working under Eila asked, "Umm... Section Chief?"

"Yes?"

"Was there really a need to get the military involved? Don't you think we're going a little too far?"

Eila glared at the man. "Tell me, what is our job?"

"Overseeing the underground, ma'am!" the man answered, standing up straight.

Eila put her hands on her hips and nodded. "That's right. If people don't take us seriously, it'll only make it harder to do that job. We need the people of the underground to be intimidated by us. Is that understood?"

"Y-yes, ma'am!"

While her subordinate trembled in fear, one of the soldiers—part of a ground force borrowed from House Banfield—approached her.

"Lady Eila, we've finished investigating this building. It's just—"

Before he could finish his report, a firefight broke out inside of it. The soldiers had apparently stormed a building where a number of underground criminals had banded together to make a stand.

Eila nodded curtly and gave the soldier his orders. "Everything's going as planned. We've got them cornered now. You're all wearing powered suits, so don't be afraid to hold back, all right? Arrest anyone who resists."

A group of underground punks were no match for a fully armed ground force.

"They claim to have connections to nobility," the soldier went on to inform Eila.

Do they, now? Eila didn't know if that was true, but she didn't care either way. "Just capture them now and we'll question them about that later."

The soldier seemed pleased by Eila's tough response. "You sound just like a friend of Lord Liam's. We'll round them all up, don't worry."

The soldier returned to his team, and Eila looked around her at the chaos. The underground had developed in a completely different way from the Capital Planet's surface, so it had been easy for things to fly under the radar here. She wondered if she could repurpose a place like this into a paradise for her and other like-minded people.

This dump interfered with LiaKur, so I'll purify it and make use of it for better purposes. I'll make the underground a place where wholesome lady deviants like me and my comrades can thrive!

Eila was formulating a plan to cleanse the underground of its illegal drug trade and turn it into an environment where people could participate in her *own* hobby instead.

I'M THE **EVIL LORD** OF AN **INTERGALACTIC EMPIRE**

3 Trouble

THE MEETING ROOM where Calvin's faction gathered was fan-shaped and multi-leveled. Many of its seats were filled, and enlarged holographic documents were displayed at the front of the auditorium-like room.

The current topic of discussion was the protests occurring within House Banfield's domain. Calvin's faction received detailed reports from the spies they sent to incite the protests. Their discussion was based on information collected from these spies, and they even had a line of communication open with one of their operatives during the meeting.

The video call showed a large-scale protest underway behind the spy. It was a pleasing sight for the nobles of Calvin's faction, but the spy himself didn't look too happy about it. In fact, he appeared rather nervous.

"The democratic movement has grown far beyond our original plans, so in that sense, we've succeeded. However, the movement's too big for us to control now."

Their plan to nudge the Union immigrants into staging protests that would disrupt the functionality of Liam's domain proved so successful that the nobles gathered for the meeting were surprised by the spy's news.

Calvin couldn't hide his own astonishment. "This is a lot more than I was expecting. Frankly, I didn't think there could *ever* be protests of this size in Liam's domain."

No one would have expected the democratic movement to grow so large in Liam's domain, which was generally considered to have a very well-liked government.

The astonished nobles all exchanged looks with each other.

"The citizens really didn't need much to inspire them, did they?"

"It disgusts me how arrogant and demanding these spoiled people are."

"Well, surely this will teach that brat Liam his lesson."

Considering the results, their plan had been a resounding success. Calvin complimented the spy. "Good work. Looks like there's no need for us to interfere any longer. Just monitor the situation from now on and report to us if there's any change."

"Yes, Your Highness!"

Calvin cut the call and stood before his faction, smiling. With these huge protests occurring in Liam's territory, there was more than enough justification for them to criticize Liam freely. At this point, their objective had been more than met.

"Liam's ability to rule will now come into question. We could easily condemn him, but there's still his military might to consider. What should we do?"

They could openly call attention to the fact that Liam wasn't ruling his territory properly, but war with the United Kingdom was still on the horizon. Calvin's faction needed Liam to exhaust the United Kingdom's forces, so they were unsure when it would be appropriate to condemn him for the protests in his domain.

One of the nobles of Calvin's faction spoke up. "We should wait until his forces either lose or narrowly win against the United Kingdom. As it is now, Liam's forces shouldn't be underestimated."

"It's not as if we couldn't take them down in the long run," said another noble, "but it's dangerous to fight them on equal footing. Liam himself is a skilled enough fighter to have defeated a Swordmaster. In fact, we should probably increase the crown prince's guard. Better safe than sorry."

"Could we make use of the Swordmasters of the two major styles?"

The nobles knew it would be foolish to take Liam on in a fair fight, so it was best to avoid direct conflict with House Banfield. After all, Liam had taken down the infamous pirate nobles all on his own. He had a habit of coming out victorious against incredible odds, so the nobles of Calvin's faction were rightly wary of him. In order to defeat Liam, they knew they'd have to let the United Kingdom deplete his forces first. In the event that he returned from that fight alive, they could then use the protests in his domain to defame him. And in the event that Liam turned to violence against Calvin in retaliation, it was best to increase Calvin's personal security.

Calvin already had his assassins and spies, but Liam still frightened him. By sheer brute strength, Liam had defeated a man who had reached the rank of Swordmaster in a fair fight. Mulling over the subject of his personal safety, Calvin decided to gather as many top sword-fighters as he could.

"Summon the top swordsmen of the Ahlen style and the Kurdan mixed fighting style. I'll put some skilled guards on the two Swordmasters as well. All of you should make sure to keep yourselves guarded as well."

Part of Calvin's success was that he didn't forget to look out for the other nobles in his faction.

The two styles he had mentioned were the Empire's major close quarters combat styles. The Ahlen style emphasized swordfighting, and the Kurdan mixed style made use of a variety of weapons. Most of the knights in the Empire were trained in one or the other. When an individual became the top fighter in either of these two styles, they were awarded the title of Swordmaster.

However, there was a political component to the title as well, which made the designation Swordmaster less than perfectly accurate. After all, there might be a problem controlling powerful fighters who reached the status of Swordmaster on their swordplay alone. Fighters who were strong but untrustworthy couldn't be given the important jobs that Swordmasters needed to take on. The practice of giving the title to the top fighters of the two official styles was a way to keep the reputation of the Swordmasters clean. If a Swordmaster should misbehave, it would call into question the authority of the Empire that gave them that title. For that reason, it was best that the two styles appointed trustworthy people for the position. Of course, the most powerful fighters of the Empire's two major styles still had to possess the skills to back up their positions. They also needed to be good leaders with master swordsmen under them as apprentices.

"Explain the situation to the two Swordmasters," Calvin instructed his people. "Make sure they know that if they ignore the rising style known as the Way of the Flash, their positions might be in danger down the line."

If the Way of the Flash caught on, it could replace one of the two major styles, displacing a current Swordmaster from their position. Calvin knew that if he made the masters of the two styles concerned about their futures, they wouldn't be able to ignore the Way of the Flash. He was sure that once he made them properly concerned, the leaders of the two major styles would give everything they had to crush the Way of the Flash before it gained any more notoriety. Damaging the emerging fighting style's reputation would diminish Liam's reputation as well.

Calvin planned on cornering Liam in every way he could, and this latest idea proved well-advised. As soon as the Swordmasters of the Empire's two official sword styles were advised about the Way of the Flash, they acted right away.

Soon, the mass media was reporting on the new sword style known as the Way of the Flash in such a way that it reached even neighboring nations.

On one channel, a guest explained that he was the very person who had introduced Yasushi to Liam. Originally, this man had been chosen to teach young Liam martial arts, but back then, House Banfield's reputation had been poor, so he had declined the position himself and volunteered Yasushi.

"Yasushi's a third-rate swordsman at best," the man said to the interviewer. *"He's barely better than an amateur— more like a street performer than an actual fighter. That's actually how he used to make his money."*

"What's the true nature of the Way of the Flash, then?" the newscaster asked.

"I'd say it's made-up party tricks. In the first place, it's impossible to strike someone without drawing your sword. It's obviously some sort of sleight of hand."

On another channel, an analyst gave commentary on the Way of the Flash. It wasn't clear how he got his information, but he was discussing the sword style's basic moves. It was the analyst's claim that Yasushi simply copied the moves of other sword styles to create his so-called original style.

"This move, supposedly original to the *Way of the Flash*, is just a technique from the Kurdan style. And this one here is from the Ahlen style. Basically, it's all just cobbled together from other styles."

"Meaning?" asked his interviewer.

"Meaning that the *Way of the Flash* is just an imitation of others. There's no basis for its claim of being a unique style."

Every program that discussed the Way of the Flash lambasted it—and glued to his screen, watching these programs, was Yasushi. The programs relentlessly disparaged him and his Way of the Flash.

The man himself was thrilled. "Good...good! More! Say more! Prove to everyone that the Way of the Flash is totally fake!"

People had started calling Yasushi a Sword God due to all the lies he'd told Liam, but Yasushi had made up the Way of the Flash entirely. He was indeed only a third-rate swordsman who couldn't perform an actual move like the so-called "Flash." Yet because of his association with Liam, he had been harassed by his reputation of being a Sword God.

Yasushi was elated at the thought of finally being freed from the deceptions he himself had perpetrated and began crying with relief. "Finally! The weight will finally be lifted!"

The sword school born of his lies would disappear from this world, and with its extinction, he'd be released from everything that troubled him.

Elsewhere, in a cheap eatery, two people sat slurping noodles. On the restaurant's mounted wall screens, the pair listened to a special news program titled *The Way of the Flash—Exposed!* Programs of that nature seemed to be airing everywhere lately.

"*The Way of the Flash, which has been the subject of much discussion lately, has recently been exposed as a complete sham,*" said one commentator.

"*It has. If what the Count said was true, then it makes no sense that such an amazing style would have been unknown all this time. It's lies, all lies.*"

All the other diners listened excitedly to the discussion. Apparently, they had their doubts about this so-called Way of the Flash and enjoyed seeing it torn down.

"Yeah, all the nobles want to do is show off," a customer said.

"The Way of the Flash is totally fake," another added.

"Only the Ahlen style and the Kurdan mixed style are the real thing. They're the best."

On the program, the commentators began speaking with some instructors of the two major styles, who also strongly disparaged the Way of the Flash. They claimed the style didn't truly exist, and that there must be some trick to the supposed "Flash" move.

The quiet pair finished their noodles, left some money, and exited the eatery. They wore sandogasa straw hats low over their faces and Japanese-style clothing. Swords sat at their hips in their scabbards. Once outside the eatery, the two stopped to chat.

"Which one do you want?" one of them asked the other, though the other seemed disinterested in the question. While they didn't show it in their words or attitude, the two of them were actually quite angry.

"I don't care. I could take either of them."

"You're right about that."

The two parted ways at the eatery and walked off in separate directions.

I'll kill them.

Each time I watched one of those news exposés, I felt as if I was being boiled alive. Loads of people associated with the two major sword styles—including the strongest of both, who each held the title of Swordmaster—mocked the Way of the Flash day in and day out. They called it phony, nonsense, nothing but copied moves. I swore to cut down each and every one of them someday, but right now, the timing was just too bad for me to do anything but suffer the humiliation.

As I fumed with rage, Ellen stepped before me.

"Master..."

Seeing my anxious apprentice there, I couldn't help taking out my frustration on her. "What? Do you doubt the Way of the Flash too?" I asked, acting completely immaturely.

Ellen shook her head emphatically, then looked me straight in the eye. "I believe in your sword, Master! I don't understand all this complicated stuff, but I know that your sword is real. To me, you're the best swordsman in the universe, Master!"

When I saw my apprentice looking up at me with tears in her eyes, I felt as though my heart was being squeezed in a vice. I was embarrassed to have a child comfort me, but at the same time it felt as if I could see Yasushi standing behind Ellen.

I knew I was just imagining it, but it seemed like my master was smiling and reassuring me.

"Lord Liam, when you are in turmoil, you must reflect

on yourself. Though your heart may burn hot, keep your head cool. You mustn't forget what's truly important."

After all, Master Yasushi said such things to me when I was young and practicing the Way of the Flash every day.

I shook my head and covered my face with one hand, chuckling. Since gaining an apprentice, she'd repeatedly helped me see what was really important. Even though I was now training a successor, I was humbled and reminded that I was nowhere near Master Yasushi's level. I was still immature as a teacher.

"You're right," I told Ellen. "There were no lies in Master's sword. What I saw with my own eyes was the truth, and the truth won't change no matter what anyone says about it."

I thought back to what I saw that first day. Master Yasushi's Flash was the real deal. I knew that for a fact, didn't I? I felt stupid for letting other people's words get to me.

"Master?" Ellen looked up at me uneasily. She was confused.

"There's something I need to deal with right now," I said to her. "I can leave crushing the other styles for later."

The more pressing matter I needed to address was those protests in my domain. The problem was, Prince Cleo had been dragged into a war between two intergalactic nations at the same time. Since I had to use my own army to assist him in the war, I wasn't even sure if I could maintain order in my own territory. I needed more people. I had an overwhelming labor shortage on my hands, and taking in refugees hadn't solved it.

"Ellen, when you're feeling frustrated...train. Work up a sweat, and—"

Ellen smiled at my words, but I was cut off by an emergency transmission notification. I opened the call and saw it was from Brian, who was minding my territory for me while I was away.

"T-terrible news, Master Liam!!!"

In House Banfield's mansion, Brian had broken out in a cold sweat.

"I can't believe the protests have spread all the way *here*!"

He had just called Liam to report that the protests had progressed so far that the entire domain was about to be plunged into chaos. At the moment, House Banfield was just barely holding things together. It seemed that if they took a single misstep, they ran the risk of completely losing control of the populace, and then chaos would reign.

Serena, the head maid, came to Brian just then with another bomb. "Brian, I have here a petition crafted by the mansion's staff. Over eighty percent of the staff have signed it."

"Nooooo!!!" Brian cried, shaking his head wildly. He gripped his stomach, feeling as if he were being physically crushed by the extreme situation they found themselves in. "O-over eighty percent?!"

"You can't overlook daily inconveniences. It seems like they've gotten caught up in the energy of the protests and are taking the opportunity to make demands."

Even the servants who worked in Liam's own mansion worked themselves up enough that they created a petition. Just the thought of the protests infiltrating the very heart of House Banfield worsened Brian's stomach pain.

"I-I only just told Master Liam about the situation! *Why?* Why do things like these keep happening?"

Brian fell to his knees.

The Guide was skipping with glee, even humming a little tune.

"Mhm-hm-hm. I didn't think it would have such a potent effect!"

Not only was Liam's domain on the verge of anarchy, but people were trashing the Way of the Flash left and right. Liam was furious about it. Things were only getting worse for House Banfield, and the Guide was so thrilled that he could hardly contain himself. The delight he felt was all the more intense due to the decades of suffering he had to endure up until this point. Right now, the Guide was experiencing the most joy he'd felt in his entire existence.

"For some reason, whenever I *help* Liam, it hurts him. It's amazing! It's perfect that my interference is indirect too. This is exactly the way I like to do things."

Due to the influence of the Guide's powers, waves of immigrants had flooded into House Banfield's domain. It seemed like great news for House Banfield at first since they needed labor and had plenty of developed territory to fill, but the immigrants brought plenty of problems with them too. In the end, Liam's good luck had turned into bad luck.

It delighted the Guide to be able to affect events indirectly and watch his target suffer from afar. He was the lowest of the low, but this was why he was missing something crucial.

"I'll keep giving Liam all the help I can! Oh no, my support's not over with yet—and that means Liam's troubles aren't over either!"

◆ ◇ ◆

There were traitors all around me.

"I never imagined the servants in my own mansion would betray me."

My servants were elite workers, handpicked from my domain. They were selected not just for their abilities, but for their loyalty as well. And yet they still betrayed me. Of all things, they came to me with a *petition*. It was just so unthinkable that I refused to read it.

Comforting me in my irritated state was a worried Rosetta. "Calm down, Darling."

"Oh, I'm calm. I'm calmer than I've ever been. In fact, I'm excited thinking about all the ways I'll punish everyone who's betrayed me once I get back to my domain."

I should start coming up with torture methods. I'll let them all know what happens when they underestimate an evil lord like me.

I must have been wearing one hell of an evil expression, because Rosetta gave me a sad look. "Darling..."

I averted my eyes from Rosetta and spoke directly to Ciel, who stood beside me. "Have you heard anything from Baron Exner, Ciel?"

Ciel's reply seemed emotionless, but I sensed the hostility she directed toward me. She was trying to hide it, but her feelings regarding me were written all over her face. It was clear she hated me.

"Both my father and brother told me to support you as much as I can through all this, my lord," she said stiffly. "My brother seems to be particularly worried. He contacts me every day...and *every day*, he asks about you."

She emphasized the words "every day" very clearly. She must be feeling frustrated about her brother's devotion to me as a friend, but she still managed to keep herself outwardly composed.

This is quite interesting. I like her. I was intrigued that Ciel was by my side not because she liked me, but because she was obligated to be.

"I'm sure Kurt's busy fulfilling his military service. Maybe I'll contact him later. Right now, is there anything you need?" I asked her this in a gentle tone, but Ciel's stony expression didn't change. She wouldn't yield to any kindness from me.

"No, nothing. Everyone here treats me very well. I'm thankful to be learning so much."

From this exchange, you might think I was looking out for Ciel—showing concern for a young noble girl training away from home with House Banfield. Ciel and I didn't have a genial relationship though, and she didn't hide her animosity toward me. Rather, it was that she *couldn't* hide it, at least not from me.

Her father Baron Exner was a fellow evil lord, but she herself had to be a fluke, raised to be pure and upstanding, unlike the rest of her family. It must be frustrating for her that she didn't have the ability to take down an evil lord like me. She had no personal fighting ability, and she didn't have the brains to outwit me either, so there was nothing she could do against me. What all this amounted to was that she was nothing more than a fun toy for me.

She wasn't a pushover like Rosetta, but a girl with a *true* steel will. She certainly couldn't be swayed by a few kind words. She was a fun girl who openly showed her disgust for me whenever I talked to her. The only problem was that she was Baron Exner's daughter, and I couldn't be too cruel to Kurt's sister. I wanted to tease her, but I'd have to strike a good balance so I didn't go too hard on her.

"That's good to hear," I told her. "It's been so hectic lately that I worried your training was being affected."

"You needn't worry about that. As I said, I'm learning a lot every day."

"If you need anything, don't hesitate to let me know. I'll always make time for you."

"Thank you very much..."

Rosetta then injected herself into our conversation. "Don't worry, Darling, I'll keep a close eye on Ciel!"

In her enthusiasm, Rosetta thrust out her chest so fast it jiggled a little. *Have a little more modesty, would you?* It was amusing how Ciel gave Rosetta's bosom a jealous look and then glanced down bitterly at her own chest, but since Rosetta interrupted my fun, I was cold toward her.

"You will, will you?" *Read the room, Rosetta! Don't get in the way of me teasing Ciel. Well, I guess I should leave her alone for now.*

In any case, if there were traitors even within my own mansion, there were sure to be more of them spreading through my domain. It didn't take a genius to realize that Calvin's faction would use this chance to sabotage me. I was sure they were up to all sorts of mischief in my domain at that very moment. I realized I should probably assume that anyone who might even dream of betraying me was already a traitor.

Dammit! Can't the Guide help me out this time? If he can't, that means I need to get through this all on my own... Hmm?

I stopped there for a moment and realized that there was a way for me to get out of this situation *and* emerge victorious in the end.

"Oh? Maybe this situation isn't as bad as I thought..."

4 Conceit

BACK AT MY WORKPLACE out in the sticks, I considered my future course of action. The office I used now once belonged to my incompetent superior's superior. Officially, I was still only a trainee, but since I'd cleaned out the upper management here, I took their place regardless. Some of the others here weren't too happy about that, but most of them accepted me and went about their work as usual.

What's this training supposed to be good for anyway? Well, I'm not gonna be here long, so I guess I don't have to think about it too much.

In any case, due to my thorough cleaning, my workplace was very comfortable now. All of my troublesome superiors and the evildoers connected to them locally had been taken care of, so my work-related problems had been solved. There had been some noisy resistance from the officials who'd benefitted in some way from my old superiors and their corrupt network of people in town, but of course when I said I'd take them on if they had any complaints, they all shut up pretty fast. I'd done a thorough investigation of everyone connected to my old superiors, and if even the slightest bit of embezzlement was found, I'd used that to have them fired. As a result, no one here got in my way anymore.

With fifteen minutes left before it was time to leave work for the day, I sat mulling over the objectives before me:

First of all, I had to be victorious in this war between intergalactic nations.

Second, I needed to quell the chaos in my realm.

Third, I had to crush everyone who ridiculed the Way of the Flash.

The first and second were absolutely necessary and time sensitive. The third I could take my time with, so I'd hold off there for now. To be honest, in my anger, I wanted to handle the third problem as soon as possible, but nothing could shake my knowledge that the Way of the Flash was the strongest sword style around. Besides, the war wouldn't wait for me.

Conflicts between intergalactic nations were such a big deal that it took a lot of time to even prepare for them.

It would be a while before we could get moving, so first we had to decide *how* to move.

"Now, who should I deploy where?"

I had to decide not only who to deploy, but who to leave behind on the Capital Planet. Due to the political strife with Calvin, I couldn't send out my entire force.

"The Capital Planet will be a real concern for me."

I didn't know what Calvin would get up to if I left the Capital Planet completely undefended, so I wouldn't be able to fight to my heart's content without leaving some trusted forces here. While I weighed my options, Kukuri materialized from the shadows.

"Do you have a moment, Master Liam?"

"What is it?" I asked.

"Terrorist attacks have been occurring on the Capital Planet lately."

"That's not unusual here."

"These acts are suspicious, however. The perpetrators claim a variety of motives, but the attacks are consistently too well-executed. The Empire isn't investigating them seriously either."

Terrorist attacks that the Empire wasn't taking seriously? *That* set off alarm bells for me. The group of assassins we went up against recently had apparently disguised themselves as terrorists. If Kukuri was bringing this up, we must be their true target, and if they managed to kill us, Calvin's faction could simply claim we were victims of a terrorist attack. It was a sneaky way to do things, but I considered taking some pointers from this prince.

"Can you guys look into it?"

"We can do our best, but we're spread thin."

"We'll leave it alone, then—I have something else I want you to handle. I want you to root out everyone important who's betrayed me. Don't do anything to them, though. I plan to make use of them later."

"Very well. Traitors... That count in the United Kingdom is suspicious, but it will take time to dispatch people there. We already have some people in the Union, however."

Kukuri's men had snuck into the Union the last time we interacted with them. His people really worked hard.

"Count Pershing? I expected him to betray me, so that's fine. You don't need to go do anything there."

"Shall we take care of him?" Kukuri asked.

"Sure, if you have the time, but he's not an immediate problem."

From what Thomas had told me about Count Pershing, I knew the man would betray me sooner or later. As a fellow evildoer, I wanted to get along with him, but I couldn't blame him if he betrayed me after seeing my situation. If our positions were reversed, I would have betrayed him too.

"Just be careful of any information coming from Count Pershing—and make sure the only info he gets from us is fake."

"We did learn that Count Pershing will be fighting in the war."

According to Thomas, Pershing didn't seem the type to make a name for himself on the battlefield. I wondered what that was about.

"Well, take care of him if you have the chance, but covering the Capital Planet is the bigger issue right now," I said.

Our enemies wouldn't have gone to the trouble of creating a mock terrorist organization if they didn't plan to throw it at us. When I considered the possibility of them sending assassins who could rival Kukuri and his men, I didn't really feel comfortable leaving *anyone* behind.

I wanted both Tia and Marie to lead on the battlefield. I could conceivably leave one of them here, but I didn't like my odds in battle if I did. Chengsi...well, she seemed best suited for combat as well. I would leave Kukuri behind on the Capital Planet, of course, but I wanted at least *one* more person I could rely on there.

Wait a second... I was thinking about this with the assumption that *I'd* be going into battle. Maybe that approach was wrong. There wasn't really a reason for me to go out and fight personally, was there? I reconsidered the deployment of my personnel under the new assumption that I'd remain on the Capital Planet.

"We'll make this work, Kukuri," I said, and told him what I had in mind.

"Yes, sir."

Claus was panicking. Oh, on the outside he appeared perfectly calm, but inwardly he was shouting to himself, *You've gotta be kidding meee!!!*

All of House Banfield's major players were gathered in a meeting room in the high-class hotel where they resided while here on the Capital Planet. Since Claus was Liam's personal guard, it was only natural that he be present, but he couldn't help but become nearly hysterical inside when he heard the plans Liam put forth regarding personnel assignments. In fact, everyone in attendance was confused.

Liam sat up front in his chair, looking perfectly satisfied with his decisions that baffled everyone else in the room.

What did he say that created such confusion?

"I've decided to put Claus in charge of Prince Cleo's forces."

Liam had always been the type to speak and act in ways that were difficult for some to comprehend, but this time, every single person in the room was stunned. He had appointed Claus, a man with no real distinguished accomplishments, as the supreme commander of a fleet of millions. Of course, Prince Cleo would be the *official* supreme commander, but he couldn't be expected to actually lead. After all, this would be Cleo's first battle, and he needed an acting commander to stand in for him.

Liam had picked Claus for that role, but the man himself spoke up to protest this decision, while still maintaining his outward composure. "Lord Liam, I have no experience commanding a fleet of millions of ships. With all due respect, I cannot serve in this role. You should choose someone else for the position."

"It isn't a problem," Liam replied, immediately rejecting Claus's suggestion.

How is it not a problem? To Claus, it was nothing *but* a problem. The supreme commander in this war would be commanding not just the Empire's regular army, but all the ships provided by participating nobles as well. House Banfield was personally contributing 60,000 ships to the fight. Well, at the very least, Claus's appointment as the top commander was proof that Liam trusted him that much.

When Liam announced his decision, Claus was pierced by the sharp, envious glares from Tia and Marie. The two of them were so strong as knights that they occupied the two highest positions in that role...but they were also problem children.

"Isn't that *wonderful* for you, Sir Claus?" Marie said, her face twitching.

Tia was also smiling, though the sentiment didn't reach her eyes. "I'd happily take your place if the burden is *too great* for you."

Claus's stomach began to hurt from their stares. *Gaaah! I can't take them glaring at me like this!!!* In terms of his individual strength and abilities as a knight, Claus didn't measure up to Tia or Marie in the slightest.

While Claus endured their resentful stares, Liam noticed this and his mood soured. He sent a sharp look of his own at Tia and Marie. "Do you have a complaint about my assignments?"

Tia and Marie immediately fell to their knees and apologized, trembling before Liam.

"O-of course not!" Tia exclaimed. "I will gladly follow your every order, Lord Liam!"

Marie had something else to say, however. She had more of a problem with Claus's abilities than with Liam's commands. "I would never complain about your orders, Lord Liam, but do you really think Sir Claus is suitable for this job? He said himself that he has no experience commanding a fleet of this size."

There were only two people in House Banfield with the experience of fighting in a war where millions clashed with millions: Tia and Marie. In her time as the so-called Princess Knight, Tia had lent her skills to another nation, fighting in a war of that scope. And two thousand years ago, when Marie was known as one of the Three Knights, she had fought in several such conflicts, commanding a large part of the Empire's forces. She had been a supreme commander herself three times, beating out Tia in terms of experience in the position.

The two of them had far more experience than Claus, and Claus himself knew that more than anyone.

"The position is simply too large a burden for me," Claus spoke up. "I again beg you to reconsider, Lord Liam."

Liam had no intention of changing his mind. "I'm certain you can do it. I'm putting Tia under your command, so feel free to put her to work. And you, Chengsi..."

Everyone's attention shifted to the woman leaning against a wall who had been playing with one of her pigtails this whole time, showing zero interest in the proceedings. As someone who had made a serious attempt to kill Liam, people considered the beautiful knight dangerously insane. Even so, Liam had forgiven her, and she was still in service to House Banfield.

When Liam called her name, Chengsi cocked her head expressionlessly. "Yes?"

With Chengsi's doll-like appearance, the gesture was almost inhuman. Tia and Marie didn't hide the hostility they directed her way.

Liam showed no sign of being bothered by Chengsi's creepiness. "You're the strongest fighter here, so I'm putting you under Claus too. You'll serve as Prince Cleo's personal guard."

Chengsi's expression didn't change as she received Liam's orders, but she did say more this time. "You trust me to do that?"

Liam threw her some bait to help motivate her. "Do the job I've assigned you, and I promise to play with you again."

The woman visibly shivered, her cheeks flushing. Now she was filled with life, no longer seeming like a blank doll. It was as if Chengsi was a different person than she had been only seconds ago.

That was when Claus realized something. *Wait, Lord Liam! You're forcing* two *problem children on me?!*

While Claus experienced more internal panic, Marie raised her hand timidly. Her name hadn't been called yet, and she had a forlorn look on her face, as if she was worried that Liam had forgotten her.

"What about me, Lord Liam?"

To dispel her worries, Liam replied, "You'll be hunting pirates with a fleet of 3,000 ships. I can't give you many forces, but the ones you have will be elites. I leave defense of my domain to you, so keep it safe, all right?"

"Y-yes, my lord!"

Since Liam himself would remain on the Capital Planet during the war, leaving the defense of his domain to Marie while he was away was a sign of his trust in her.

"Lord Liam, how many troops do you intend to station at the Capital Planet?" Claus asked.

"I believe 3,000 ships should be enough."

When Tia heard that number, it was her turn to panic. "That's not enough, Lord Liam! Calvin's faction won't overlook this opportunity! You should leave at least 10,000 ships behind!"

Liam seemed confident, unconcerned by Tia's worries. "All you guys need to focus on is winning. Meanwhile, I'll kick back on the Capital Planet and watch."

He spoke as if he'd only be taking it easy, but everyone knew the Capital Plant was just as likely to turn into a battlefield itself. Leaving him virtually alone there while the vast majority of his fighting forces were elsewhere seemed just too dangerous. Even if Liam was setting up the situation as bait for Calvin's faction, the threat seemed too great.

"B-but..." Tia persisted, still not convinced.

"Enough!"

"A-ah! I apologize, my lord."

No one would dare talk back to Liam once he shouted, so it was clear that they had all just better do as he said.

Considering the matter settled, Liam shifted to a new topic. "Anyway, what's Eulisia up to? I have work for her too."

Claus cocked his head when Liam asked after her, since she wasn't present at the meeting. "Err, I believe Lady Rosetta said something about having Lady Eulisia return to the military. Something about her recent conduct..."

Liam's eyebrows shot up at that. "At a time like this? Hurry up and call her back! My domain's a mess right now and I've got work for her to do!"

Had Liam actually forgotten about Eulisia until this very moment? Claus doubted his master for a moment before realizing that Liam didn't even see Eulisia as a woman.

I suppose she'll never find her way into Lord Liam's bed. Hmm...the problem of his successor remains.

As soon as I left the meeting room, I headed for a dressing room to meet up with Patrice of the Newlands Company. Patrice was one of my personal merchants, part of the large merchant house's upper management. She was a voluptuous woman with dark skin, and today she wore a suit that exposed her cleavage. Right now, she was having Rosetta try on dresses that she'd brought.

"That looks amazing on you, Lady Rosetta," Patrice was saying. As soon as Rosetta tried on a dress, Patrice complimented her and recommended another.

"Wh-what am I going to do with this many dresses?" Rosetta said. "This is the thirtieth one!" She was starting to look a little tired after trying on so many.

"They're for parties," Patrice replied simply.

"Parties? This many dresses should last me for decades of parties." Rosetta smiled awkwardly at the huge pile of dresses she tried on.

Patrice corrected her misunderstanding. "Well...you won't be wearing any of the dresses more than once, so I believe these will only last you a month or so."

"Huh? Oh, are they all reasonably priced then? I see—they're disposable. Phew... I thought they might be expensive."

Patrice explained further. "This would be the general price, yes." She held out her tablet and the average price per dress was displayed as a hologram above it.

Rosetta's eyes bulged when she saw the number. "Th-that's a lot! Well, I suppose thirty dresses *would* cost this much..."

"Oh, that's just for one dress."

"Huh?" Rosetta gaped in surprise. Beside her, her personal maid Ciel was equally stunned.

Ciel would also be attending the parties, so there were dresses for her as well. There were fewer than those for Rosetta, but still a decent number. I figured the overly serious Ciel probably wouldn't want to attend parties in expensive dresses, but to me, it was a necessity.

I like parties, and wasteful spending is what being an evil lord is all about!

I planned on holding parties almost every day here on the Capital Planet while my troops went out and fought. Naturally, I expected my enemies to make a move during this time, but it wasn't my style to sneak around and nervously look for them. I figured I'd just let them come to me.

I also planned on actually enjoying these parties, since I missed out on so much fun in college. Wallace wasn't doing anything worthwhile with his time, so I'd have him organize the events while I merely attended and enjoyed myself.

Patrice approached to tell me why she called to meet with me. "Lord Liam, I have a message for you from the leaders of the Union. They insist they have nothing to do with the protests. Actually, they were surprised to learn of them. They could hardly believe their citizens started protesting as soon as they arrived in your domain."

I gave those immigrants a warm welcome, but they betrayed my kindness. Well, I was sure they were mostly confused idiots instigated by Calvin's spies and didn't think the Union was involved in the first place. I imagined they had spies within my territory, but every nation did that.

"I didn't suspect the Union."

Patrice gave me a solemn look. "What do you plan to do with the protesters? Most Imperial rulers would raze an entire planet to eradicate them. That's what the Union is worried you'll do."

"Awfully concerned about their former citizens, aren't they? I'm not gonna burn it all down. That's my precious territory after all, and they're my subjects now...

My human resources. The organizers are gonna have to be punished though." The ringleaders wouldn't get away with causing so much chaos in my domain.

"Anyway," Patrice went on, "do you believe you can win the war with the United Kingdom? And even if you do win, your faction's power will be severely compromised, won't it? You have a bit of a personnel shortage already..."

Patrice worried that I didn't have enough talent, but I just smiled.

"Investment is important."

"Do you mean you have some connections you can make use of?"

"I've got something I can finally collect on, that's all."

I'd been sending the young people of my domain to study abroad for no real reason other than that it was tradition, but now it was time for them to do some work for me in return. As for the military and government bureaucrats...many of them had benefited from my support over the years. I'd supported them in case they might come in handy, but mostly it was just that I tended to throw my money around liberally. In fact, I'd pretty much forgotten about a lot of the people I'd helped until now.

"I'm calling in favors. There won't be any problems with our numbers. Patrice, I'm winning this one."

At my cocky attitude, she crossed her arms under her large chest and sighed. "Well, it would be bad for me if you lost. You really must be victorious against the United Kingdom—and you'll have to fight Calvin's faction after that, so it would be best if you could succeed in the war without losing too many of your forces."

Patrice didn't understand what I meant. The adversary I said I would beat *was* Calvin. Calvin was careless, thinking there was no way he could lose against me. I didn't think he'd make a move so soon, but the confidence I showed Patrice wasn't just posturing.

As I watched Rosetta and Ciel try on more dresses, I looked forward to the fun that would soon await me.

The Empire's Seventh Weapons Factory was experiencing a boom the likes of which it had never seen before.

"Ah ha ha ha—I can't stop laughing!"

Drawn into the international conflict, Cleo's faction had commissioned new heavy equipment from the Third, Sixth, and Ninth Weapons Factories. They didn't order anything from the Seventh, but Liam sent in a huge order instead.

Standing beside the guffawing Nias was one of her subordinates, who looked upon the factory in full operation mode with a smile on his face as well. He turned to her. "We'll be changing out all the weapons for Baron Exner's house as well, I hear. Count Banfield sure is generous, isn't he?"

Liam was sponsoring all the nobles in his faction who hadn't been sure their forces could cut it, outfitting them with state-of-the-art battleships, mobile knights, and anything else they might need.

Since Cleo would be defending them in an international conflict, the Empire had promised him its full support—at least, on the surface. As far as the Seventh Weapons Factory was concerned, they didn't want to incur the wrath of Calvin's faction by favoring Cleo's faction, but their pragmatic attitude was that they simply sold their battleships and such to whoever was buying. And right now, the more they manufactured, the more they sold. They were even selling off their old stock, so this situation was extremely lucrative for them.

"Intergalactic war sure is good for sales," Nias observed. "Not that the war has started yet. But..."

Of course, before production really geared up, some matters had to be addressed. Although the new machines the Seventh Weapons Factory produced were top-grade, they had all been heavily modified after complaints from House Banfield. They didn't like the designs. They didn't like the interiors. They didn't want the functional specs to be altered, but they requested so many extra features that ultimately the machines weren't the Seventh's original creations at all. The Seventh would have preferred not to make all those changes, but their traditional models just wouldn't sell. No one liked them. They received no orders for anything but the units modified to House Banfield's tastes.

"We've only sold a few of our unmodified units," Nias's subordinate sighed. "My pride's in tatters."

Nias was unbothered. "I didn't design them, so personally? I don't care."

Liam was making all sorts of bold moves. He was providing for Cleo's fighting forces pretty much all on his own, and he was lending money to the faction's nobles too. Nias figured that by powering up Cleo's faction, Liam was strengthening his own position within it. In the end, even after the war, Cleo would be left with a formidable military force.

Grinning and drunk with excitement, Nias gestured at the ship under construction directly in front of her. "What I do care about is my own special project. Just look at it!"

The three-thousand-meter flagship Nias was custommaking for Liam would be the ultimate battleship, crafted with an abundance of rare materials.

"I even used rare metals in the engine. Its output is going to be something else! The gun barrel is arondite, and the thermal conductors..."

She had always had plans in the back of her mind for the ultimate ship. Plenty of engineers did, but they were always held back by realistic concerns such as budget and acquiring rare metals. Liam's backing had made that dream possible for Nias, and she was using this opportunity to really show what she was capable of putting together.

Nias still wore a dopey smile on her face, and it didn't seem like she'd be coming back to reality anytime soon. Her subordinate decided it was time to return to work.

"Well, I'm just happy we're making so much money," he said before stepping away. "And for their part, Lord Liam is outfitting Prince Cleo at the perfect time."

The latest generation of craft had just come out, so obviously all the ships currently being utilized would be the next to become outdated. That meant the fighters of Cleo's faction would be the first ones to use the craft of the coming generation.

I'M THE EVIL LORD OF AN INTERGALACTIC EMPIRE

134

5 Wallace's Awakening

IF I WERE TO EVALUATE Wallace, I would say that he did no harm, but he did no good either. Even though he was born a son of the emperor, he was past the hundredth place in the line of succession. It was hard to say if his royal blood had any value at all. His abilities were generally lower than average, and his college scores were in the forties in every subject. That wasn't failing, but he was hardly excelling.

House Banfield supported Wallace simply because I liked having a royal as my lackey. Officially I was his patron, but since he insisted on being useless, I had to order him around.

"Wallace, I plan on throwing parties every day here on the Capital Planet, and I'm appointing you their organizer."

It was finally time for me to indulge myself in the notion that nobles should throw lavish events. However, if I had to go through the work of organizing them myself, then I wouldn't really be able to enjoy them. Thus, I had chosen to make use of Wallace for that purpose.

He immediately had complaints about the assignment. "You want me to organize parties? There's no way I'm doing something that annoying." Wallace rejected my order outright, brushing his hair back from his face haughtily, so I slugged him.

"Hey, that hurt!" he yelped, holding his head.

"Listen, Wallace, I'm busy right now. I'm having to hunt down Eulisia just to help get things together around here. I don't want to screw up and miss this chance."

Rosetta had sent Eulisia back to the military as a consequence for fooling around day after day. My having to go get her back just went to show how critical House Banfield's current situation was. House Banfield was stretched to its very limits, but Wallace didn't seem to understand that.

"Chance? Sure you don't mean *crisis*?" Wallace cocked his head, confused.

Just looking at him made me feel like I was getting stupid myself. "No, this is an opportunity," I said. "I'm this close to seizing good fortune."

Wallace looked like he wanted to ask, *"What are you even talking about?"* but more than anything, it was obvious he just didn't want to be bothered with work. "Why can't you organize these parties yourself?" he said.

"Because then I'll be too busy to enjoy them. And just so you know, I expect you to come up with something different each time. It'll be boring if every party is just like the next."

"Well, that's just unreasonable," Wallace complained. "I can't come up with something new every single day. If I have to do that, can the parties at least be low-key?"

I explained my feelings to him. "Listen, I'm picky about parties. I won't allow you to cut any corners. I'll give you all the people and money you need, so do your best."

"At least give me some ideas for the kind of parties you want!"

"I told you—if I'm involved in the planning at all, I won't have as much fun!" I barked.

Wallace reluctantly accepted his fate. "Looks like there's no point in arguing with you... I'll do it, but don't expect much, okay? And if you like parties so much, then you should be the one planning them in the first place."

"How many times do I have to tell you—"

"You really are selfish."

If I planned everything myself, there would be no surprises, and I'd have to worry about making sure everyone else was enjoying themselves. I hated doing that.

Now, the question was...what kind of parties would Wallace plan for me? In my head, I was already working on how I'd blow off some steam and berate him if the parties he delivered weren't any fun.

A discussion on recent developments at House Banfield was underway in Calvin's faction's meeting room. Upon hearing the latest news, everyone in attendance raised their voices in surprise.

"Liam doesn't plan on fighting in the engagement himself?" one of the nobles cried out.

"Why not? Is he running away?" said another.

"He's going to dispatch his most trusted knights in his place. His elite fighters will all be concentrated around Prince Cleo. He's also sending out that quiet knight he's been seen with on the Capital Planet... I believe his name is Claus?"

"I haven't heard that name before. Is he close to Liam?"

"I can't imagine he's holding anything back, but it's strange he will remain on the Capital Planet."

The fleet's supreme commander would be Prince Cleo—in name only, of course—but everyone had expected Liam would be the one actually commanding it. His announcement that he intended to remain on the Capital Planet was surprising.

Calvin smiled. "We've won."

The nobles' eyes turned to him when he proclaimed their victory. "Your Highness?"

"There will be rumors that Liam remained behind out of fear of the enemy. No—we'll spread those rumors ourselves. Even if Cleo's forces are victorious against the United Kingdom, Liam's reputation will suffer regardless."

"Well...I suppose it will." The nobles seemed to agree with Calvin, but they still had their concerns. "Your Highness, do you believe Liam is staying behind without some hidden motive? His deployment plans have been announced, but he's out there throwing parties every day and showing everyone how unconcerned he is."

Calvin was also curious about Liam's daily events. "That bothers me too, but it's likely just poor judgment. Whatever the case, there's no way for his reputation to recover from this. The truth is that he's sending Prince Cleo to the battlefield and staying behind. Even if he scrambles to fix things now, he missed his chance to shine."

The inexperienced Cleo would be going out to fight as the supreme commander. It was just ridiculous that the head of the prince's faction would remain home during such a conflict, and especially so for a man like Liam, whose military exploits were precisely what had won him his reputation in the first place.

What would people think of him when they heard he wasn't joining the fight? They would doubtlessly believe he'd avoided the battle out of fear. Even if there was no actual need for Liam himself to fight, it just looked bad for him to stay at home. Then, there was the fact that while his subordinates were out there fighting, Liam would be enjoying himself by partying every day. His reputation up until now had been sterling, but this would send it plummeting.

Of course, Calvin had *also* run from the battle and pushed it all onto Cleo, but that was before the official announcement of who the supreme commander would be was public. He had a number of excuses to use for things turning out that way, and he knew the nobles in his own faction would only deflect any criticism onto Liam.

Right now, those nobles continued to be baffled by Liam's apparent poor decision-making. "Did we go too far? This is a rather strange way for him to ensure his failure."

Calvin cautioned his followers. "It's not over yet, so we can't let our guards down. Even if it is over for Liam's reputation, he's still trouble as long as he breathes."

Even with his reputation in shambles, Liam's very existence vexed Calvin. One just had to look at the trouble Liam caused during his training out in the boonies. Even though he was a mere trainee, he carried out workplace reforms that removed every corrupt official from the area. That demonstrated a lot of ability and a spirit that was entirely too upstanding. Therefore, it was clear Liam was bound to cause Calvin trouble sooner or later if he stuck around.

Calvin made a decision. "Let's use what we prepared for combating him."

The nobles all nodded silently at his announcement. Calvin was confident of victory, but he didn't forget that it was Liam who took down his brother, Linus. Calvin wanted to get rid of Liam while he still had the chance, before he caused any more problems.

Calvin said aloud, "You've let your guard down because you're too strong, Liam."

To Calvin, it appeared that Liam had become careless because of his overconfidence in his superior capabilities.

The venue for House Banfield's party was abuzz with excitement. Throughout the hall, the impressed nobles in attendance oohed and aahed. It was a standing buffet party with various pieces of art—mostly statues—prominently displayed. Up-and-coming artists were summoned to present their new works, even standing beside the artworks to explain them. Nobles who appreciated art, as well as those who collected it as an investment, were very interested in the pieces on display.

"My, this is magnificent!" said one partygoer.

"I'd love to own this piece," another gushed. "I think it would look splendid in my mansion."

"I've already reserved that one. It's been a while since I've been to a party, let alone one with such an interesting theme. The last party I attended was so eccentric, I couldn't enjoy it."

The guests consisted mostly of the nobles in my faction and their family members. I invited those close to me so I could show off my wealth, but it was also good to simply make sure the people in my faction were happy.

I chatted up the nobles with Rosetta in tow. I noticed she was wearing one of her expensive new dresses. Then, Baron Exner's representative—a uniformed Kurt—made his appearance. The people around us excused themselves courteously and Kurt waved his hand as he approached me.

"Liam!"

"You're here. Welcome."

Accompanying Kurt was Princess Cecilia, to whom he'd just become engaged. Princess Cecilia and Prince Cleo were half-siblings, sharing the same mother. The couple seemed to be getting along fine, but when I started talking to Kurt, Rosetta pulled Princess Cecilia aside to talk with her privately. Was she being considerate of Kurt and me? *Hm, that's nice of her.*

Surprised at Rosetta's thoughtfulness, I started to chat with Kurt. "Haven't seen you in a while. How's the military treating you?"

Kurt was taller than the last time I saw him, and he was bulkier too. He looked more like a military man now, but his pretty face hadn't changed one bit. His personality seemed the same as when we first met too.

"To be honest, it's tough. I don't mean bad though. It's easier to get used to military life than serving as an official on the Capital Planet was."

It seemed the military life suited him, so I asked about his placement in the coming war. "You'll be defending the Capital Planet, I heard?"

"That's right. It's all just paperwork for now, though. Once I receive my official assignment, I'm sure it'll be on a patrol fleet."

"Want me to introduce you to a regular army fleet? I got Cedric promoted to lieutenant general. You'd do well in his fleet."

Cedric was Wallace's brother—another prince, but one who pursued the life of a soldier. I was supporting him too, and I'd gotten him promoted. He'd been surprised by the sudden change, but I told him it was a down payment for the future work he would do for me. He'd looked fearful, no doubt wondering just what it was I intended to make him do.

Kurt smiled wryly. "You haven't changed, Liam...but that doesn't sound too bad though."

"Consider it done, then."

Seeing Kurt looking so happy about this really made me feel like he was another evil lord just like me. *Looks like he's taking after Baron Exner, just as he should.*

Ciel, on the other hand, was different. Standing with Rosetta, she watched her happy-looking brother with a troubled expression. She was Rosetta's maid at this time, so even here she was on the clock. That meant she couldn't talk freely to a guest like Kurt now, even if he was her brother. She seemed awfully disheartened to see her brother growing into another evil lord just like his father. Or was the look on her face more complicated than that?

I decided to tease her a bit. "Kurt, it looks like Ciel wants to talk to you."

"Is that okay? She's busy acting as Rosetta's maid, isn't she?"

"We're friends, aren't we? I don't care about something like that."

I tapped the overly serious Kurt on the chest with my fist and he blushed. Maybe he was embarrassed to go speak to his sister.

"I-in that case, I'll take you up on that." Kurt stepped closer to his sister. "Ciel, how have you been? You're not causing any trouble for Liam, are you?"

Ciel could only return her brother's polite smile with an awkward look. This was supposed to be a chat between siblings, but they exchanged pleasantries as if they were merely two noble acquaintances.

"No. The count and Lady Rosetta treat me very well."

"I'm glad to hear it," he said. "Oh? Liam didn't give you that dress, did he?"

Kurt had noticed Ciel's elegant new outfit. I'd purchased a whole new wardrobe of dresses for her, enjoying the fact that she wouldn't like to receive expensive gifts from me. She looked good tonight, but I knew she resented it. I bragged about it all to Kurt in front of her.

"I hired a bunch of popular designers on the Capital Planet to design some dresses for her. I think there were around sixty, all custom-made for Ciel."

As long as these parties went on, Ciel would need to wear a new dress every night, and she wouldn't wear any a second time. I savored this feeling of wanton wastefulness, but I wondered if Ciel actually hated these extravagant gifts.

"I-I said that I didn't need them," she told Kurt. "But... th-the count insisted..."

Ciel looked frustrated, not at all thankful to me for the dresses, but that was good! It was great! Actually, I was really fond of Ciel because the way she felt about me was exactly how I hoped Rosetta would feel. If she didn't like these dresses, you could bet I would order hundreds more for her.

In any case, Kurt wasn't pleased by Ciel's reaction. "Ciel, you don't seem happy about Liam giving you these presents."

Kurt was smiling to maintain appearances, but he seemed a bit irritated with Ciel, like it offended his personal sense of honor that she didn't like me. They were still siblings, though, and he just scolded her lightly for being rude.

Ciel sensed his irritation as well and hung her head,

apologizing. "I'm sorry. I just wasn't sure how to feel since I've never owned so many expensive outfits before. I'm very grateful to the count—really."

I was quite amused, seeing Ciel apologize to me after Kurt had chastised her. "There's no need to apologize," I said. "I still hope you'll come to me if there's anything else you need, Ciel."

"O-of course," she responded with a fake smile.

Kurt sighed. "You're sweet, Liam."

"I'm not sweet."

When the conversation came to a good stopping point, Rosetta rejoined us after her friendly chat with Princess Cecilia. "You really are splendid, Darling. I couldn't even imagine throwing away dresses after only wearing them once. I'd at least like to keep my favorites."

Rosetta's family was so poor that she couldn't stop trying to save money, even now. I couldn't believe she would want to save old dresses. Didn't she have any self-awareness as the fiancée of an evil lord? I couldn't understand it at all.

"I can buy as many dresses as you could possibly want," I said.

"I just want to keep some of them..."

While we talked, some noble kids walked over to us. The fathers of these girls weren't attending the party themselves. If there were any children here, they were either accompanied by their mothers, other relatives, or servants. The reason their fathers weren't here was because they were away from the Capital Planet, mobilizing for the war.

I was looking after the kids of all the nobles who went off to fight in the war, making sure their families were well taken care of so they wouldn't worry and be distracted from their duties. It might have looked like I was keeping them hostage, but it was more to reassure the nobles.

The approaching young girls greeted us. "Your dress is beautiful again today, Lady Rosetta." They seemed greatly interested in dressing up for social occasions.

"Oh, thank you," Rosetta replied.

One girl chirped, "Where did you buy them all?"

"Ah, we ordered them."

"R-really?"

The other kids looked with exasperation at the girl who had asked Rosetta where she had bought her dress. "It's custom-made, of course!" one of them chided her.

"Where are you from, the sticks?" another scolded.

"Ready-made items aren't fashionable at all. You have to get your dresses made-to-order by a popular designer."

Man, girls are scary, even when they're kids.

Kurt smiled awkwardly as he listened to their conversation, and Ciel's cheeks were twitching. Ciel had probably also been surprised to learn that such dresses were typically custom-made. Princess Cecilia watched quietly with a hand on her cheek. She looked a little troubled too.

Rosetta comforted the inquisitive girl, who suddenly looked sad. "Don't let it bother you."

Seeing that the girl was about to cry, an adult came hurrying over. He seemed to be the guardian of one of the others who made fun of the girl for being from the boonies. He looked nervous. "I-I apologize, Lord Liam. You kids, go back to your families."

"Okay," the kids said obediently.

The man bowed his head low to me after they left. "I'm terribly sorry; they should never have spoken like that in front of you, my lord. I'll be sure to discipline them later."

Well, I am a country bumpkin lord from the sticks myself. And Rosetta used to be so poor that she couldn't even buy nice dresses. The man must have been worried that the kids' innocent comments had offended us. I was pretty annoyed by their attitude, to be honest, but I contained my feelings. "It doesn't bother me," I said.

Everyone here was a part of Cleo's faction, so I couldn't let my temper get the better of me or treat anyone poorly.

I turned to the remaining girl, the one who was ridiculed for being from the sticks. "Don't cry. If you like, I'll order a custom-made dress for you. You'll come to another party if I do that, won't you?"

The girl was surprised by my offer and quickly stopped crying. Looking ecstatic now, she asked, "Would you really?"

"I promise you, on my honor."

Good! Now she won't refuse to come again because she got her feelings hurt.

Her family came over to thank me, then led the girl away. Watching all this, Kurt and Princess Cecilia chatted about me excitedly.

"Liam's always been nice," Kurt said.

"I'm sure he has."

Kurt's making sure to give Princess Cecilia the impression that I'm a good guy. Evil lords really love playing their little games.

Ciel was watching me suspiciously, so I smiled at her. She quickly turned her face away. *What a fun reaction!* It made me want to tease her even more.

While I was enjoying the moment, Rosetta expressed her gratitude to me. "Thank you, Darling."

"I haven't done anything to be thanked for." *Why is she thanking me? I didn't do anything for her.*

Rosetta shook her head. "I'm just happy about the way you treated that girl. It felt like I was looking at myself back in my own childhood."

"I see."

Watching me being nice to that girl, Rosetta had imagined what it would have been like if someone had done the same for her when she was young. She really was too easy to please. With my wealth, a single dress for that child didn't even amount to pocket change for me.

I couldn't look directly at Rosetta as she smiled at me in her adoring way, so I averted my gaze and scratched my head. "Well, whatever."

I turned my thoughts to the fact that I might have hit upon a hidden talent of Wallace's. We were having these parties every night now, and I was honestly enjoying each and every one of them without becoming bored. Tonight's party's theme was even tailored to the specific guests that had been invited.

Maybe he's actually pretty good at this.

Outside the party venue, Kukuri appeared in a dark alleyway. As a large man in black wearing a mask, he gave off a strange aura of bloodlust.

He spread his strangely overgrown arms and chuckled ominously. "So you've finally decided to appear."

As soon as he spoke, several shuriken came flying at him. He deflected the throwing stars, which then burst into flames. What had been solid blades a moment ago had burned away as if they were only an illusion.

Other masked men appeared around Kukuri, and at the same time, their enemies revealed themselves. At first, black flames appeared before Kukuri and his men, but these flames took on the shape of human figures. These figures quickly solidified into weapon-wielding ninjas.

"Kill."

With that short, whispered command, the ninjas lunged forward. A fierce battle broke out in the narrow alleyway.

Two ninjas leaped at Kukuri. He swept his hands through them, but he didn't feel anything when he touched them. His hands merely passed through air, and the outlines of the two ninjas quivered. They lost their shapes and reverted back to black flames, but Kukuri didn't panic. Lightning-fast, he grabbed the cores at the centers of the two flames and crushed them in his fists like eggs. The moment he crushed the cores—small glass spheres—the flames flared up for a second before sputtering out.

"Hee hee hee hee! That's two down," he said.

Seeing two of their allies killed so easily, the rest of the ninjas immediately backed away from Kukuri and his men. They were uneasy at the realization that Kukuri knew the secrets behind their abilities.

"This brings me back," Kukuri said to them. "Your clan always was a nuisance. I can't have you losing your nerve so quickly, though. Your ancestors wouldn't have done that."

"Who are you?" one of the ninjas asked Kukuri.

Kukuri spread his large arms wide and introduced himself. "It's a pleasure to meet you...and a pleasure to see you again. Some used to call us the Shadows. We're part of the darkness of the Empire...but of course, that was merely what others called us."

When the ninjas heard this, they tried to flee, feeling they were at a disadvantage. Kukuri wasn't about to let them go so easily. Black thorns sprouted from his shadow and shot at the fleeing ninjas like darts, piercing their vulnerable cores. The dozen or so ninjas all vanished instantly, and Kukuri's subordinates slid back into their own shadows.

Kukuri remained alone in the alley, calling out to the presence he knew was still observing the scene. "Two thousand years. We have waited two thousand years for this. We will have our revenge. Tell your masters...they can blame this on their ancestors."

With that, Kukuri vanished into his own shadow as well.

"Wallace!"

"Liam, my own talent... It frightens me."

Liam, wearing his party clothes more casually now that the event was over, had come to thank Wallace. Rosetta dropped into a chair, exhausted after the string of parties she'd been to by now. Ciel brought her a drink, giving Liam and Wallace's farcical conversation the side-eye.

"I thought you were a total good-for-nothing, Wallace, but now I'm thankful for you! These parties have been killer!"

"That was really mean, but thanks. I had no idea I had a talent like this either."

Liam brought Wallace some drinks, and they sat to enjoy them together.

Everyone was surprised by how well-received Wallace's daily parties were. Liam expected him to fail, and even arranged to replace him right away if he couldn't do the job, but Wallace had totally surprised him with his talent.

Under other circumstances, this kind of skill would be useless, but...

Liam was spending his money lavishly, and it looked to everyone around him as though he was simply goofing off every day, but he was truly enjoying himself. Rosetta, on the other hand, was worn out from engaging with all these guests in a diplomatic role.

Ciel was worried about her. "Why not take the night off tomorrow, Lady Rosetta? You must be getting tired of attending these parties every day."

Rosetta shook her head. "I can't do that. People will be worried if I don't show up. Many brave nobles have gone off to fight in the war. I need to help ease their worries as much as I can."

"I suppose so, but..."

What were these nobles who were fighting in the war afraid of? Obviously, their enemy the United Kingdom, for one thing, but the nobles of Cleo's faction also had to fear Calvin's faction. What if their families were taken hostage while they were fighting? Many nobles had left their loved ones in Liam's care on the Capital Planet so they could go join the fight without sparing too much worry about those back home.

In a way, their families also served as hostages for Liam. The nobles of Cleo's faction had sworn not to betray him, and their families being here ensured that promise. If the nobles betrayed Liam's trust, Liam was in a position to kill their families, but as long as they didn't move against him, their families would be under his protection. The nobles still had to worry about Calvin even while they were off at war.

Ciel sighed. "Don't you feel the count should be fighting in the war himself?" she asked Rosetta quietly. "I think that would put everyone at ease."

Rosetta frowned, unable to dispute Ciel's stance. "Yes, I think normally we would have taken everyone's families to House Banfield's domain rather than on the Capital Planet, and Darling would have gone to the battlefield himself. But...with the way our territory is right now..."

Large-scale protests had broken out all over House Banfield's domain. In this climate, House Banfield couldn't properly care for the families of the nobles in Cleo's faction there.

Ciel heaved a sigh, remembering the protest situation. "I can't believe they're protesting about such a stupid thing now... They're being worse than our subjects."

As things developed, the big protests throughout House Banfield's domain were not focused on democracy. Only a small group continued protesting for political change—so few, relatively speaking, that they hardly registered among the whole.

So what, then, were the majority of people protesting about?

The issue of Liam's heir, or his lack thereof.

The people of House Banfield's domain were holding massive protests to essentially send Liam the message of "Hurry up and make an heir already!"

It was unprecedented.

Ciel's head hurt just thinking about the situation. *In my domain, people get into a tizzy about when my father will release a nude photo collection...but this is even more absurd.*

The petitions from the servants of House Banfield's mansion were all appeals to Liam—who had staunchly refused to lay a hand on any one of them—stressing that they were ready for him to do what he wished with them anywhere, anytime. The mansion's maids were begging him to make a move on them so as to produce an heir, and similarly, the other mansion staff members, both male and female, were all urging Liam to sire an heir sooner rather than later.

The stupidity of the situation exasperated Ciel. *All nobles are trash, aren't they? Of course...and I'm one of those nobles myself. But if those are the kind of problems our people have to focus on, I guess our domains are making their lives easier than they appreciate.*

Meanwhile, Liam and Wallace were toasting the party's success.

"I can't wait for the next one!"

"Look forward to it, Liam! I'm confident the next one will be just as great!"

"That just makes me more excited. I know—plan a bucket party, would you? Even if we only do it once, I want House Banfield to throw one at some point."

Wallace's expression suddenly grew grim at Liam's excited request. "I'm sorry, but that's a bit too much. I can't do that."

"I-I see... Oh well." Liam was deflated. He then changed the subject, as if he suddenly remembered something. "We can talk about bucket parties later, but I haven't seen Eila around lately. Have you been inviting her?" Liam was worried about his friend, since she hadn't yet attended any parties.

Wallace's face clouded over. "Eila's been running wild in the underground."

"That's right... Didn't she borrow some of my soldiers recently for a 'purification mission' or something?"

Ciel stiffened at the mention of Eila's name. She recalled the day she'd confided in the woman, expressing her worry that her brother would soon become her sister. Eila had looked at her gravely and said, *"It's better when they're both boys!"*

Eila scared her, but Ciel was curious what the other woman was doing, so she listened in on the boys' conversation.

Wallace told Liam about Eila's activities in the Capital Planet's underground. "I hear she's getting involved in areas outside her jurisdiction. They call her the Queen of the Underground these days."

Liam was surprised to hear that. "Isn't she taking her job a little too seriously? Guess I should tell her not to push herself so much."

Liam worried that Eila was working too hard, but Wallace shook his head, indicating that wasn't the case. "She's enjoying herself, so she's fine. If anyone has a problem, it's the residents of the underground."

When Ciel heard that Eila was running wild there, she recalled something. *Come to think of it, she sent me a message recently saying she was going to "root out the source of the problem," but...it couldn't be. Right?*

Meanwhile in the underground, two groups of officials

in black suits stood glaring at one another. To an outsider, the scene might have looked like a faceoff between mafia gangs. Tough-looking men shouted at a woman in a black suit as if to intimidate her.

"This area's under the jurisdiction of Section 8! What's the chief of Section 4 doing here?"

The woman in black was Eila, and standing behind her was her own group of serious-faced officials. Behind them were armed soldiers.

Eila was finishing a lollipop, and when she was done, she pulled the stick out of her mouth and smiled at the officials accusing her of infringing on their turf. "You lot were accepting bribes from the people here and overlooking their crimes."

"Wh-where's your proof, huh?"

"Oh, I've got proof, but it involves alllll kinds of annoying paperwork. I figured I'd just capture you now and then deal with that part later." Eila had become used to being forceful. The smug smile dropped from her face as she ordered her subordinates, "Arrest these corrupt officials."

Her tough-looking men and the House Banfield soldiers that she'd borrowed from Liam rushed at the corrupt officials. When the two groups started fighting in the middle of a major street in the middle of the underground, onlookers talked amongst themselves.

"So that's the Berman I've heard so many rumors about."

"She's basically the leader of the underground now."

"She's got a cute face for someone trying to clean up all the corruption here."

Among the people of the underground, some knew more about her than others.

"You don't know? She's friends with Count Banfield."

"Banfield? No wonder she's such a stickler for the rules. So she's friends with that upstanding noble, eh?"

Even in the underground, House Banfield had a reputation for being a family of virtuous nobles who wouldn't tolerate any injustice. If this woman and her team had something to do with the head of that house, it made sense to the people here that they would take their jobs seriously.

The men of Section 8 were overwhelmed and arrested.

"It's over, Section Chief," reported one of Eila's subordinates.

She relaxed at that. "I see that. Now, let's head to the area Section 12 is in charge of. We'll take care of the last two sections today."

Determined to wipe out the entire trade of illegal sex-change drugs and round up all corrupt officials while she was at it, Eila pushed forward.

I'M THE **EVIL LORD** OF AN **INTERGALACTIC EMPIRE**

6 The Expeditionary Army

A FLEET OF OVER six million ships had gathered in a sector of space within the Empire's territory. It was a grand sight, but mobilizing a force of this size cost no small amount of money. Even for an intergalactic nation like the massive Empire, it was difficult to muster such funds. This was a fight to eliminate the forces of the United Kingdom of Oxys from the Empire's territory, though, so they couldn't skimp on expenses. In other words, they *had* to be victorious here.

On the bridge of the three-thousand-meter-class superdreadnought serving as the force's flagship, Claus, the acting supreme commander, endured the pain in his stomach as he stood beside Prince Cleo.

Numbers alone aren't enough in a huge fight like this. Can we really win?

Just in terms of fleet size, they had gathered twice the fighting power of their enemy, but they couldn't focus all their ships on one battle. Space was vast and their enemy would split its forces, so the Empire had to do the same. That would mean managing multiple battle-fields at once—and not just two or three, but hundreds or thousands of fronts. If one counted small skirmishes individually, the number of engagements might even be in the tens of thousands. If the Empire forces lost in some areas, it would be all right as long as they won the larger conflicts, but it was impossible for one person to effectively keep track of that much fighting.

A number of bridge operators shouted out messages.

"Standing Supreme Commander Claus! We're getting complaints that supplies aren't reaching our patrol fleets!"

"Standing Supreme Commander Claus! The patrol fleet nobles are demanding that we hold a banquet before they commence activities!"

"Standing Supreme Commander Claus! One of the patrol squads is fighting amongst themselves! They're firing on their own allies!"

Complaints were coming in from the patrol fleets that had been scraped together for the war. They were commanded by useless nobles that Calvin's faction had known would get in Cleo's way. Anyone in the force who wasn't in Cleo's faction was basically just there to be a liability, likely an arrangement with Calvin's faction. These patrol squads were already causing problems and holding their own army back.

The nobles in charge didn't really care if they won or lost the war, and if things started looking bad for them, they would no doubt find some excuse to flee the fight. Desertion was an offense punishable by death, even for nobles, but Calvin's faction likely planned to make Cleo—or Liam, rather—take responsibility for any deserters to help tear Cleo's faction down.

If the war was lost, it would be the end of House Banfield. Knowing this, Claus felt crushed by the weight of the responsibility sitting on his shoulders.

Oh, my stomach hurts! I figure only half the force—three million—is on our side, and the rest are enemies!

The United Kingdom of Oxys's ships numbered about three million, and the Algrand Empire's numbered six million—but half of the latter were essentially enemy craft too. It wasn't an advantageous engagement of six million versus three million, but a precarious fight of three million versus six million.

Claus's one solace was the fact that they even *had* three million allied ships, which was all thanks to Liam. Liam had convinced many Imperial nobles to join his forces and was making use of his personal merchants to help keep his ships supplied during the war. He may not be joining the fight himself, but he was certainly doing his part by supporting the force from the rear.

It's all thanks to Lord Liam's support. I suppose that isn't a bad tactic for him...but why am I here again?

Seated next to Cleo on the bridge was the knight Lysithea. A short distance away sat his bodyguard Chengsi, who was buffing her nails as though she wasn't the least bit worried.

Prince Cleo has never commanded a fleet before, and this is Princess Lysithea's first battle of this scale. Not to mention mine as well. And Chengsi doesn't seem interested at all.

If Liam were here, Claus wouldn't have to worry about anything either, not besides simply following orders. But Liam *wasn't* there. The only way they even managed to gather a fleet of this size was because of Liam's remote support. Things in the rear were stable because Liam was taking care of supplies and everything else of that nature.

If Liam were here in command instead of on the Capital Planet, Claus had no doubt that Calvin's faction would be sabotaging their supply lines. When Claus thought of things that way, Liam was right about his own placement. If he miscalculated at all, it was in making Claus the acting supreme commander of the fleet.

Clutching his stomach, Claus turned to Tia. The woman's eyes shimmered dangerously.

"I see the idiots are still making noise. Operators, just add those complaints to the list. None of them concern us right now," she said.

Liam was far from stupid, and he wouldn't expect Claus to command the fleet all by himself. Therefore, he dispatched Tia to work under Claus. Still, Claus decided to think of himself as Tia's observer rather than as her commander.

Lady Christiana said she's had experience with wars of this scale. If that's the case, I should be supporting her instead of the other way around. What could I achieve on my own anyway?

Tia tended to ignore busywork, so the fastidious Claus ended up doing it for her. Tia had noticed this, so she'd stopped complaining about it to Claus and behaved as though she was the actual supreme commander.

"Do you have a strategy to use against the United Kingdom, Lady Tia?" Cleo asked nervously. Claus had met with Cleo previously in private, but he hadn't been able to come up with any kind of real beginning strategy.

Smiling, Tia replied, "We'll play it by ear. Nothing will go as planned in a war of this scale, anyway."

That answer made Lysithea nervous. "Can we really win this? We're effectively outnumbered two to one..." Like Claus, Lysithea didn't feel all their allies could be trusted to work in harmony with them.

Tia cocked her head and smiled at Lysithea. "Two to one? You have to think about this the right way, Your Highness. From our perspective, there are indeed three sides to this fight...but the United Kingdom won't distinguish between us and Prince Calvin's allies when they see Imperial ships."

A visual representation of their fleet of six million ships appeared on the bridge's main screen before them. There, they could see numerous ships moving about, ignoring orders and breaking formation before the battle even started. These were the uncooperative ships of the main fleet, plus the patrol fleets. While half of their ships were now setting forth toward their specified destinations, the other half were obviously moving wherever they pleased.

Tia watched them with some amusement. "Ah, the traitors are showing themselves already. Well, let's start by taking care of them."

Tia opened a communication channel and sent out orders to the trusted ships of the fleet. "We fight for Lord Liam's victory! Let's put those traitors to good use!"

The last thing she said before signing off was said in such a cold tone that it startled everyone around her. "Pershing... You'll regret betraying Lord Liam."

The fleet of 60,000 ships commanded by Count Pershing in the United Kingdom's army was but one part of a larger fleet of ships belonging to other nobles. Altogether, their force numbered 100,000 ships, and they were currently stationed at a planet that belonged to the Algrand Empire.

The personnel of this combined fleet were all citizens of one of the nations that comprised the United Kingdom. During the United Kingdom's recent internal conflict, this nation had risen up against its rulers. Normally for such a betrayal these people would be forced to fight on the frontlines, but they made a deal with the United Kingdom to avoid that fate.

The Empire withdrew from the vicinity of this planet when the invading force arrived, so the fleet already managed to achieve something without causing or suffering any damage.

Smoking a cigar on the bridge of his ship, Count Pershing was notified of a communication from the Imperial Army.

"It's our regular update from the Imperial Army, my lord," one of his operators announced. "It details their next moves."

Pershing received the report from his subordinate and examined its contents. "Hmm... Prince Cleo's flagship is secretly moving with a small number of ships? So they want to trick us into thinking he's still with the main force, eh? Looks like the Imperial Army has no idea how to fight."

Pershing suspected that a dummy flagship with the main force was being used to make it seem as though Cleo was there. This strategy had been used in the past. Several nations had even been defeated by thinking their enemy wouldn't possibly send out their flagship with so few ships to defend it. This strategy was a gamble, though, because if their enemy found out what they were up to, the small group would be in jeopardy. Count Pershing decided to forward this information to his superiors.

"Report this to our sovereign. It's nice and easy just sitting back to watch this war, isn't it? I pity those who actually have to kill one another out there."

Count Pershing fully intended to wait out the whole war here without once going to the front lines. The other nobles in his fleet were the same—they had no intention of fighting.

"Don't think too poorly of me."

Was he saying that to Liam, or to his allies? His staff on the bridge had no idea.

Meanwhile, the Imperial Army's commanding flagship received a new report.

"300,000 United Kingdom ships have met the mixed fleet! Our side just lost 60,000 ships!"

Tia acted devastated to hear the news. She held one hand to her chest and covered her face with the other. "What terrible news. I ordered them to quickly return to their posts too...but they just wouldn't listen."

That one report confirmed the elimination of a good number of delinquent nobles and their soldiers who were only getting in Tia's way. Most of them were related to Calvin's faction in some way. To put it simply, they were fellow soldiers in the Imperial Army, but they were all Liam's enemies. Tia eliminated them by sharing misleading information, and her display of sadness was simply an act. Behind the hand that covered her face, Tia wore a dark smile, knowing that she sent so many of Liam's enemies right into the jaws of doom.

Claus felt a chill run through him when he caught her expression. *She really did that!*

They lost 60,000 allied ships in the blink of an eye, but Tia felt no remorse. After all, they had only done away with some traitors.

Cleo looked frightened as he watched Tia. "Should we really be sabotaging our own allies...?" The prince couldn't understand why they should fight amongst themselves when they had a real enemy to face, and he didn't seem to approve of Tia's glee from annihilating their own troops.

Tia, on the other hand, actually found it charming that Cleo reacted with such disgust to her actions. "I used to think the same way you do, Your Highness, but life-or-death conflicts with your own allies are exactly what ends up happening in wars of this scale. One small mistake and we could have been the ones eliminated instead of that mixed fleet."

If they didn't outmaneuver their enemies first, they eventually would be the ones to become space dust. When Tia helped Cleo see this, he held his tongue. Beside him, Lysithea couldn't say anything to refute Tia's logic either.

Seated nearby, Chengsi just looked up from her nails to smirk. Perhaps Tia's style of command appealed to her—her cheeks were flushed with excitement over what was transpiring on the battlefield.

"Now *this* is war," Chengsi said. "No—this is humanity itself. The battlefield is where humans shine the most beautifully and act the most repulsively. Ahh... Our homeland truly is wonderful."

Tia stared at the elated Chengsi with chilly eyes—not as one would look at an ally, but as one would a detestable foe. The reason for that was because Chengsi had made an attempt on Liam's life to see if she could beat him in personal combat...and because *after* that, Liam had taken an interest in Chengsi and forgiven her. House Banfield's knights didn't feel the same way about the bloodthirsty woman as Liam did, however, and Tia would happily kill Chengsi as soon as she got the chance.

Tia spoke indifferently to her with undisguised hostility. "Why not die on the battlefield yourself, then? Give your life for your beloved homeland."

At Tia's words, Chengsi tapped a finger against her lips and narrowed her eyes. Tia was completely open about her desire to see her dead, and yet she was still smiling casually. "It's too bad I can't kill you right here," Chengsi replied. "But if I fool around too much, Liam won't play with me again, will he?"

Chengsi was plainly stating that if not for Liam, she would have taken out Tia at that very moment.

The other knights on the bridge were filled with rage, Tia foremost among them. "You're just a savage berserker who was only spared because of the mercy in Lord Liam's heart," she spat back.

Things were getting dangerous, so Claus intervened. "That's enough, both of you. Lady Christiana, this is no time for us to be fighting amongst ourselves."

Claus pointed out that there was a bigger battle to be fought, and Tia looked away from Chengsi. "I suppose you're right." Tia still didn't hide her contempt for the other woman, however, and gave off the vibe that she was just waiting for the right time to kill her.

Claus cautioned Chengsi as well. "And Chengsi, if you're bored, I'll give you an opportunity to fight. Be ready to sortie."

Chengsi was supposed to be acting as Cleo's personal guard, but Claus decided to use his authority to send her into the field instead.

The woman smiled, her expression both bewitching and ominous. "I bet it'll be fun to test out my new toy." The "new toy" Chengsi referred to was a customized mobile knight.

She left the bridge to prepare to sortie, and the tension in the air immediately lessened. Everyone around him relaxed, but for Claus, the pain in his stomach had intensified.

Why are there so few normal knights in our order? Anyway... Since I reassigned Prince Cleo's bodyguard, I guess I'll have to write a report to explain that later.

While Claus nursed his aching stomach, Tia announced her next strategy. As she had done with the traitors in their own force, her aim was to transmit misinformation for Count Pershing to intercept that would lead to more losses—but this time, on the United Kingdom's side.

"Now, let's see if we can get Count Pershing to dance for us too."

Claus watched Tia manipulate the battlefield like a gameboard. *Lady Christiana definitely should have been made acting supreme commander from the start.*

The flagship of the United Kingdom's forces was a type of vessel called a fortress-class ship. This mobile fortress was housed within an asteroid—the latter of which was outfitted with powerful engines for propulsion—and therefore boasted a command center far larger than a superdreadnought could support.

In addition to the supreme commander, dozens of generals and hundreds of staff officers and operators occupied the fortress' command center. Information on every battle occurring in every location was gathered there. In addition, information provided by Calvin's faction regarding the movement of Prince Cleo's forces was displayed alongside it.

From taking in all this data, some of those in the command center noticed the situation looked very unusual in several locations. Still, the team couldn't hide their excitement as reports of their allies' accomplishments poured in.

One of the operators shouted, "Our ground forces have captured the enemy base on Planet Two!"

To better organize things, they numbered the planets in the sector of space serving as the battlefield. A landing force had been dispatched to a world in the battle zone called Planet Two, which had a livable atmosphere, and they had overwhelmed the Imperial forces there and captured their base. The planet was now under United Kingdom control. It was a great victory to be sure, but that wasn't the only good news the bridge operators had to share.

"The Eighth Roaming Fleet encountered an enemy fleet and completely destroyed it!"

"The Second Fleet just won a battle against a fleet of over 100,000 ships!"

"Report from Fleet Thirty-Nine! An enemy fortress has surrendered, and now our people are occupying it!"

Morale was high as the United Kingdom's forces pushed into Imperial territory with incredible momentum. Everyone other than the flagship's officers were surprised to hear these reports. However, the operators didn't know that their allies had connections in the enemy army—specifically, to Calvin's faction. They believed these victories were solely due to their army's own abilities.

Secret information or no, one cool-headed staff officer was becoming suspicious. "This is too easy," he observed aloud.

It was practically a miracle to win on so many fronts so quickly in a war of this scope. This staff officer was wary, knowing that they should expect some losses of their own.

The supreme commander of the United Kingdom's forces, a female general, was nothing but pleased by their victories. "This is a good thing," she said.

"Supreme Commander?"

"If they have traitors on their side, they won't be able to fight at their full strength. Let's keep our momentum going, and victory will be within our grasp. It was frustrating that their supreme commander eluded us in that first battle, but other than that, the Empire's practically handing us victory. We just need to keep racking up the wins."

If they were triumphant in this war, the supreme commander would be promoted to field marshal, becoming the youngest person ever to hold the position. That glory seemed so attainable to her now, and she was blinded by it.

"It's just too unnatural," the staff officer persisted. "Shouldn't we pull back for a bit to get a better perspective of the war as a whole?"

The supreme commander wasn't listening. "If we pull back now, we'll lose our momentum. Not to mention, I want my people to win some achievements of their own. If I'm the only one promoted after this, they'll be jealous."

The supreme commander wasn't about to be swayed, and the staff officer's brow furrowed.

The supreme commander laughed as she gazed upon the holographic overview of the battleground projected before her. "If I carve out enough of the Empire's territory, my name will go down in history."

She fantasized about how her name would be passed down—the great general who led the United Kingdom to victory.

Things were going so well for Count Pershing that it was actually creating problems for him. Chief among these was a request from other nobles in the same fleet he was a part of.

"Can't you consider it, Count Pershing?"

"I'm not sure what to tell you."

Faces of other nobles were projected all around him on his ship's bridge. Surrounded this way by his fellow nobles, he suffered under the pressure of their demands.

"We don't desire any sort of grand victory; we just want to be able to say that we fought against the Empire ourselves. With our allies winning so many battles, our own achievements will pale in comparison."

Other fleets of the United Kingdom were achieving so much success that these nobles, who'd previously decided to wait out the war, now wanted to fight so they could have some victories to their names as well.

"Our sovereign commands this fleet," Pershing replied. "We can't very well bring our sovereign to the battlefield, can we? We may be in a superior position, but danger still remains."

"But our sovereign is the one who wants to fight! Count Pershing, your information network can find us a suitable foe to engage, can't it?"

"Well...I suppose so."

Count Pershing didn't anticipate something like this happening. *The Cleo faction is worthless. I heard that Count Banfield was an accomplished fighter, so I didn't expect his force to be so weak. You really can't trust the rumors, I suppose.*

Count Pershing was disillusioned with House Banfield after having heard so much about their pirate-hunting exploits. At the same time, he couldn't help but feel his own aspirations rising.

I suppose if I don't make a name for myself here, I'll regret it when I get back. There shouldn't be any problem if we find some small fleets and overwhelm them, right?

The United Kingdom nobles were getting restless, seeing the steady progress their allies were making in the war.

Count Pershing made his decision. "Very well. I'll find a suitable enemy for our sovereign's forces to fight."

"We're looking forward to it, Count Pershing."

On the bridge of the Imperial Army's flagship, Tia stood imposingly with her arms crossed. Her face remained expressionless as she heard each new report of the Empire's losses.

Cleo and Lysithea had gone to their rooms to rest for the time being, so she was alone on the bridge with two female knights who served as her adjutants.

Tia asked, "Where might the acting supreme commander be?"

"Sir Claus is resting. You should take a break as well, Lady Christiana."

"I can't rest right now."

Tia continued to monitor the status of the war. The Imperial Army was losing battles or being pushed back in various areas. The bridge operators reported each new piece of information with professional indifference, but more blood seemed to drain from their faces with each new report of a loss.

Tia was waiting for the right time to mobilize their forces. *We're almost there...*

The door to the bridge opened and a refreshed Claus entered. "What's the situation?" he asked.

"No change," one of Tia's adjutants responded curtly.

"I see."

It was a rude way to speak to the acting supreme commander, but Claus didn't reproach the officer.

This adjutant seemed irritated at the current state of affairs, and whispered to the other adjutant, "Why did Lord Liam appoint Sir Claus as acting supreme commander and not Lady Christiana? I still can't under-stand it."

She was obviously displeased that Claus wasn't as talented as her own superior. Tia, however, was uncon-cerned. She was just waiting for the opportunity she needed.

Then, one operator called out an urgent report. "A new enemy fleet has appeared, headed in our direction. They are 100,000 in number!"

Tia smiled. "It's time to make our move. Deploy the ships on standby."

While the operators hurriedly contacted the sister fleets, the adjutant sighed, "We sure did put out plenty of bait for them."

"And managed to eliminate a lot of traitors in the Imperial Army," said the other adjutant. "We should be thankful to the United Kingdom's forces."

Tia's strategy to use misinformation to pit Calvin's faction's forces against the United Kingdom's army had reaped great success. When the fleets of Calvin's faction clashed with the United Kingdom's, they must have realized they'd been betrayed. They tried to defend themselves against the United Kingdom's army, but they were easily overwhelmed thanks to the information Tia had allowed Count Pershing to intercept, even though

Count Pershing had no idea he was also being played that way.

Pershing was under the impression that Tia and her allies were members of Calvin's faction, but it was actually Cleo's faction that he was going up against. Tia had pitted their two enemies against one another, and in the process, reduced their forces...while her own faction hung back and maintained its full fighting strength.

"I feel sorry for the soldiers fighting for Calvin's faction," Claus said.

The nobles and officers who actually opposed Cleo's faction only made up a small proportion of Calvin's forces. Many common soldiers who were merely following orders were sacrificed in Tia's plan.

"Would you prefer it were our subordinates dying?" Tia replied. "I chose this plan to make sure as few of *our* people as possible would be killed. Do you disagree with my thinking, *Sir* Claus?"

Tia addressed him without using the title "Acting Supreme Commander," and Claus sensed something dangerous in her tone. Tia must have felt that Claus was criticizing her plan, because she was giving him a fierce glare.

Claus shrugged to play down his comment. "I was the one who approved your plan. The responsibility lies with me too. Still, I intend to respond to any distress calls, regardless of the faction they come from."

What Claus was saying was that now that her plan had served its purpose, he intended to assist any allies he could. Even if requests for help came from Calvin's faction, he intended to act on them.

Tia didn't contest him. "Of course, *Acting Supreme Commander.*"

A special craft waited in the flagship's hangar. Its distinctive red paint job was Chengsi's signature color, and the unit was her personal mobile knight. House Banfield commissioned it for her from the Seventh Weapons Factory since she possessed incredible talent as a knight. A one-of-a-kind machine for a one-of-a-kind knight: the Ericius.

The Ericius had a slender frame and conical shoulders. There were firing lenses for beam weapons all over it, so it was amply armed, but the Ericius had no weapons that it could hold in its hands like other mobile knights. The machine's long and slender claw-like fingers weren't suited to holding weapons. Because of the firing lenses all over its body, it would be difficult to equip the machine with optional weaponry as well. That fact seemed to confuse several of the maintenance techs, and they could often be seen staring at the atypical machine with puzzlement. Even so, this was the way the craft was designed to be.

"It's finally time to shine, my cute little hedgehog."

Wearing a red-and-white pilot suit and with helmet in hand, Chengsi drifted over to her machine in the gravity-free hangar. She had taken the mobile knight for a few test drives since receiving it, but this would be its first real battle.

Chengsi opened the hatch and boarded the craft she'd nicknamed her "hedgehog." The cockpit was decorated in a traditional design, to her tastes. Hovering paper lanterns illuminated the space, set in spots where they wouldn't obstruct visibility.

Chengsi settled into the pilot's seat, and the control sticks and pedals shifted to the perfect positions for her to make use of them. Clasping her hands together and stretching her arms out, she checked the Ericius's various control panels.

In exchange for not having a rifle or close-proximity weapon, the Ericius was fully loaded with firing weapons, their controls arrayed before her. Thanks to this arrangement, her mobile knight had almost no armor, so if the exposed frame took a direct hit, it could be seriously damaged. However, Chengsi felt that she didn't need defense. She directed all the energy that would normally be used for defense to offense instead. The frame did make use of rare metals in its construction that bolstered its strength, but it was a craft that didn't seem very practical for real battles. However, that was exactly what Chengsi had asked for.

"I could fight forever like this."

Chengsi waited for her orders to sortie, her eyes narrowed into blissful slits.

Information on both allies and disoriented enemies came flooding into the bridge of the Empire's flagship. Even as they struggled to process it all, the operators made their reports without emotion.

"The enemy landing force on Planet Two has retreated, and we've retaken our base there."

"An allied fleet just reported that they've driven off the enemy's Eighth Roaming Fleet."

"Remnants of some decimated enemy fleets are trying to reform. Our allies request permission to engage before that happens."

All reports indicated that their previously inferior position had reversed completely, and their allies were now fighting with a clear advantage over their foes.

As Claus listened to the reports, he reflected on Tia's plan. *She lured the enemy into our territory, then threw our forces at them after they expended a good deal of their fighting strength on the traitors.*

The United Kingdom's army had been advancing steadily, fighting against Calvin's faction, which should have been on their side. Though the Kingdom had won many battles, their forces were still depleted in the process. Cleo's faction waited for the perfect moment to strike—when the Kingdom's numbers had dwindled, and they were running low on ammunition, supplies, and energy.

Claus was secretly terrified of Tia. *I don't know how she got false information out there to get them to believe we were Calvin's force. Anyone can come up with the idea to manipulate the enemy's intel, but it's impressive that she actually pulled it off. That being said, Calvin's people are still officially our allies and they've taken too many losses.*

Tia was showing no mercy toward their opposing faction. The severity of her ruthlessness was unimaginable when one considered her regular behavior. Tia often acted rather ditzy when Liam was nearby, though Claus had been under the impression that in general she was a good-natured knight. However, when faced with enemies, she apparently became a different person. Even now, when she received the reports on how Calvin's forces had been reduced, she simply smiled coldly with satisfaction that her plan had proved successful.

I've heard that the more talented a knight is, the more darkness they hold in their heart. Does Lady Christiana possess that darkness at her core?

If Claus had any hint as to the reason for those feelings, it was the knowledge that she had once been captured by pirates. He heard that she'd been subjected to torments the likes of which he couldn't even imagine until she was finally rescued by Liam. Tia and the other knights who had been captured along with her didn't like to talk about the experience, but they felt deeply indebted to Liam for saving them and expressed that feeling through unflinching loyalty.

In a way, it was more unusual that Tia, someone who could slaughter her enemies mercilessly, became so emotional when she was in front of Liam. Some part of Tia's humanity was broken, and Liam brought out her vulnerabilities. She could still be human, at least around Liam. And Marie—despite always fighting with Tia—was the same way.

While considering how dangerous Tia was, Claus was thankful that they weren't enemies. *If she was all on her own, she could either go down in history as a great hero...or as a demon. But I should stop doubting my comrades. For now, I need to focus only on the battle ahead.*

Tia suddenly turned to face Claus, her eyes glittering. Her lips were curved upward in a crescent-moon grin. "Acting Supreme Commander Claus, what would you say to using this fleet to attack the enemy's main force at this time?"

Claus was taken aback by Tia's suggestion that they pit the supreme commanders of both sides against each other to decide the outcome of the war. It didn't show in his face, but on the inside, he wanted to reject Tia's suggestion. Still, based on her strategies thus far, if Tia believed they could win the battle, he decided he should take that chance.

Still keeping his expression stoic, Claus nodded at Tia. "Very well."

Lady Christiana is the real supreme commander here. All I can do is go along with her decisions and support her in whatever way I'm able. I can't say I expected her to suggest we attack the enemy's main force ourselves...

The United Kingdom's main force was called the First Fleet. It was made up of some 300,000 ships—a tenth of the entire army—though its numbers were currently divided. Its ships were scattered, providing aid to other fleets, as the situation for their army had worsened.

Currently, some 100,000 ships guarded the fortress-class flagship, and within its command center, the supreme commander was seething. She didn't show it on her face, but her arms were tightly crossed and her pointer finger tapping.

"Why is our army suddenly losing?"

From her tone, which was more tightly wound than usual, her staff officers knew she was in quite a foul mood.

"The Imperial Army has bolstered its forces," a female staff officer answered. "Supreme Commander, I suggest we fall back and regroup."

The supreme commander didn't approve of the staff officer's reasonable suggestion, however. No, she couldn't back off like that, and it wasn't just because of her ambitions.

"It will only confuse our allies if we show our backs to our enemy now. Not to mention that most of our fleets have pushed too far into Imperial territory."

Hearing this, the staff officer grimaced with dread.

The supreme commander went on, "The fleets who got greedy and rushed in too recklessly are probably going through hell right now."

It was the supreme commander herself who had ordered her forces to advance, but some fleets ignored her specific orders and pushed in too far. The First Fleet ordered them to return, but the overeager fleets found some reason or other not to.

"Communication failure..." "We're already in pursuit of an enemy fleet..." "We're going to the aid of some allies..."

"If they're so far in," the staff officer suggested, "why not have them chain a series of short-distance warps to meet up with our main force?"

"Do you want to lead the enemy straight to us?" the supreme commander snapped back. "Fleets chaining warps will just call attention to themselves."

In a universe with widely separated intergalactic nations, simply cruising through space wouldn't get anyone anywhere. For that reason, ships were designed to jump instantaneously between two points, but their warp engines were meant only for short distances. Special structures were required for long-distance warping: enormous rings that floated stationary in space, connected to one another by wormholes. Only by moving between those rings could ships perform long-distance warps.

Thus, if a ship fled by using its warp engine, an enemy could do the same and follow it. Short-distance warps also required a huge amount of energy. It wasn't uncommon for a ship to flee from a threat via warp only to run out of energy immediately and become a sitting duck. So, even if these ships *were* able to meet up with the First Fleet, they would be useless by the time they got there.

The staff officer understood all this, but she was anguished, unable to simply abandon her allies. "At this rate, they'll be wiped out..."

"I know that. We'll send aid and rescue them—"

Before the supreme commander could finish, an operator raised a panicked cry. "Allied fleet approaching via short-distance warp! Message from the fleet: 'Encountered the enemy, requesting aid.'"

The supreme commander and all her staff officers tensed up. Outwardly, they tried to remain calm in front of their subordinates, but their expressions turned grave when they heard the bad news.

"Who *are* these idiots?" one of the staff officers shouted.

The operator identified the approaching allied fleet. "It's the Dahl Principality's fleet!"

The Dahl Principality—the same nation Count Pershing served.

Just what is going on? Seated on the bridge of his battleship, Count Pershing trembled uncontrollably. *It was supposed to be a simple win. How did this happen?*

As the ship powered down its warp engine, an operator yelled, "The Imperial Army is in pursuit!"

The Dahl Principality's fleet had successfully completed its warp, but an Imperial Army fleet followed right behind them. Count Pershing was terrified by the sight of the pursuing Imperial Army on the monitor before him. Within the enemy fleet was a group of ships with the crest of House Banfield displayed on them.

"Eeek!"

The reason he covered his face with his arms in terror was because they'd already just fought a battle with the Imperial Army. Out of a sense of ambition, the Dahl Principality had decided to go on the offensive and attack the Empire, targeting a small fleet numbering fewer than 10,000 ships. The enemy fleet was made up of old ships that could hardly put up any resistance, so the Principality's 100,000 ships easily annihilated them.

Sovereign Dahl was pleased by this...that is, until a fleet of 30,000 Imperial ships suddenly appeared out of nowhere. The Imperial fleet did heavy damage to their forces. The enemy fleet only had a third of their numbers, but they quickly destroyed half of the Dahl Principality's fleet. The Dahl flagship had also been eliminated; their sovereign died in battle. The surviving nobles were in the process of fleeing to save their own skins.

In a panic, Pershing fled in the direction of the United Kingdom's main force, the First Fleet.

"Can you see the main fleet yet?" Count Pershing shouted.

"We're approaching visual range!" an operator answered.

Out of fear for his own life, Count Pershing led the great Imperial fleet right to the United Kingdom's main force. Imperial ships now appeared one after another behind them—almost 300,000 of them. Attacks from the rear picked off Pershing's allies one by one. He had no idea when he would be caught up in an explosion himself.

A red mobile knight suddenly began to approach from behind them. Seeing this on the bridge's main screen, Pershing trembled even harder.

"I-it's her!"

The slender red mobile knight had uniquely flared shoulders. Particles of red light emitted from these cone-shaped parts, trailing behind the mobile knight as it moved. When the red craft caught up to one of the Dahl ships, it fired powerful lasers from the lenses set into its body. Pierced by the laser beams, the ship burst into pieces.

The red mobile knight came swooping out of the explosion, setting its sights on its next victim. It pointed one large arm ahead of its body and its claws glowed gold, a beam forming at their tips. This energy beam took the form of a giant set of claws, which the unit swung down at the ship it had targeted. Slashed by the mobile knight's energy claw, the ship burst into bits.

The sight of a single mobile knight destroying one ship after another was like something out of a nightmare.

"Is that thing a monster?" Count Pershing cried. "Deploy all our mobile knights to slow it down!"

Count Pershing was hoping to survive long enough to reach the main fleet by sacrificing all the knights who served him.

The Dahl Principality deployed its mobile knights. Giant, human-shaped craft spilled from each ship, forming a loose unit. The mobile knights' heads had the bucket-like look of great helms, and many of them featured horns to mark them as the elite commanders.

Leading the mobile knights with their ominous glowing eyes was a female knight who was a top ace in the United Kingdom's army. A veteran of the frontlines, she had already taken out more than ten enemy units in this battle. This top ace held the current record for the most craft taken down in the Dahl Principality, but it reassured her to know that other Dahl knights with admirable reputations fought alongside her in their own cockpits.

"Our orders are to defeat the red craft," she barked over her communication system. "Take it down no matter what you have to do! If you go after any other unit, I'll take you out myself!"

Sufficiently intimidated, all her subordinates answered, "Yes, ma'am!" And indeed, they couldn't afford to look anywhere else right now. After all, they were up against—

"Now these are some lively foes."

The beautiful face that appeared on every communication screen, enemy and ally alike, was one that was well known, even in the United Kingdom.

"It's the Empire's Red Devil! Spread out!"

The Principality's mobile knights maneuvered to surround Chengsi's red mobile knight. Their deft movements marked each and every one of them as ace fighters, but the woman grinned fervidly nonetheless.

A chill ran down the top ace's spine, and a second later the red mobile knight demolished one of her allies. The red craft carried no physical weapons, instead lashing out at the machine with its gold, glowing claws. The Dahl unit tried to block the attack with the huge sword it held, but the blade shattered instantly, and the unit was torn in two.

Chengsi ripped her claws out of the mobile knight's wreckage, tossing aside its ruined halves.

"I'm impressed you could react to the Ericius's movements at all. I'd prefer it if you people put up a bit more of a fight, though." Chengsi sighed, clearly unsatisfied, but she continued on to crush more of the mobile knights.

The top ace ground her teeth as she watched the Dahl Principality's top fighters go down one after another. She swung her craft about, firing beam weapons at the red mobile knight, but none of her attacks found their marks.

The red mobile knight exhibited a shocking range of movement for such a machine. It dodged the many attacks launched at it as if it were putting on an acrobatics display. The craft had been made with mobility in mind, forgoing bulky armor. It seemed like an absurd design, but with Chengsi as its pilot, it was a frightening threat.

"I'll stop you here, even if I have to give my life to do it!" The top ace's mobile knight tossed aside its rifle and took up a blade instead. It became difficult to pilot her craft well as she accelerated toward Chengsi, her body pressing back into her seat, but the female knight didn't care about that. Instead, she intended to ram her unit into the enemy and go down together.

As the top ace chased after the red craft, dodging its attacks, Chengsi laughed wildly. *"Good! Oh, you're very good! And ready to lay down your life, too! Wonderful! It's too bad about that poor machine you're piloting, though."*

A moment later, the top ace's mobile knight was bisected by a blow from Chengsi. The attack rocked the ace's cockpit, causing jagged shrapnel to fly about the chamber. One chunk of metal impaled the female knight through her guts.

"You monster..." she rasped, coughing up blood. She heard Chengsi's voice through her failing control systems in return.

"Unfortunately, I'm just human. There are stronger monsters than me out there in the universe."

"The universe...truly is...a vast...place."

"I agree."

To ensure the female knight's death, the red craft pierced the ace's cockpit with an energy claw.

In the cockpit of the Ericius, Chengsi was elated. Her cheeks were bright red, and she panted with excitement.

Letting out a satisfied sigh, she smiled at the next wave of enemy mobile knights approaching her. "You've given me such a warm welcome. I suppose I have to live up to your expectations, don't I?"

Chengsi pressed down on the acceleration pedals and expertly manipulated the control sticks. She was enjoying herself, and not just because she was piloting her custom-made mobile knight. She was enjoying killing people.

The nuclear reactors in the Ericius's shoulders emitted their trails of red particles, and the beam weapons built into the machine's body began to glow. Then, the Ericius went into a spin as it plunged into a group of enemy mobile knights. The enemy craft burst apart, pierced by the Ericius's many lasers. Chengsi had hacked into the enemy's communications channel so she heard the anguished cries of the pilots in their cockpits. That, more than anything else, excited her.

One pilot shouted, *"How can a mobile knight have lasers that powerful?"*

"It'll run out of energy in no time! We just have to endure!"

"Th-there's no way! My energy shield was destroyed in one hit!"

The unique thing about the Ericius was that it utilized almost all of its energy for offense. The beam weapons built into its body were as powerful as those normally used by battleships.

Chengsi's unit stopped spinning and reached out with its golden claws to grab the head of a mobile knight that had gotten too close.

"I have more than just lasers," Chengsi said, and the Ericius's hand began to vibrate. Aided by this high-powered oscillation, the claw easily ripped through the enemy craft's head. The claws utilized a combination of physical blades and beam weapons, making them as versatile as they were deadly.

The Ericius's other hand plunged mercilessly into the enemy's cockpit. The sharp claws slashed through the enemy mobile knight like it was made of paper.

Her unit then kicked the destroyed craft away. Other enemy mobile knights surrounded it, aiming their guns at Chengsi. A rain of lasers and projectiles flew at her craft, but Chengsi piloted through it all, avoiding any strikes without breaking a sweat.

"That's good. You should collaborate and come up with a strategy."

Needles made of light materialized from the firing lenses of the Ericius's beam weapons. They all fired at once, streaking toward enemy units. The enemies tried to evade them, but the needles followed their movements and exploded when they found their targets.

"I believe they're called needle missiles..." Chengsi said casually over the open communication line. "They're not bad, but the name could use some work." She sighed at that, but she was satisfied by their performance.

Chengsi had destroyed dozens of enemy mobile knights by now, but others still kept coming. "I'd like to play with you more, really, but Claus told me to take down some *ships*," she said reluctantly. "Sorry, but I need to finish up here quickly."

Suddenly, the Ericius manifested energy swords from various points on its exterior. With these long energy blades poking out from its body like the spines of a hedgehog, the unit began to spin. The energy blades slashed through her enemies like a whirling sawblade, leaving them shredded in her wake.

Spinning so fast it looked like a glowing orb, the Ericius reduced everything it struck to scrap. Not only mobile knights, but even some enemy ships were caught up in the chaos and destroyed.

"Oh, I like you, Ericius! Let's have some more fun!"

This mobile knight had just the sort of functionality Chengsi had hoped for, and she was growing quite fond of it. To her enemies, though, the craft only inspired terror.

Chengsi laughed gleefully as she instilled fear into the hearts of the Dahl Principality's army.

"It's hard to understand what a berserker is thinking."

"You said it."

On the bridge of the Imperial Army's flagship, Tia and one of her adjutants were appalled as they watched Chengsi fight.

The lone knight pushed deep into the enemy ranks, having left her allies far behind. Her red craft, which looked unarmed but actually housed weapons all over its body, seemed like the perfect machine for Chengsi, a woman with a penchant for using hidden weapons. Her allies, meanwhile, kept far enough away from Chengsi's Ericius to avoid friendly fire.

The Imperial fleet continued chasing the Dahl Principality's army as it fled. House Banfield's ships led the charge, shooting down the fleeing ships without mercy.

As Lysithea stood beside Cleo, her face grew more and more pale as she watched the situation unfold. *House Banfield's top knights are terrifying—no, the entire army is. With every instant this fight goes on, tens of thousands of lives are being lost on both sides. But they're so calm watching it, as if none of that death is really happening.*

From Lysithea's point of view, Tia was just as fearsome as the berserker Chengsi. She had been the architect of this hell, and she watched over it as if it didn't affect her in the slightest. Even Claus, the acting supreme commander of their force, kept watch over the battle with a complete lack of expression on his face.

That man is just as fearsome in his own way. He seems to be around my level when it comes to his abilities as a knight, but he's completely unfazed by the situation we've found ourselves in...and he agreed to Tia's plan in the first place.

She glanced over at Cleo, who was just as pale as she was. The prince looked horrified by the battle that raged before them but was doing his best to wear a brave face.

"We've located Count Pershing's ship," one of the operators reported to Tia.

Lysithea clenched her fists at this information, but not out of anger. Rather, she was terrified to find out what sort of retribution Tia and Claus had in mind for their traitorous enemy. She prepared herself to hear something truly horrifying, but it seemed Tia had more mercy in her heart than Lysithea expected.

"Notify all ships. They are not to attack Count Pershing's ship, nor any other vessel in the fleet he commands. I want them spared."

"You're not attacking them?!" Lysithea couldn't help exclaiming upon hearing Tia's unexpected command.

She slapped a hand over her mouth after blurting this comment, but Cleo looked at her with exasperation. "Please keep your voice down, Lysithea."

"I-I apologize."

Tia turned around to face them with a sunny smile on her face. "Don't worry...Count Pershing's fate is already set in stone," she said with an eerily happy tone.

On board the fortress-class ship serving as the United Kingdom's flagship, the staff officers were clamoring.

"Spread out! Try to surround the enemy fleet and take them out!"

"Call back the fleets we dispatched elsewhere—we need reinforcements!"

They began to engage directly with the enemy's main force, which their allies had brought right to their doorstep. The First Fleet's response to the unexpected situation had been swift, but the enemy's forces were three times the size of their own.

They'd considered retreating, of course, but the immense size of fortress-class ships made it very difficult to maneuver them quickly. They turned slowly, they cruised slowly, and they even warped slowly.

"The fleets we dispatched are already engaged and can't return!" one of the operators shouted.

"What?"

"All of our fleets throughout the zone are under fire from the Empire! No one can spare ships to send as reinforcements!"

Listening to the conversation between the operator and staff officer, the supreme commander crossed her arms tensely. "Those incompetent fools led the enemy right to us... Hmm? What's that?"

She noticed something on the main screen. "Zoom in on Count Pershing's fleet! Hurry!"

One of the staff officers manipulated the screen, focusing on Count Pershing's warship. The approaching Kingdom fleet was surrounded by Imperial ships, but Count Pershing's forces alone were taking no attacks from the enemy. Their other Kingdom allies were being shot down without mercy, but the Imperial Army was leaving Count Pershing's fleet untouched.

The supreme commander lowered her brows in anger and spat out words of loathing. "You've betrayed us, Dahl Principality—no, wait. *Pershing!!!*"

To the United Kingdom's supreme commander, there was no other possible explanation. Pershing had clearly betrayed them and was leading the Imperial Army straight to them.

As the two nations' main forces clashed, Claus monitored each individual report that came into the flagship's bridge.

Ships that were low on energy from performing short-distance warps requested instructions, so he had them switch positions with less-depleted ships. He sent resupply ships to the rear of the battle so they could safely reorganize. He found himself managing the particulars of fewer than two thousand ships. It was far too small a task for an acting supreme commander to be bothered with, but Tia was busy, so Claus was taking care of it as if they'd reversed roles.

I'll put the refueled ships on cleanup, I suppose. Hmm... the United Kingdom's flagship definitely is impressive, isn't it? It's like a mobile military base.

The Empire had fortress-class ships of its own, but theirs were smaller than the United Kingdom's. By now, the United Kingdom's army was fighting a force three times its size, but they were holding their own thanks to the impressive power of their fortress-class flagship. The Imperial Army was taking increased losses, and more and more ships were being sent to the rear to regroup, but Tia was too focused on maintaining the offensive to concern herself with damaged or exhausted ships falling back.

"They're tough," she remarked to her adjutant about the fortress-class ship.

The adjutant displayed data on the enemy's supreme commander and her staff officers. "Their commander is known for being the youngest person ever to be promoted to general within the United Kingdom's army."

Tia narrowed her eyes when she heard that, a smile forming on her lips. "She sounds very aggressive. I like that, but she's still Lord Liam's enemy. I'll have to destroy her myself."

Her adjutant raised her eyebrows. "You plan to enter the fray yourself, Lady Christiana?"

"I want to take care of that fortress-class ship as soon as possible. If we let this drag on too long, the rest of their main force will return and surround us."

"Still, the commander can't go out and fight herself," her adjutant protested.

Tia smiled again. "I'm just following Lord Liam's example. Honestly, I would send Chengsi in to take care of this, but it's too much responsibility for that berserker."

The adjutant gave up on trying to convince Tia to stay behind. She pressed two fingers to her ear and opened a communication line to the hangar. "Prepare Lady Christiana's craft for launch."

As Tia left the bridge, the woman shot a look at Claus. "You can take care of the rest, can't you? I'll leave you my adjutant, so you can rely on her for anything you might need."

"I'll do that," Claus replied, keeping his opinions on the matter to himself.

I really don't think the person who's actually command-ing the fleet should go out in a mobile knight, but... Lord Liam's the same way. There's not much I can say about it, is there?

In that regard, if he said anything to criticize Tina's decision, it could be taken as criticism of Liam as well.

Well, I'm sure Lady Christiana will be fine. She's a talented commander, but in a mobile knight, she's a first-class ace. I don't need to worry about her.

Claus felt a bit disheartened whenever he compared himself to Tia, but he shook off the feeling and concentrated on the matters at hand.

Now, I should get aid to the wounded and continue reorganizing our forces.

A squad of mobile knights, led by a white-colored Nemain-class unit, charged through space toward the fortress-class ship. Commanding the team from her cockpit, Tia gave orders to the ace pilots she'd selected for her entourage.

"Our task is to capture the fortress-class ship. We'll need to secure a path for the landing force."

Hundreds of Nemains followed after her with the cape-shaped boosters at their backs spread wide. Behind these came small troop-carrier craft with the landing force on board, guarded by Raccoons with large shields. These Raccoons were heavily armored mobile knights with more rounded frames.

"We're in interception range, ma'am."

Tia moved her control sticks in response to the report. As they approached the asteroid, lasers rained down on the Nemains, but the pilots skillfully wove through these attacks and accelerated toward the fortress-class ship instead, switching their boosters to reverse thrust when they closed in.

Lowering their speed, the human-shaped units alighted on the surface of the fortress-class ship. At first, there appeared to be nothing but barren rock all around them, but suddenly, various weapons and mobile knight guards popped up out of hidden trapdoors. Tia's fellow pilots were ready for this, however. Rifles in hand, the Imperial mobile knights eliminated all nearby threats, and then proceeded to search for a secret access point for the fortress.

"Over here, ma'am!"

Tia's Nemain used its massive sword to slash at a non-descript-looking area of rock, breaking right through it and exposing a path to the inside.

"There you are..." Tia sneered.

She and her elite pilots then infiltrated the base.

Inside the huge fortress-class flagship, the Imperial Army's landing force approached the command center.

The United Kingdom at least had foot soldiers of their own, and for now, the command center was still heavily fortified.

Keeping track of the situation on various monitors, the supreme commander gritted her teeth. "So they got inside."

The staff officers were anxious that the enemy invaded their fortress. "Supreme Commander, you're in danger here. You should get to safety."

The supreme commander shook her head. "It will only plunge our allies into chaos if I flee. The command center is still secure and functioning. If I can just help the First Fleet hold its own against the Imperial Army until reinforcements arrive, we can still win this."

The enemy was already inside their fortress, so it seemed their chances of victory were slim at this point. Even so, the supreme commander insisted on remaining in the command center and presiding over the battle until the very end—if only for the sake of their allies.

Her staff officers were moved, but they were still crushed by the situation they found themselves in. "If not for Pershing..." one of them murmured bitterly.

The supreme commander knew better than to focus on what couldn't be changed now. "What's done is done. The enemy was one step ahead of us...and I was too hasty in dispersing the First Fleet's forces. You were right."

"No..."

The supreme commander regretted not listening to the others' opinions, but it was too late for that. "I want you to escape," she said to her staff.

"Supreme Commander?"

"It'll be better for our nation in the long run if *you* survive, not me. Our ground forces will defend you until you can escape from this ship."

"Supreme Commander!"

The staff officers resisted, but members of the ground forces were already stepping forward to escort them out of the command center.

"Now then," the supreme commander muttered to herself. "I'm going to take every Imperial down with me that I can. But there's someone else who has to pay too..."

Within a single extensive battle zone, a fight raged between millions of ships. Perhaps it was more fitting to describe it as a strategy game set against the vast backdrop of space. Planets were captured, bases were constructed and then lost. Allies betrayed allies and found themselves betrayed again. An incredible story was unfolding here. Had certain things not gone the way they did, this war could have lasted hundreds of years, but it was coming to its conclusion far sooner than anyone anticipated.

As for Count Pershing... At the moment, he was so tightly surrounded by Imperial Army ships, his fleet couldn't even move from their current position.

"What's going on? What is happening?" he cried in frustration.

The sixty-thousand-ship fleet he commanded was now a mere several hundred. All the Dahl Principality's allies had been wiped out, and the only ships remaining were those under Count Pershing's direct command. With Imperial Army mobile knights pointing guns at them, Pershing's ships were completely immobilized.

It was at that point that Pershing received a communication on his monitor.

"Things are working out well for you, aren't they? You traitorous bastard."

Pershing had played both sides—the United Kingdom Army and the Imperial Army—and now the supreme commander of his own forces called him out on it.

"S-Supreme Commander? Y-you're wrong! There's been some kind of mistake!"

"I'm not listening to the words of a turncoat," the supreme commander snapped, contempt plain on her face. *"I have two things to tell you. One: I'll make sure every person in*

the Kingdom knows what you've done. And two: I under-estimated you. I thought you were nothing more than a typical greedy noble. I had no idea you would continue to ally yourself with House Banfield, even now."

"Wh-what are you talking about?"

"Don't play dumb. You tricked us into taking out Calvin's forces instead of Cleo's, weakening ourselves in the process."

Count Pershing didn't understand what the supreme commander was saying. How could he have betrayed the United Kingdom and Calvin's faction? The one he betrayed was Count Banfield...or at least, that's how it should have been.

The supreme commander's anger was only growing. *"I hate the Empire, but I loathe you even more. On my name as a general of the United Kingdom's army, I swear I will crush you if it's the last thing I do. That is all."*

The supreme commander cut off communications and Pershing's complexion went from flushed to ashen. He slid from his seat onto the floor, trembling feverishly.

"What in the world is happening? I knew I was getting information from Imperial spies, yes, but it was *House Banfield* I aimed to betray! How could I have betrayed my allies instead?"

Pershing had spies in the Empire who had been feeding him information, which he diligently passed on to those above him. For a while, everything had been going wonderfully. So how come now, all of a sudden, he was being treated as a traitor?

While Pershing struggled to comprehend the situation he found himself in, a lone mobile knight flew up to his ship. The unusual red craft made a hard landing on the ship's hull. It was the Ericius, piloted by Chengsi.

As soon as she touched down, Chengsi opened a line of communication and her face appeared on Pershing's monitor. There was a strange sensuality to her breathlessness, but Count Pershing couldn't appreciate that at the moment.

"I had a little too much fun back there," Chengsi rasped. *"I need to take a break. Oh, right... Sir Claus ordered me to serve as your guard, Count Pershing, all right?"*

This red mobile knight had decimated the Dahl Principality's ships along with the United Kingdom Army's fleet...and yet here was its pilot, proclaiming that she was here to act as *his* guard.

Count Pershing covered his ears and rolled onto his side on the floor, not even wanting to understand anymore. "This can't be. It can't be! Why is this happening to me?"

Chengsi laughed at the sight of him. *"Oh, wait... Were you tricked? Aw, you poor baby!"*

A short while after that, the fortress-class flagship was completely overrun and fell into the possession of the invading forces. With that great loss, the United Kingdom's army was defeated, and its remaining forces retreated from the Empire's territory.

Tia returned to the Imperial flagship after driving off the last of the United Kingdom's fleet.

By herself, she entered a dimly lit room. Waiting inside were several spies from Calvin's faction. Tia smiled at them, not with aggression, but with simple gratitude.

"You've done very well. I'm grateful to all of you."

The spies' bodies suddenly appeared to be swallowed up by a black liquid. The unnerving liquid columns changed shape, eventually transforming into a group of masked men dressed in black. These were Kukuri's people who performed House Banfield's dirty work.

One of the enigmatic operatives stepped forward to represent the group. "We only did as Master Liam ordered."

"Still, our victory couldn't have been assured without your hard work. I'll be sure to report as much to Lord Liam myself."

"We appreciate that. Of course, in reality it was Pershing who did most of the work."

Tia could only feel anger toward Pershing, who had betrayed House Banfield and hence Liam. Her expression grew dangerous at the thought of the man. "What a fool he was. He was the perfect pawn to manipulate, though."

From the moment House Banfield became certain that Pershing would betray them, they decided to make use of him and remove him after he served his purpose. To implement that plan, they replaced the spies who relayed information to him with Kukuri's shape-shifting operatives. Pershing fell for the ploy hook, line, and sinker, and happily went on to destroy Calvin's faction's forces for them by feeding his own people false intel.

"Master Liam was certain that Pershing would move against him," Kukuri's subordinate said.

Tia smiled. "Of course he was. The whole reason he allied himself with that scum was just for this moment. That snake was never fit to be anywhere near Lord Liam, but I'm glad he was useful for something." Tia's cheeks flushed with admiration for the count, who had predicted Pershing's betrayal and made productive use of him.

"What do you intend to do now?" asked Kukuri's subordinate.

Tia's head was filled with thoughts of Liam, but she still had a job to do. She quickly moved on to the matters at hand. "The United Kingdom's asking for a cease-fire. It's been about three months since the start of the war, hasn't it? I didn't expect it to end this soon."

"Considering the scale, it was incredibly quick, yes. I'm sure Master Liam will be pleased."

Tia beamed like a child at the thought. Clasping her hands together, she spoke her true feelings. "Oh, I'm looking forward to making the report to him! Do you think he'll praise me directly? Ahh, I can hardly wait!"

Kukuri's men exchanged glances among themselves and shrugged.

Overall, the Empire lost about one million of its ships, and something like 20,000 ships had deserted the fight, but they came out victorious in the end. A portion of those losses did belong to Cleo's faction, but they were more than satisfied with the results of the war. After all, the great majority of the losses were taken by Calvin's faction, and most of the deserters were theirs too.

One of Kukuri's men chuckled. "If you only see the numbers, it looks like we took serious losses."

From the statistics alone, the Empire's heavy losses seemed regrettable, but Tia was entirely unbothered.

"*Our* losses were few, so it's fine. And by the way, we'll have to make sure that any idiots who deserted the fight are punished accordingly, won't we?"

From the standpoint of the Empire, it was a hard-won victory, but for House Banfield, the war was an overwhelming success.

"We can use this as ammo against Calvin's faction when we're back," Tia gushed. "Ahh, I can see Lord Liam's victory now! And I'll be right there at his side for it!"

Tia returned to her fantasy realm, so Kukuri's men left her to it and faded into the shadows.

"Ahh, I can see Liam's defeat now!"

On the Empire's Capital Planet, the Guide—who had been in a fantastic mood lately—watched the news of the Imperial Army's victory in high spirits. He wasn't pleased that the Empire had been victorious, but he liked that they suffered such heavy penalties in the process.

"While Liam was fooling around partying every day, the Imperial Army suffered terrible losses. He's sure to get in trouble for this!"

The Guide couldn't stop smiling, reflecting on how Liam had become more and more troubled recently. His body still burned constantly from Liam's ever-present gratitude, but he could grin through the pain now. After all, Liam's fury was building by the day—he'd been smoldering with rage ever since he first started getting word from his domain. Large-scale protests were still breaking out all over Liam's territories, and because of that his ability to rule was coming into question. The Empire's opinion of Liam was on the decline, and the Guide was so thrilled about that he could hardly contain himself.

"Soon! Soon, everything Liam has gained will crumble!"

The Guide skipped around the city, feeding on unhappiness as he went. In the heavily populated capital of a vast intergalactic nation like the Empire, deep stores of misfortune were everywhere, and he absorbed as much as he liked from the citizens he passed by.

"The Capital Planet is great! It's the center of everything, so its misfortune has the most profound flavor." He spoke of it as if he were tasting a fine wine.

In his happy wanderings, he came upon a man who sat in an alleyway drinking liquor with a dour look on his face. "Dammit!" this man was grumbling to himself. "No matter what I do, it never goes well. Why do I—"

The Guide sucked up the man's discontent to nourish himself. "Oh, that man's despair was quite good. Mmm, the misfortune is so tasty today!"

A call came in on the tablet in the man's breast pocket, and he answered it with irritation. "What? It's just more bad news, isn't—huh? R-really? You say a noble really likes the clothes I design?"

A second ago, that man was a designer with zero prospects, but apparently, he'd just won himself a client—and a very well-paying one at that. However, the Guide had no interest in his good fortune.

"This always happens when I suck out someone's unhappiness: they're left with only positivity. Ugh, it's just terrible. I need to go on now and continue making Liam unhappy. Oh, I mean, make him *happy*."

The more the Guide worked to make Liam happy, the unhappier the young man became. It appeared to be working perfectly, and the Guide meant to continue in this way.

But as the Guide stepped away, a dog poked its head out from behind a garbage can in the alleyway. It cocked its head, watching the Guide secretively. Meanwhile, the drunk man expressed his eagerness for the work that was being requested of him.

"House Banfield's mistress and her attendant, yes? You want me to design dresses for them? How many? At least *ten*? Wh-what's the pay? Oh yes... I'll do it! I'll make ten dresses...or twenty! This is great... I can support my whole family with this order alone!"

Crying tears of joy, the designer jumped up and ran off. The dog followed after him, looking back again and again at the Guide as it went.

I'M THE **EVIL LORD** OF AN **INTERGALACTIC EMPIRE**

7 House Banfield's Protest Problem

"**E**VEN DRESSES must be practical! It's not enough for them to be simply *worn*. 'True beauty lies in functionality' is my motto!"

I entered the hotel dressing room to find that the interesting designer I called for had already arrived first thing in the morning. Thanks to the daily parties we were throwing, Rosetta was running out of dresses she hadn't already worn. One or two designers just couldn't cut it, so I sent requests to a good number of people. Now, one of those designers was going on about functionality, even for single-use dresses. *What's with this idiot?*

"Just look at these embellishments!" he raved. "A normal dress would utilize a disposable shield energy generator, but mine has one with heightened functionality. It's heavier because of that, but I'm sure as nobles, that won't be an issue for you."

Most nobles wore accessories that could deploy a protective field out of fear of assassination attempts. Such accessories produced a barrier when they sensed danger nearby, but a lot of these field generators were one-use only. After all, proper generators were heavy and costly.

Some people repurposed their shield accessories, but we couldn't do that since each accessory was carefully tailored to a specific dress. Besides, reusing these devices wouldn't be properly *evil*. Being economical was good, and if I wanted to be evil I had to spend as lavishly as I could!

It was hard for me to decipher the looks on Rosetta's and Ciel's faces as they listened to the man. I wasn't sure they could accept the designer's notions of enhanced functionality over convenience. We were requesting disposable dresses from him, but he meant to jack up costs by giving his garments the functionality of combat gear. The two of them were dubious about spending so much money on something they would wear only once, but I myself liked frivolous spending. As an evil lord, it was my duty to use the tax money I wrung out of my subjects to live lavishly. That went for disposable dresses just like everything else. In fact, it was *great* that I could spend so much tax revenue on something so pointless.

I applauded the man's passionate speech. "Wonderful! I like it."

"Th-thank you very much!" The man bowed deeply.

I decided to request something else of him. "I've got another job for you. Amagi?"

"Yes, Master?"

I called my maid over from the corner of the room and introduced her to the designer. "This is my Amagi. I've been thinking she needs something else to wear other than maid uniforms. She should have a dress too, right? I want you to make Amagi something too."

The designer wasn't sure how to respond to my request, given that he must have recognized Amagi was a robot. I was sure my knights standing guard nearby would draw their swords and cut him down if he said the wrong thing. Heck, I fully intended to kill him myself if he said anything to disparage Amagi, but apparently the guy wasn't a total idiot.

"W-well, I have no experience designing clothes for androids...but with some time and thought, I believe I can fulfill your request. Just please understand that this is somewhat outside my area of expertise."

I liked him even more after hearing his response. One of the designers I spoke to earlier about making an outfit for Amagi had sneered and said, *We do not make clothing for dolls.* I decided never to order anything from him again after that. Lucky for him that we were only communicating over a video call at the time, because I wanted to kill him for his disrespect. Amagi convinced me not to though, since some noble or another was fond of him, and it would have been an issue. I almost sent Kukuri and his men after him anyway, but I knew Amagi would find out if I went that route, so I gave up on it in the end...for now. I had my hands full right now, but I still hoped to find time to get back at that designer in some way in the future. It'd be fine as long as Amagi didn't find out about it, right?

At the moment, I had to focus on this more cooperative designer. I told him, "That's fine. I'll send you the particulars. You're free to decide the budget."

"Yes, sir!"

When the designer accepted my request, Amagi gave me a reproachful look. "Master, I do not require any dresses."

"Consider it an order, then."

"But..."

Amagi opened her mouth to persist with her disapproval, but Rosetta joined me in trying to convince her. I was actually a little touched by the gesture.

"You could wear a nice dress every once in a while, couldn't you, Amagi? I'm sure it would look good on you."

With even Rosetta siding against her, Amagi couldn't very well continue to argue. "Very well. However, I could not stand to dispose of a garment after a single use, so please allow me to keep it after wearing it."

Yes! Amagi finally gave in!

"Of course!" I said, then I addressed the designer again. "I want this to be the best dress you've ever made—got it? Whatever the cost, you name it. This better be a masterpiece...but I don't want it looking gaudy either. And make sure it doesn't expose *too* much skin!"

"Y-yes, sir!"

As I watched the designer get to work entering notes on his tablet, I received a call from Brian. It seemed like lately he was reporting nothing but bad news to me. I imagined the look on my face was less than enthusiastic as I opened the communication on my own tablet. And sure enough...

"Master Liaaam!!!"

My mood soured in an instant. And I was in such a good mood a second ago. Brian was always ruining things for me. I told myself that if he was anyone else, I'd have the guy tortured right about now.

"What is it?"

"The protests! The protests have grown even larger!"

"What? I thought I had Eulisia on that! What happened

to her? Isn't she supposed to be good at cracking down on troublemakers?"

Eulisia was supposed to be an elite soldier, but she couldn't even quell some simple nonviolent protests? Well, I had to admit, it wasn't like my elite soldiers should have to be used for such things in the first place...

House Banfield's domain contained several planets with habitable environments, and once again, there were protests on every one of them today. The general atmosphere of the protests was unusual, though.

"Takoyaki! Who wants takoyaki?"

"We got yakisoba over here!"

"Get your protest placards here!"

Stalls that provided various foods and services were set up everywhere. Soldiers performed traffic control, and medics were on hand.

A soldier who noticed some people straying from the march's designated course reprimanded them gently.

"This isn't the designated march route. Get back on course, would you?"

"I'm sorry, but is there a bathroom nearby?"

"Right over there."

"Thank you."

These were supposed to be protests, but the atmosphere was more like that of a festival. Alex, the leader of the democracy movement, was watching the proceedings, dumbfounded.

Alex had been a college student back on his home planet, which was part of the Rustwarr Union. He made it to graduation day, but he had never taken his first step into adult society. Instead, he joined the rebel forces that opposed the Union, armed with knowledge and youthful passion. He planned to help make the rebellion succeed and secure a good position for himself in the new nation they meant to create in the process. Unfortunately, the rebellion was suppressed before he could make anything of himself, and he was now a refugee.

When he ended up in the Empire, he thought of a new way to make a name for himself: launching a democratic movement in a different nation. The method was merely a method to Alex, not a goal. He was aware that House Banfield ruled benevolently and was good to its people, but he took advantage of that to begin his movement. If House Banfield attempted to suppress his protests, he planned on leveraging that fact to accuse them of being no better than any other noble house. If they opposed him too strongly, he would start up an anti-government army and lead it himself. Thankfully, though, plenty of people came forward to support him, so he was certain that his movement would succeed.

That is, until...

"Why are protests that have nothing to do with my movement breaking out everywhere?"

Alex shouted in frustration, because the people he watched marching by with placards were advocating for something completely unrelated to what he thought he was organizing.

"Don't forget your heir!" a protestor cried.

"Fulfill your duty as the lord!"

"Lady Rosetta deserves happiness!"

Liam, the lord of House Banfield, didn't have any children to inherit his position, so the people of his domain were concerned—especially since an international war had just taken place. The people realized that in a conflict of that scale, their lord could perish at any moment. Thus, what the citizens of his domain demanded...was for Liam to sire a child.

Alex was infuriated that his own movement wasn't gaining any ground, while these baby-making protests were growing explosively. "You've gotta be kidding me! This is their chance to gain some rights for themselves within the Empire's dictatorship!"

"Calm down, Alex." His companions attempted to pacify him.

"How am I supposed to calm down? Why does no one understand? Is everyone on this planet a complete idiot?!"

A college student carrying a sign with a picture of a baby on it walked by Alex's group. He gave them an openly judgmental look when he saw their own placards extolling the virtues of democracy. He stopped to talk to them, though he didn't look too happy about it.

"You guys are immigrants, right? Do you have a permit for your protest?" the student asked. "We're holding a pro-heir protest here, so if you want to talk about your own stuff, do it somewhere else."

Alex did not in fact have a permit for his protest, but he argued with the man anyway. "We're advocating for people's human rights—"

The college student interrupted him with a sigh. "Yeah, there's no need for that. To be perfectly honest, you guys and your democracy movement are just a nuisance here. If you want democracy, could you advocate for it on a different planet?"

Alex was indignant at the college student's attitude. "What? Oh, I see... You're a spy for the nobility, aren't you? It'd be too weird for a citizen not to want rights. You're just an agent working for the lord, right?"

The college student replied to the enraged Alex calmly. "Nope, I'm just a normal citizen, but I *did* just get back from studying abroad. You guys don't know anything about how things work in the Empire, do you?"

"How things work?"

The college student furrowed his brow at Alex's ignorant reaction. He swept a chilly look over the other youths advocating for democracy as well. "What do you think the Empire does when movements for democracy get off the ground?"

"Well, I'm sure they put the pressure on to suppress them, but that's no reason to—"

"The typical noble's response is to *burn the entire planet to ash* to save them the trouble of rooting out all the rebels. So now you know why we'd rather not go down with you for your stupid movement, yeah?"

"B-burn?" stammered Alex. "They wouldn't go that far, would they?"

"Of *course* they would. There are plenty of examples from the past."

The worldly college student knew of several planets that had been utterly destroyed because of growing democratic movements. In his history lessons, he learned of planets turned into seas of flame to serve as examples. In fact, some nobles went even further in their efforts to nip rebellion in the bud and saw to it that their people's education was so limited that thoughts of democracy would never enter their heads in the first place.

"Listen, we're provided a full education here," the college student went on. "We can even study abroad. Do you really want those rights taken away from us because of what you're doing?"

Alex still couldn't accept what the student was saying. "You're no better than livestock! You want to spend your lives sucking up to the nobility? If you're human, you should think for yourself a little more. Besides, who's to say the next noble who takes over here won't make everything worse? Aren't you worried about that? You want to live your whole lives according to someone else's whims?"

The college student was disgusted with Alex. "According to someone else's whims, eh? And things were different for you back in the Union?"

"What was that?"

"For example, lots of people are killed in space pirate attacks, right? In that sense, we're all basically at the mercy of someone else's whims. To me, the current lord's rule isn't bad at all. What guarantee do you have that things would be better after people gained independence?"

"I see it's not just the nobility that's the problem. Everyone here has stopped thinking. You're all rotten."

"Then why did you even come here? If you want to preach democracy, move somewhere else. No one's gonna stop you from leaving."

Alex was astounded. He couldn't comprehend the people of House Banfield, who didn't advocate at all for their own rights.

While he stewed, someone who was obviously important in the domain appeared at the protest. A large number of soldiers accompanied her as her guard, and mobile knights cruised in the sky, keeping an eye out from above.

"Looks like something's starting," one of Alex's friends said to him.

The college student walked away, and Alex shifted his attention to the arrival of this big shot. "Wonder who that is. Let's see what's going on."

As they edged closer to get a better look, Alex thought: *Okay, so this is a planet full of idiots, but I should consider it a good thing that I've found out how easy they are to manipulate. If this important person is about to make a speech, I'll just look for all the holes in it, then get more people to join my cause by refuting their words.* He wanted to use this as an opportunity to draw more attention to himself and recruit more people to his cause.

Standing atop a floating armored vehicle was a woman in a military uniform holding a microphone.

She then addressed the crowd. "Protesters! There is no need to make such a fuss over the lord's bedtime affairs! Break it up, everyone!"

Alex realized who this beautiful blonde woman was. "Hey, isn't that the lord's concubine or mistress or something...?"

One of his friends looked her up on a tablet and nodded. "It sure is. There's plenty of information on her."

Alex wondered what kind of speech she would give, but apparently, she was only here to break up the protest. Thus, the crowd booed her.

"Lord Liam needs to fulfill his duties as a noble!"

"We're serious about this!"

"Hey, aren't you his concubine? This is on you too!"

News of Liam pulling Eulisia out of the military for his own purposes had spread throughout the domain, making the people assume she was now Liam's lover. However, in response to the words they shouted, Eulisia trembled. Tears filled her eyes.

"I-it's not like I..." Eulisia's job should have been to call on the protesters to disperse, but instead, what she shouted into the microphone came straight from her heart. "It's not like I haven't tried! I did everything I could to get Lord Liam to make a move on me, but he won't show any interest!!!"

The crowd quieted down when they heard that.

One anxious citizen mumbled, "What... Does the lord hate women or something?"

Eulisia heard the man and cried even harder into the microphone. "I would have been able to give up if he did! But... But he says he likes women fine! I devoted my whole youth to becoming his secretary! Just recently, I had to go retrain with the military...and he said he didn't even know that was where I was! And then he told me to come back here and quell the protests! Did he forget about me altogether after not seeing me for a few years?!"

The hard work she performed every day seemed to be pushing Eulisia to her limits. More than anything else, she couldn't forgive Liam for just forgetting about her.

She clutched the microphone in both hands. "I want to... I want to go on dates too! He takes Lady Rosetta to parties every day now, but *I* have to work? Why? Can't I just have some fun for one day? Late at night, I cry when I think about how I'm only getting older... I get more and more anxious every night, lying there thinking about it!"

The protesters exchanged looks with each other. Eulisia was sobbing into the microphone now, so the protesters began to console her. Some young girls even cheered her on.

"Y-you can do it!"

"You'll get there someday, Miss Eulisia!"

"I-it's all right! You're pretty! You're so pretty!"

Eulisia continued venting her pent-up frustrations. "I want him to make a move on me too, but he won't! What am I supposed to do about it? I'd do anything if it'd get him interested, but nothing I've done has worked! It's not my fault!!!"

"After that, the 'Don't Forget About Miss Eulisia Either' protests started, in addition to the 'Treat Lady Rosetta Right' protests. I will say that Lady Rosetta still commands most of the populace's attention, however. Her popularity is really something else. Why, it moves me to tears!"

As Brian reported to me on the state of the protests, and a little too joyfully for my tastes, my fists trembled at my sides. What in the world had Eulisia done? She completely ruined my image as an evil lord. My carefully cultivated image of being viciously villainous was reduced to merely that of a commonplace bad guy. The current perception of me seemed to be that I was just a stingy jerk who wasn't feeding a mutt he took in. *I can't let this stand!*

"Incidentally, there are also those calling for you to take on a new concubine," Brian continued.

"Why the hell do my subjects think they can tell me what to do? My harem is my concern alone! I'm not taking orders from anyone, okay?!"

Brian's eyes became cold, and seeing that made me all the angrier. *H-hey! If it weren't you, Brian, I'd cut your head off for that, you know!*

"Your number currently stands at zero, Master Liam."

"Huh? What number?"

"From the day you first stated that you intended to form a harem, up until today... Your total count of kept women currently stands at zero."

"Huh? I-it does not!" I protested. "I have Amagi! She counts!!!"

"Even if she did, she would only count as one. You have yet to lay a hand on Lady Rosetta, and you've completely neglected Lady Eulisia, a woman you pulled from a promising career in the military. I have to admit—I've seriously considered joining these protests myself."

"Screw you! I don't take orders from anyone! I have my own tastes, okay?!"

I'm just supposed to put together a harem because everyone around me tells me to? I'm expected to take a woman to bed because I have some duty to do so? What a load of bull!

I'll only bed who I want to bed, when I want to bed them! I'm not backing down on that!!!

"*Your preferred tastes can be considered after the more pressing issue of your heir is resolved.*"

I was at a disadvantage against Brian and his sound arguments, but that didn't mean I wasn't thinking about ways to get back at my subjects for pulling this crap with me.

"Just wait 'til I get back home," I said. "I'll tax the living daylights out of those good-for-nothings. They won't even be able to *think* about holding protests when I'm done with them."

Brian didn't react to that, ignoring it like I was only ranting. Instead he resumed his report. *Hey, isn't this guy a little* too *rude to me?*

"*Ah... I look forward to it. Anyway, on the other hand, the democracy movement didn't gain nearly as much traction as I feared it might. That fire may as well be extinguished by now.*"

Well, I was thankful *those* protests had quieted down, at least. "Democracy, eh? Make sure you figure out who the idiots were behind that movement. They're my enemies. Human rights, my ass. All they want is my authority for themselves."

"*Master Liam?*"

Brian gave me a questioning look, but I went on without waiting for him to catch up. "Whether or not nobility exists, there will always be people in a role of authority," I said.

No matter what the system of government was, there were always rulers and there were always subjects. A world without a class system? Something like that couldn't exist. Without nobles, politicians would just have all the power. Then, you had the gap between the rich and the poor to consider too. There was always a minority with all the power to rule over the masses.

To be honest, I supposed democracy *would* have been a better system than a hereditary nobility system, but I didn't plan on giving my authority to anyone else and I didn't care what happened to the masses. And neither did the people who clamored for democracy. Only a tiny fraction of them truly cared about fairness, and I was sure the rest just wanted to seize the authority I wielded for themselves.

No, even if they started out with pure ideals, once they *had* authority, those rebels would inevitably be corrupted by it. I understood that well, having risen to a position of power myself. Authority was alluring and led people astray. I didn't think that was necessarily a bad thing though, not when it came to myself. In fact, I *wanted* to be led astray by authority. I wanted to drown in its allure. After all, I was an evil lord.

"If they want to depose me and rule in my stead, then they need to show they're more powerful than I am. If they can do that, then they can have my power. If they can't...then they should be treated as the losers that they are, right?"

If they wanted to overthrow me, I invited them to try, but they had better be ready for the consequences when they failed. I wasn't kind to my enemies. I would crush these people thoroughly.

8 Their Names

THE NOBLES OF Calvin's faction weren't happy.

One of them, face red with rage, pounded his fist on the table in front of him, drawing the attention of everyone else in the meeting room. "Over one hundred members of my household died! One hundred sons and family members!"

"We were the only ones who suffered losses? Damn it!!! If we had known how skilled that man of Liam's was..."

"Claus, was it? He's completely unknown, but he must be incredibly talented. And cold as ice too, to eliminate so many of his own forces just because of a difference between factions."

The war with the United Kingdom had ended all too soon. Though they assumed it would last for decades, the entire conflict concluded well within a single year. Thanks to this swift victory, Cleo's reputation was soaring, even though there had been many losses on the Empire's side. However, the great majority of those were from Calvin's forces, who rushed out to meet the fight while Cleo's faction hung back to wait for the perfect time to strike.

The forces Calvin's faction contributed to the war didn't represent the entirety of their military strength, so it shouldn't have affected them much to lose a small number of ships. However, the fact that they had all been wiped out made it a different story.

A noble seated near Calvin wore a bitter scowl. "Your Highness, because of the war, Prince Cleo's forces are now almost entirely outfitted with next-generation weapons. Most of the weapons factories we asked not to supply them ignored our requests."

"Indeed. It seems my name doesn't amount to much, does it..."

The Empire had given their approval to make updating the expeditionary army's weaponry the highest priority at any weapons factories that supplied them. To undermine Cleo, Calvin's faction had contacted the weapons factories and asked them to give Cleo's faction only the minimum of support. Unfortunately, the factories that already had a relationship with Liam ignored that request. Of the factories Calvin's faction had contacted, the Third, Sixth, Ninth, and the Seventh—all of which were intimately involved with Liam—had given Cleo's faction their full support instead.

As a result, the expeditionary army had placed the majority of their orders with those four weapons factories and the other factories hadn't been able to profit from the conflict, so now they were irritated with Calvin—just like the nobles in his own faction.

"So the factories ignored the crown prince's request and sided with Cleo's faction. The nerve of them." Calvin said this, but he could imagine why the weapons factories had ignored his request. "I suppose they thought they'd get more out of it in the end if Liam stood at the top."

One of the nobles noted, "The Empire has always favored the First and Second Weapons Factories. I wouldn't be surprised if the others have been nursing resentment for a long time now, and figured they'd benefit more from siding with Cleo's faction."

"That's troubling. It's not as if it's *my* policy."

The reason the Empire favored the First and Second Weapons Factories was because they tended to be repositories for the highest-quality military technology. When they were first established, each individual weapons factory would share whatever technology they developed for themselves with the First and Second, since their goal was to create the best-performing weaponry for the

Imperial Army. As the years went by, though, eventually the First and Second Weapons Factories basically just profited from the technology of the other factories without innovating much on their own. The Empire left that situation as it was for so long that the other weapons factories came to hold a grudge. These other factories doubtlessly gave their assistance to Cleo's faction due to the influence of Liam, who was their regular patron. The other factories probably hoped that if Cleo became emperor, he would improve the situation they currently found themselves in.

Calvin changed the topic of conversation to the weaponry itself. "So Cleo's faction has armed itself with the latest weaponry, eh? I'd like for us to do the same. Would that be difficult?"

He looked at the nobles around him, and from their sour expressions he surmised that the answer was yes.

"It might be possible for *some* of our forces," one of them replied, "but with the losses we sustained in the war, our finances are dire at the moment. The United Kingdom will be paying the Empire reparations, but I doubt the prime minister will allow us to make use of them for such purposes."

The prime minister would likely use the conflict's heavy expenses as a reason to cut back on military spending, leaving Calvin unable to use the Empire's money to strengthen his own faction.

This led the other nobles to return to the subject of Liam.

"That boy used Empire money to strengthen *his* faction though!"

"No, the brat spent a good deal of his own money, as I understand it."

"So is he out of funds now too?"

Liam had spent quite a lot of his own wealth to fund his war efforts, but he got a good return on his investment by bolstering the military might of Cleo's faction. They also improved their ability to work together as a unit.

I messed up, Calvin thought. *Liam didn't stay behind just to party and play it safe.*

Liam remained behind on the Capital Planet so he could focus on supporting his troops from the rear. Because of him overseeing logistics, Cleo's army had suffered no setbacks in that area. It could even be said they succeeded *because* Liam wasn't with them. He took a slight hit to his reputation for not going to the frontlines himself, but the benefits far outweighed the costs.

Now my faction's military strength is in question, by comparison.

Calvin's forces in the expeditionary army had suffered severe losses, and they wouldn't be able to upgrade the weaponry of their remaining forces for some time. They were in a bad position, and the prime minister was sure to reject any attempts to use the Empire's money to fix that now that the war was over.

The momentum's with Cleo now, but it can't end like this.

If this were enough to get Calvin to give up, then he would already have dropped out of the race for the throne by now. He would even already be dead.

"We allowed Liam to walk away with most of the glory, but we can't let things stand the way they are."

The gathered nobles added their input.

"Let's do all we can to ruin Liam's reputation."

"I'll admit he's skilled at logistics, but it still doesn't look good that he didn't fight on the frontlines himself."

"To defeat Cleo, what we really need to do is defeat Liam. But how?"

Even if they were to go after Liam's associates instead of him directly, he protected those associates diligently. He also had a very skilled underground organization working for him that had thwarted all of Calvin's moves against him while he remained on the Capital Planet.

In Calvin's eyes, Liam was finally a formidable enemy. The other nobles of his faction didn't underestimate him any longer either. He wasn't just a boy who got lucky and was full of himself because of his personal strength as a fighter. No—he was truly an enemy to contend with.

We realized Liam's strengths too late... Was this how it was for you, Linus?

Had Calvin's brother lost to Liam because he underestimated him in the same way?

Calvin pulled himself together and gave his faction a new order. "Let's call those two Swordmasters to the Capital Planet."

The nobles all exchanged nervous glances, but they accepted his suggestion as unavoidable.

"Will you send them to face Liam directly?"

Calvin shook his head. "No, I want them with me, just in case. I think things are about to get messy on the Capital Planet, so I want them to serve as my guards."

If they couldn't deal with Liam on the battlefield, then they'd have to deal with him right here. Still, Calvin knew it would be a bad move to just send the Swordmasters to deal with him directly. It would be more beneficial to show people that the Swordmasters were aligned with him than to send them to assassinate Liam.

There are other ways to get to the count. Political moves, financial moves...any number of approaches. Military strength isn't all there is.

After conferring about it, Calvin and his noble allies decided to use whatever methods they could to deal with Liam.

He really must have some sort of divine force on his side if he was able to turn the situation around on the battlefield the way he did. Unfortunately for him, the real battle's not over yet.

The planet where the Ahlen sword style had its headquarters was ruled by the Swordmaster serving as the style's current head. This fact showed just how much weight the Ahlen style carried in the Empire. Many powerful nobles were counted among its students, including Imperial royalty. As one of the two major fighting styles utilized throughout the Empire, it was rivaled only by the Kurdan mixed fighting style.

At the headquarters, the Ahlen style's Swordmaster was in the process of preparing for a trip to the Capital Planet. He was a muscular man dressed in a suit and a coat. He was also wearing sunglasses and had his trusty sword in hand.

"We're all ready, sir."

His students stood in a line in front of the car that

waited to take him to the spaceport. They bowed as he approached.

Walking beside him, the Swordmaster's son said, "Who does the crown prince think he is? Summoning you to protect him just 'cause he's scared of Liam."

The headquarters of the Ahlen style actually had more power than many noble houses, so the Swordmaster's son spoke like a noble himself. Essentially, they *were* nobles. They earned their position teaching their sword style across the Empire. Their unique position allowed them to speak with some authority.

"I've never even *heard* of the Way of the Flash," the son said. "It's laughable that the crown prince is so scared of a sham. Well, I guess it's a good opportunity to give him some more training."

The family had grown arrogant since so many Imperial nobles practically revered the instructors. They had grown used to being held as masters of swordsmanship. Their abilities with the blade were real, and the authority their family commanded rivaled other noble houses. Making an enemy of the Ahlen sword style essentially meant making enemies of all the nobles trained in that style. The school was much more powerful than many noble houses themselves.

"Count Banfield is full of himself for defeating Swordmaster Gerut, but all he really did was beat one self-taught swordsman," the son went on. "Banfield's nothing for the Ahlen style to be worried about."

"True enough," the Ahlen Swordmaster said, nodding. "The Way of the Flash is just like any other wannabe sword style that will fade away in an instant."

The Swordmaster was about to get into the car, but suddenly he froze and leaped away from it. Many of his students did the same, but those less skilled among them must have been cut by something. Blood spurted from their bodies as they cried out in surprise.

The Swordmaster's son drew his sword and took a fighting stance even before his father could. "Who's there?"

Suddenly, the car itself was bisected vertically.

Standing before the Swordmaster and his son was a young woman holding a sword in each hand. She was dressed in a light kimono-like garment that showed off her body shape with no sign that she wore any sort of powered suit beneath it. Her eyes were hidden by the brim of her straw hat, but her mouth was curved in a smile.

"How did you get here?" the son blurted out.

The Swordmaster knew his son was panicking, but he couldn't blame him. There were a lot of reckless young people out there, and many of them infiltrated the Ahlen style's headquarters every year in a show of bravado. That was why there were strict checks in place if one wished to come to their planet. The fact that this woman had gotten through those security measures was proof of her skill.

The woman brought a hand up to her hat, and a group of master swordsmen with the rank of assistant instructor rushed at her, seeing this as a moment of vulnerability. The Swordmaster called out to taunt the woman, assuming she was about to die at their hands.

"For someone infiltrating enemy territory, you were much too relaxed. If you're going to attack someone, you need to— Wha?!"

One second, the Swordmaster saw his assistant instructors rushing at the girl, and then the next, he saw them all flying away—each one missing a limb. They all fell to the ground, their lives spared, but clutching their injuries. He hadn't even seen the woman *move*.

His son stepped in front of the Swordmaster. "Are you an assassin? But then, why wouldn't you—"

Why isn't she killing her victims? Naturally this question came to the Swordmaster's mind too, even as he marveled at the woman's skill. *Just now... What did she even do?*

He didn't see the woman's sword move at all. Was she using some sort of magic? A new type of weapon?

As the Swordmaster stared at her in awe, the woman threw her hat aside and showed him her face. Her wild orange hair was long, tied back behind her head. It swayed in the wind, billowing out for a second like a lion's mane. The main reason he was able to instantly identify her as a woman without seeing her face was because of her large breasts, which her clothing couldn't disguise. For all her untamed unruliness, she had a strange sex appeal...but she also seemed very young to him, as if she'd only just become an adult.

Who is this woman? What is she? And...what school does she belong to?

The Swordmaster was sweating heavily. At last he drew his own sword, and when she saw that, the woman finally identified herself.

"I'll give you my name. If I don't, you're liable to say you don't know who took you down, right? The name's Fuka Shishikami—and my school is the Way of the Flash."

The Swordmaster leaped back when he heard that. His son, however, stepped forward instead. "So you and your fake school have finally shown yourselves! I'll put you in your place!"

The Swordmaster reached out desperately as his young, impetuous son rushed forward. "You idiot! Get back!"

"Father, there's no need for you to draw your sword against one measly—"

Before he could finish, something strange happened to his son's body. The Swordmaster's eyes widened at what he saw take place right in front of him.

A-again! What happened? What did she do?

The most talented of his children had both of his arms lopped off like a complete rookie. As his blood sprayed into the air, the young man cried. "My arms... My aaarms!!!"

A crimson pool began to spread on the ground around him as blood gushed from the stumps of both limbs.

"You're in my way. Move." Fuka kicked the son out of her way and walked up to the Swordmaster. Her swords were back in their scabbards, and her hands weren't even touching their handles. She spread her arms wide, as if to show that she had no intention whatsoever of drawing them. "I've been wanting to meet the Swordmaster of this pathetic little school. Actually, I wanted to bring your head as a gift when I go to challenge the senior pupil to a fight."

Seeing this woman who invaded the headquarters of the Ahlen style and cut down all his strongest fighters without breaking a sweat before him, the Swordmaster instinctively realized...

I'm no match for her.

He was chosen as a Swordmaster mostly for political reasons, but he still stood at the top of a renowned school of swordsmanship. He definitely had the abilities to back up his title. Unfortunately, it was those very abilities that allowed him to gauge the strength of his opponent and determine that he couldn't beat her.

The Swordmaster smiled, even though he knew he couldn't defeat her himself. "It's lucky that we met here, and not elsewhere. Here, it doesn't really matter how I take you down."

"Huh?"

Fuka gave him a questioning look, but before she could say anything the Swordmaster shouted, "Do it!"

Armed soldiers charged out of the headquarters building, and floating tanks appeared in the air above them. The soldiers surrounded the young woman, pointing their guns at her. Fuka shrugged.

The Swordmaster pointed his sword at her. "Did you think I'd grace you with a fair fight? No matter how strong the Way of the Flash is, if you lose here, it's all over. No one will learn the truth. The only thing anyone will hear of is your defeat. This is the end for your school."

Witnesses here would only spread the tale of an Ahlen Swordmaster defeating a student of the Way of the Flash, keeping the full details of the encounter a secret. If they did that, all anyone would ever know was that the Ahlen style was victorious over the Way of the Flash.

Fuka's eyes went deadly cold. The expression on her face was one of disgust, as if she was disappointed to learn the true nature of this Swordmaster. Even so, her lips wore a smile.

"I only need to win!" the Swordmaster continued to rant triumphantly. "Winning is all that matters in any kind of fight. Coming up with a strategy that allows you to win is nothing to be ashamed of. Now disappear, Way of the Flash!"

Fuka scratched her head. She had lost all interest in the Swordmaster. "Oh, whatever. I just want to be able to say I beat you. You need to pay for trash-talking my master though. Your only purpose from now on is to live a life of shame and to spread the word of how strong the Way of the Flash is."

Enraged by Fuka's arrogance, the Swordmaster shouted to the soldiers around him, "Hurry up and shoot her!" At the same instant he did this, though, the soldiers and their weapons all went flying—each one of them slashed to pieces.

The Swordmaster couldn't move. After all, Fuka had been thirty meters away from him a second ago, but now she stood right in front of him with the tip of her sword pressed to his gut.

"I'm going to take a little time now to show you just how frightening the Way of the Flash is. Oh, and I'd like to take that title of yours while I'm at it. It's kind of cool."

Did she really not understand the steps one had to go through before they could officially call themselves a Swordmaster? She thought she could assume that title just because she thought it was "kind of cool"? The Swordmaster felt her words were an insult to his entire life.

Enraged with Fuka, he tried to open his mouth to say something, but what came out was only a pained "Gah!!!"

"Really, I wanted to just squish you all like bugs, but you need to suffer longer than that for badmouthing my master."

The Swordmaster trembled when he looked into Fuka's eyes from up close. *Th-this little girl is stronger than me? What is this Way of the Flash? Why is it only making itself known now? Why?!*

"K-kill her!!!" the Swordmaster yelled, and even more soldiers appeared around them. "Kill her! I don't care if I get caught in the crossfire! If you don't kill her, the Ahlen style is—"

If she escaped and boasted about this, the Ahlen style's reputation would be destroyed. He was so terrified of this prospect that he was willing to sacrifice himself to erase her.

Surrounded by hundreds of soldiers, Fuka held her two swords up and smiled again. "My blades will drink from each and every one of you."

That day, it was as though the headquarters of the Ahlen sword style was hit by a hurricane. Thankfully, somehow, not a single person died in the attack. Everyone unrelated to the school saw that as good thing... but everyone associated with the school bemoaned it as the worst possible outcome.

On the planet that was home to the school of the Kurdan mixed fighting style, a female swordsman sat on the head of a mobile knight she had just bisected with her longsword. From this perch, she looked down at the Swordmaster of the Kurdan style and his best students. The Kurdan Swordmaster was naked, and "The Way of the Flash was here" was burned into his back. Just for fun, the female swordsman had marked him that way with a laser gun.

"Well, that turned out nicely, didn't it?" she said. "I guess it's not so bad using a gun every once in a while. Now I'm in a much better mood."

The students were terrified, but it was understandable. After all, the female swordsman, Riho Satsuki, had charged into the Kurdan style's headquarters and defeated the head of the school, a Swordmaster...even toying with him in the process. The Swordmaster and his instructors had thought that if they killed her on their own turf they could keep it under wraps—even if they used a mobile knight to do it—but the young woman had cut the machine down as easily as anything.

The young woman had long, deep blue hair and pink eyes. She laughed innocently at the tormented Swordmaster. She was thin and dainty-looking, with a feminine figure, but there was a childishness to her as well, as if she had only just reached adulthood. Despite her youth, even the school's best students hadn't been able to so much as touch her.

On top of the mobile knight, Riho swung her legs back and forth playfully, losing interest in the Kurdan Swordmaster as he lost consciousness. "Aw, now what was that you said about the Way of the Flash again?"

The students stared up at her, frozen with terror.

Suddenly, one student's arm fell to the floor with a thud, like it simply dropped off on its own. "Yeeaaaaarrgh!"

It was impossible—no one had seen Riho make a move.

With a sadistic smile on her face, Riho said, "I won't kill you. It's much better for you to live on, marked with shame. That's what you get for acting like you were so strong when in reality, you're just weaklings. Did you really think I'd let you get away with ridiculing my master's Way of the Flash?"

Finally, the gathered students turned and fled, without giving a thought to how pathetic they looked.

Riho jumped down from the mobile knight to chase them. "Ah ha ha ha! You want to play tag? Are you serious? Oh my god, you guys are hilarious!!!"

As she ran after them, she slashed at their ankles. The students tumbled down around her. Then, she turned to the terrified rookie students who were cowering off to the side.

"You guys will remember this, right?" she said. "The Way of the Flash is the strongest sword style in the universe, and the strongest swordsman in the universe is my master—Yasushi the Sword God! If you get too full of yourselves like these guys, then..."

"S-stop! Aaaaaaaaaah!!!"

The lower students trembled as they watched one of the school's top students scream under Riho's boot.

The smile vanished from Riho's face. "Well, I have a nice present to give my senior pupil when I go to kill him now... Hmm, I should broadcast this scene across the Empire—no, across the whole universe, so Master can see it too! Just gimme a second, all right?"

She took a tablet out of her pocket, so as to make a video of her surroundings. The tablet floated up and hovered on its own, turning to include Riho in the shot. Recently she'd taken to livestreaming what she was up to.

"Hey, guys! It's Riho, your idol swordsman here! Today, I crashed the HQ of the Kurdan mixed fighting style! Tee hee!"

She smiled and struck a cute pose despite the sea of blood around her. The people sprawled on the ground around her were just barely alive. In her streams, she always called herself "the bloodiest idol swordsman in the Empire," and she was living up to that today.

"I beat these guys like this 'cause they were saying mean things about my sword style. It wasn't very satisfying to leave them breathing, but I'll just consider it a warmup exercise before I go kill my senior in my fighting style.

He's supposed to be really strong, so I'm looking forward to it! You guys should get excited for my next stream too! Next time, I'll even show you Liam's severed head!"

The two powerful swordsmen of the Way of the Flash that Yasushi had trained were now finally ready to go after Liam himself.

But in just one day, Yasushi became the sworn enemy of both of the Empire's major sword schools.

9 The Formula for Victory

*H*UH? *Isn't this a little strange?*

The Guide cocked his head as he contemplated the present state of things. Liam was nervous. He definitely was suffering; that much was true. The Guide could also sense Liam's intense anger. The count had been busy lately, though he made it look like he was merely fooling around every day. His army won the war, but at the cost of a large number of the Empire's forces. Cleo's faction must've been far weaker now, but the Guide couldn't shake the feeling that somehow the opposite was true.

"Is it just my imagination...? No, wait!" The Guide suddenly came to a realization. "I see! I just haven't given Liam enough assistance yet!"

Back when he tried everything he could think of to drive Liam into a corner, the boy only caused him endless grief in turn. If only he had known how much easier it would be to assist Liam instead. He was simply feeling some self-doubt now because he hadn't put in enough work yet.

Or at least that was the conclusion the Guide arrived at.

"I just need to work harder to make Liam happy! But... is that really right? I'm not making some kind of huge mistake, am I?"

The Guide was at his wits' end as doubt reared its ugly head again. Suddenly, he found himself wondering what the two feral kids he gave to Yasushi to raise to kill Liam were up to. He'd supported Eulisia in the past, and that woman still betrayed him. The Guide was starting to worry that Yasushi's pupils would fail him in the same way. He wished he could look into it right now, but he just didn't have enough power to spare.

After all, these days, every time he was able to save up a little power, he needed to use it to support Liam. When he did that, it made Liam suffer for some reason. Thus, the Guide went on struggling every day to make Liam happy. Now that he had so little extra strength, he mostly got his information from whatever newspapers he could find lying around.

Happening upon just such a discarded periodical, the Guide stooped for it and grumbled. "Ugh! I used too much power to support Liam. It was so much easier to get my information before..."

Right away, he found exactly what he was looking for. It was strange how it had just fallen into his lap like this. The newspaper had digital pages, and Riho's video started playing when he arrived at a relevant article. *"Are you watching, senior pupil? I'm coming to kill you now!"* Behind her were the Kurdan style's Swordmaster and his top students, lying semiconscious in a pool of blood. It warmed the Guide's heart to see how abnormal Riho was, declaring she was going to kill Liam while wearing such a sunny smile. The Guide marveled at how those two savage, boyish brats could grow up to become such impressive women.

"Ahh! What a pure specimen of swordsmanship! She'll surely be able to kill Liam! And what of the other one?"

He flipped to the next page and saw that the other of Yasushi's wonderfully transformed pupils recently assaulted the headquarters of the Ahlen sword style. She wreaked havoc using the techniques of the Way of the Flash as well.

"I knew I could believe in you, Yasushi. You trained up those two secret weapons perfectly." Yasushi had fled from the Empire, but the Guide sent his gratitude to the man, wherever he was now. "Unfortunately, once everything is over, I plan to go make sure that you're unhappy too. After all, I wouldn't have had to go through all this trouble in the first place if you hadn't made Liam so strong."

The Guide sauntered away, tossing the digital paper aside as he went. An oddly half-transparent dog watched as it hit the ground. The dog glanced down at the articles, picked up the paper, and ran off somewhere.

I chatted with Elliot from the Clave Firm as I relaxed in a little side room. We were waiting for the party to celebrate the expeditionary army's victory.

"Congratulations on your victory, Count Banfield!" Elliot told me. "Is the Empire throwing a celebration as well?"

Elliot had gifted me with heaps of gold and expensive alcohol to celebrate the expeditionary army's—no, *my* complete victory. Man, I loved blatant brownnosers like him.

"We're just celebrating on our own here. After all, the Empire's losses were quite significant. The United Kingdom was a powerful foe, it seems." I smirked as I said this, and Elliot caught on to my true meaning.

"I'm sure Prince Cleo's chances of succession have improved considerably now that he's defeated such a powerful foe. Similarly, the crown prince who forced responsibility for this crisis on his brother has no doubt lost a fair degree of his standing as well…"

"Things seem to have really ended up in my favor, didn't they? So, what is Calvin up to now?" I asked.

"Those around him seem rather nervous, but he himself remains calm. Of course, it could just be that he's projecting that image," remarked Elliot.

I would have preferred Calvin to panic and do something careless. After all, as long as he didn't make any moves, there was nothing I could really do against him. At least we'd eliminated a good amount of Calvin's firepower in this conflict, while my own faction had become much stronger.

I also extended my reach by lending money to other nobles in need. I wanted to play rough with that, loanshark style, but Cleo's faction was nothing but other evil lords like me, so we had to stick together. We could save petty squabbles for after we destroyed our enemies. I decided to play nice until we took Calvin down, so for now, I was only charging them a little bit of interest.

As I chatted with Elliot, Wallace came in with a harried look on his face.

"Liam, it's terrible!" he yelled.

"What is it? Isn't the party ready yet?" Wallace was pale and anxious, so it made me concerned.

"The *party* is the problem! You wanted to change the theme into a celebration of the army's victory, right? Well, there's a lot of stuff we're missing. Actually, we pretty much have to redo the preparations completely!"

"What?" On a whim, I changed the theme of tonight's party, without thinking through the consequences, and I guess...

Wallace held his head in his hands. "We can't do this! We can't celebrate our victory without a major overhaul!!!"

Wallace was still in charge of all the parties I was throwing to entertain myself. Honestly, he was proving himself to be a lot more dependable with this new job, so I decided to listen to his concerns.

I turned to address the merchant. "Elliot, work with Wallace to get everything we need."

"Just leave it to me. Procuring everything on such short notice will incur quite a cost, of course..."

"Are you stupid? This is my party! I don't care what it costs!" *Dammit! I should have thought this through a little more.*

Anyway, the damage was done, so I set Wallace up with Elliot to overcome this setback. Still, Wallace continued to fret. "We'll have to change all the fixtures in the venue, too. It's not set up for a victory celebration at all..."

Watching Wallace really got me thinking. His concern for the quality of these parties was so genuine. Society might look at him and think his talents were pointless, but I appreciated what he did.

He's really made something of himself, huh?

Back when I first met him in primary school, I never thought he'd amount to anything, but he was coming in plenty handy now. It had been a good decision as an evil lord to take him in. As it was now, Wallace's abilities were indispensable if I wanted to enjoy parties like a villain should. I wanted to pat myself on the back for having such good instincts back then. *Good job, me!*

At the same time, the nobles closest to Calvin were gathered in the palace on the Capital Planet. Each and every one of them was plainly nervous.

"Your Highness!" one of the nobles reported. "A small group is planning an attack on Count Banfield!"

"That's not good." Right now, that was genuinely bad news for Calvin. "Who?"

"Relatives of nobles who died in the expeditionary army. Some of them even lost their heirs. They said they can't leave things as they are, and they're all worked up about getting revenge...even if they have to leave your faction to do so."

Calvin's faction was large, and there were many short-sighted people among them. Managing this varied bunch was one of Calvin's duties as their leader, but it could be an exhausting task, especially now with so many nobles upset over losing family members in the war. There were likely more than a few who were genuinely grief-stricken, but the majority were just upset about the damage to their reputations. Of course, there was also the matter of the large number of ships they lost. Some nobles simply couldn't accept that they lost so much.

I'd like to stop them, but if I do, they'll turn their complaints toward me. The vengeful nobles were taking their frustrations out on Liam, but if Calvin interfered with their plan, *he* would be the one to earn their ire. He could just picture them saying, "You said we'd come out of this okay!" and "What are you going to do to make it up to us?"

All of those in the faction were equally responsible, but these people were looking for someone to pin their anger on. Emotions were at play, not logic. Many nobles didn't have very good self-control due to their insulated and privileged upbringings. Primary school and military service could alleviate some of that, but certainly not all.

The more responsible nobles were just as upset as Calvin and voiced their objections.

"This is hardly the time..."

"They don't understand the ramifications..."

"It will only serve to harm His Highness's reputation if they pull something now..."

Calvin sighed. "Let them leave the faction, then."

"Are you sure, Your Highness?" one noble asked. "I hardly think that will benefit your reputation."

"We should consider this an opportunity to get rid of the more troublesome members of the group. The faction has gotten too big, too unruly. If we're going to fight Liam, we should be at our best."

The nobles all agreed and soon departed from the room. When Calvin confirmed that he was alone, he snapped his fingers and a small flame appeared in the air. The flame swelled and changed shape several times until a large man kneeled before him. The man was a ninja, and a symbol on his clothing identified him as holding a higher rank than the men who fought Kukuri some time ago.

"What do you require?" the ninja asked.

"It seems some idiots are about to cause a scene. If you get an opportunity, use it to erase at least some of Liam's operatives. Did you get any information on them, by the way?"

The ninja explained what he knew of Kukuri and his men. "Based on our clan's records, we believe they may be a group called the Shadows, thought to be destroyed 2,000 years ago."

"The Shadows?"

"An organization that served the emperor at the time, 2,000 years ago. That was just what others called them, however. No one knows their true name."

"There were a lot of clans like yours at work back then, weren't there? Do you suppose House Banfield has been harboring them all this time?"

"No."

"You don't?"

The ninja produced a shuriken and threw it at the wall. It turned to flame, which spread out into a screen that displayed an image of one of these so-called "Shadows." The man on the screen was Kukuri.

"This man was one of the most feared of his kind at the time. He worked for the emperor, and in the end, it was said that he was turned to stone and left to erode."

If the man pictured was the most feared, that meant he was the most powerful of those secret operatives back then. This news did not sit well with Calvin.

"But he lived?" the prince asked. "It seems more likely that someone just inherited his role."

"That's not possible."

"Why?"

"Their whole clan was rooted out by the other organizations. My own predecessors participated as well. It was the emperor's orders not to leave a single one of them alive," the ninja explained.

The emperor at that time gathered up Kukuri and his men and had them all turned to stone. It was hard to believe their clan could have survived all this time, and even if they had, it was even harder to believe their unique skills could have been passed down. Maintaining an organization like that wasn't cheap. It would have been almost impossible for both the organization and their techniques to survive all this time in secret.

"Your Highness, they are intimately familiar with the palace."

"That's not good. It's not as if the palace is completely unchanged from 2,000 years ago, but it'll be trouble if any passageways remain that only they know about."

There had been plenty of renovations to the palace over the years, and they were always discovering old sections that had become walled up and forgotten over time. It wouldn't surprise Calvin at all if there were secret passages from ages past that were still usable now.

"From what we can tell, they've revived in the present with all the power they possessed in the past. I can't imagine there are that many of them, though."

So they were highly skilled, but few.

Well, there's no reason to go out of our way to fight them right now.

Still, an incredibly powerful organization from the past had been revived in the present, and that made Calvin uneasy. It unnerved him that he didn't know when these "Shadows" might come after him. Having grown up in the palace, he knew full well how frightening people of that nature were, and it made him nervous. It made him want to take care of the problem sooner rather than later.

"Can you get rid of them?"

The ninja turned to flame and vanished, leaving behind only the reply, "As you wish."

Concealed within elaborate decorations designed for tonight's big party were several hoodlums, hired by the vengeful nobles to attack Liam. These heavy decorations were currently in the process of being moved.

"Nobles just throw parties every day, eh?" one man whispered to his partner.

"They spend enough money in one night that a commoner could use to live it up over their entire life."

"Well, I hope they enjoy themselves, since this night could be their last."

Normally, hired goons like these would never have been able to make it into such a party undetected, but they received assistance from the nobles who hired them in order to slip past security and make it into the venue.

They were prepared to attack when the time was right, though right now, they couldn't see outside their tight hiding places. The decorations were equipped with cameras so they could see outside, but they were covered by cloth before the party began. Within the decorations, the men were being jostled about.

"They've been moving us around a lot..."

"Have they noticed us?"

"They would've killed us in an instant if they did. There must have been some change in their plans."

It wasn't just these two; a good number of other hired goons were hidden inside decorations for tonight's party. Even if they didn't manage to kill Liam, they were sure to cause damage one way or another. Or at least, that was the plan. One thing they knew for sure was that if they failed and were captured, a punishment worse than death awaited them. This was why these would-be killers were prepared to blow themselves up if it looked as though they were going to be apprehended. If it came to that, then one way or another, they would be sure to cause chaos.

The jostling finally stopped, and the hoodlums waited for the party to begin...but no matter how long they waited, the cloths that covered the decorations were never removed.

"Did they bring the decorations into the venue and then take them out?"

"Damnit! Come on, we're getting out of here. The venue should at least be nearby!"

"Contact the others!"

The men leaped out from their hiding places, finding themselves in some sort of warehouse. The other infiltrators also came out into the open, shocked and speechless.

"Wh-what...?"

"What's going on?"

"Wh-whatever... Let's just get to the venue!"

The men left the warehouse, only to realize they were a considerable distance away from the party itself. They hurried in its direction, but Liam's knights who were guarding the venue spotted them easily.

10 Assassination

"**W**ERE THEY STUPID or something?"

Apparently, there was an incident outside the party venue the night before. My knights spotted a group of armed ruffians running toward the venue. My knights moved in to apprehend them, but apparently the hooligans blew themselves up before my knights could even open fire on them. Either that, or the explosives they carried accidentally went off when they were shot. Regardless, it was unclear, so the incident was under investigation.

Considering their destination, they were likely after me, but the attempt was just so sloppy. I mean, did they really think they were going to just run past my security? Come on now.

I was alone in my office, but Kukuri suddenly emerged from my own shadow. "Master Liam, I have a report."

"Let's hear it."

"It's in regard to the attackers last night."

"You figured something out about them?"

"It appears they meant to sneak into the venue concealed within the party decorations. When the party's theme was changed, the original ones were moved to a different location. The problem is that they had to have assistance. In addition, it's likely such crude attackers were likely just a diversion."

Apparently, quite a surprise had been planned for my party the night before.

"I should have caught it earlier and told you to cancel the party," Kukuri continued, "but fortunately, Lord Wallace happened to remove all of their hiding places instead."

Wallace's sudden rearrangement of the venue managed to prevent a bunch of hoodlums from sneaking into my party. Well, even if he hadn't, Kukuri would no doubt have stopped them before they could strike, so I was sure things would have been okay in the end.

"I've got a weird feeling about this," I said. "I mean, it's just uncanny that Wallace could be so useful."

Of course, I was thankful his actions led to my party going off without a hitch, but wasn't it kind of creepy? I never thought that *Wallace* would ever be so useful.

I mean, a capable Wallace practically wasn't Wallace at all.

"Well, never mind that," I said. "Anything else?"

"I've lost two of my men. We're being targeted by some rather skilled operatives." Though two of his people had been killed, Kukuri's voice betrayed no anger. He instead spoke of their deaths as if reporting today's weather.

"I see. How did they die?"

"They were looking into the origins of last night's attackers when they were taken out by enemy operatives," he explained.

I'd lost some of Kukuri's highly skilled men... There weren't a lot of them in the first place, so just a few losses among them meant a drastic decrease in their strength. Part of me was angry the men went and got themselves killed, but these were valuable assets of mine and worth too much for me to treat poorly.

"Are you all right handling this on your own? I don't mind helping you out one bit if you want my assistance."

Apparently Kukuri didn't want my help, though. "We can't have you doing our job for us. All I ask is that you please give the bodies of any enemy operatives to us. Even those can provide valuable information."

"So passionate about your work," I commented. "Very well. If I get ahold of any, they're all yours."

"Master Liam, there are many skilled operatives after you right now. I would suggest being especially cautious."

Kukuri clearly worried about me, but I wasn't concerned. "It's not a problem; I'm favored by fortune. And besides, if any assassins come after me, I'd enjoy taking them on. It might be fun—I've always wanted to fend off some assassins. Anyway, if any interesting types show up, you just send them my way."

"I'm afraid that won't be possible, as our job is to prevent such people from ever getting near you."

He takes his work so seriously. This is what I'm talking about! I wish Tia and Marie would take a page out of Kukuri's book.

"That's too bad. Well, I'll leave the assassins to you as well, then. I'll be throwing another big party tonight, so I'm sure my enemies will be all over it."

"Yes, sir." And with that, Kukuri sank back into my shadow and disappeared.

Ciel plodded through the hotel corridors, exhausted from the daily parties.

"I think I've been to a lifetime's worth of parties already..."

It wasn't just the number either. The parties were also

extremely varied in theme. They hadn't gone as far as holding a bucket party yet, but there was a truly staggering variety in the types of party hosted day after day by House Banfield.

"I... I can't let this wear me down. I have to expose Liam's true character and free my brother from the illusion he's under."

Unfortunately, it was taking the young woman all she had just to get through each day.

"I can't forgive that Liam for making my father and everyone else fight in the war while he lived it up every day on the Capital Planet... I can't believe my father was okay with that!"

Ciel had no idea that Liam had been handling logistics during the war and looking after the families of the people fighting in the expeditionary army. Ciel hadn't even been to primary school yet, so her knowledge of such things was decidedly lacking. She relied purely on her instincts, and her instincts told her that Liam was just running from the battle.

"One day...I'll unmask Liam!" Even staggering around exhausted, Ciel was still fired up with hostility toward him.

Suddenly, out of the corner of her eye, she could have sworn she spotted an animal. "Huh?" She heard the patter of feet too, so it couldn't have just been her imagination. "Wh-who the heck would let an animal run around on this floor? It must have been Liam!"

Security on the floor where Liam stayed was strict, so a stray couldn't possibly have just wandered in. Also, Liam was probably the only person who could get away with bringing a pet up here.

Ciel ran in the direction she saw the animal go in, but it ended up being an empty dead end. "I guess I lost it. I should report this to Lady Rosetta..."

While she stood dreading this new task thrust on her, she spotted something on the floor—a newspaper.

"What is such a cheap thing doing here? Wait, this is..."

After reading one of the articles, Ciel rushed to Rosetta to show her the news.

"Darling, it's terrible!"

Rosetta burst into my room, making a racket. I was in the middle of instructing Ellen, and the young girl was blindfolded and standing on a ball. Ellen was breathing hard and looked as though she was about to lose her balance at any second. Sweat beaded on her forehead as she neared the point of exhaustion, but I wasn't ready to let her stop yet.

I left Ellen to her training and dealt with Rosetta myself. "What is it?"

Clutched in her hands was a disposable digital newspaper. I hadn't read many of them myself since I was rich—I typically got my news from my subordinates.

Rosetta caught her breath and then showed me a video embedded in one article. "L-look at this!"

"What is it? W-wait... What *is* this?" I snatched the paper out of Rosetta's hands and trembled with rage when I saw its contents.

The article was about an attack on the Ahlen sword style's headquarters. However, it wasn't the attack that had surprised me as much as the attacker.

"Someone's claiming they practice the Way of the Flash, huh..."

Anger welled up within me. The attacker apparently named herself a practitioner of the Way of the Flash and defeated the head of the Ahlen style, another Swordmaster. I didn't care about the Swordmaster; I just cared about how the attacker identified herself. Squabbles between opposing sword schools were beneath me. My issue was the attacker claiming to practice the Way of the Flash.

"So there are finally some pretenders, I guess."

To have defeated a Swordmaster, this person must have had some skill. I glanced at my trusty blade. It was a trophy from my fight with the Goaz Pirate Gang, and I hadn't encountered a sword that surpassed it since then. It was still my very favorite sword.

"I won't let anyone try and pass themselves off as a practitioner of the Way of the Flash. I'll cut them down myself."

Rosetta cocked her head. "Are there no other members of the Way of the Flash besides you, Darling? Couldn't she really be one?"

"What? I've never met another one before. N-no, wait a second..."

Master's face came to mind. He told me that he was looking for new students, so I supposed it wasn't impossible that there could be more out there... Plus, there must've been someone who taught Master in the first place. If that person had apprentices of their own, then it really *was* possible there could be more of us out there somewhere.

"I guess I have to find out for myself."

I decided to keep my favorite sword with me at all times. At the moment, though, Ellen was about to fall. I got behind her and caught her as she stumbled.

"I-I'm sorry, Master."

"You still rely on eyesight a lot, don't you, Ellen? Your eyes are sharp, but you need to polish your other senses too."

"Yes, sir!"

Rosetta had a strange look on her face as she watched the young girl's enthusiastic response. "The Way of the Flash is a very strict style, isn't it, Darling?" she commented. "I'm impressed that anyone could manage to pass it down."

It was practically a miracle that I even came across it myself. I couldn't help but wonder what Master was up to these days...

At about that same time, Yasushi was being chased around by a woman.

"You think you can get rid of me that easily?"

His pursuer was a beautiful woman with glasses and lustrous long black hair in a disheveled state. When she wasn't angry, she must have looked like an intellectual beauty, but there was no trace of that at the moment. With a horrifying look on her face, the normally beautiful woman hurried after Yasushi.

For his part, Yasushi was running as fast as he could. After all, the woman had a knife in her hand.

"I-I didn't mean to deceive youuu!!!" he cried out.

"Get back heeere!"

The woman almost resembled Nias. Yasushi had come to this planet by chance. He met the woman and seduced her in a moment of weakness. She was his type, so he got carried away before realizing that the woman was looking for something far more serious than he was.

The problem was that he used up all his money and ended up relying entirely on the woman to support him. Eventually, she began to pester him to get a job and marry her. To make matters worse...a baby was strapped to her back. Even through all the commotion, the infant slept peacefully. While Yasushi irresponsibly let things progress between them, the two of them had a child. He missed his chance to escape, but today, he was finally ready. However, when he finally made his attempt, the woman realized what he was up to.

"I'm not letting you get away!"

"Gimme a break!"

Yasushi tried to run from the responsibility of family life, but she wasn't about to let him escape.

Then suddenly, he tripped. "Ah—"

Yasushi fell flat on his face in a rather spectacular fashion, and at last, the woman caught up to him.

"You enemy of women!!!" she yelled.

"Nooooo!!!"

The woman's knife sped down toward Yasushi...

I sat in the usual side room, waiting for another fun party to begin. Was I tired of this yet? Of course not. Even if I was, it was my duty as an evil lord to live the high life. My mood soared whenever I thought about how I was indulging in luxury on my taxpayers' dime! On top of all that, something I was particularly excited about was going to happen this time.

"You're beautiful as always, Amagi."

Amagi would be attending tonight's party in her new custom-designed dress. My heart pounded as I saw her standing before me in something so extravagant, rather than her usual maid uniform. I had been looking forward to this for a long time. I sidled up to her.

"Master, I believe you promised *not* to take me to any parties."

"Don't worry—the venue will be dimly lit tonight, so no one will recognize you. Boy, am I glad Wallace came up with that idea! I never considered keeping the venue dark. Now I can take you out without worrying about what anyone will think."

"And your promise?"

"Y-you can come to one party, can't you?" I asked.

"For goodness' sake. Just this one time, all right?"

"Yes!"

I was satisfied that I was finally getting to bring Amagi to an event. I was looking forward to it so much that I was barely able to sleep the night before.

"Why do you wish to take me to a party?"

"Because I want to enjoy myself with you."

To Amagi, I was comfortable saying all sorts of embarrassing lines. Why was that? Because they came from the heart. I didn't care for flesh-and-blood women because they could betray you. Rosetta was a good example of that. I thought she was a woman with a steel will, but the moment I'd made her mine, she mellowed out completely. What was that, if not a betrayal? Frankly, lately I was having more fun teasing the truly steel-willed Ciel instead.

Wallace entered the waiting room. "Liam, it's time to get things started."

"Got it. Come on, Amagi."

I reached out and she took my hand, though hesitantly. My heart warmed as I walked to the venue beside her, hand in hand.

"This is my first time taking you to a party, Amagi."

"It is the only time it will happen," she replied.

In contrast to my excitement, Amagi was rather exasperated, but it seemed to me she was secretly happy in her new dress too. That made *me* happy, but...

"This sucks," I said, stopping in my tracks.

"Master?" Amagi cocked her head.

Today, of all days? This guy has the worst timing.

"Calvin. Why did it have to be today?"

Amagi still didn't understand what was happening and found my behavior confusing. "Master, what is it?"

Wallace hadn't noticed either. "Something wrong, Liam?"

"We've got incoming."

"Huh?"

I slowly let go of Amagi's hand and called, "Kukuri."

Kukuri rose up from my shadow, holding my favorite sword, and reported to me as I took it from him.

"Multiple enemies incoming, Master Liam. Our communications are being jammed as well, so we can't call for reinforcements."

"Got it. Take care of the enemies outside."

Kukuri disappeared back into my shadow, and Wallace began to panic.

"Wait, Liam! We have strong security, and everyone's identity is checked at the door. No one could possibly get into this venue with a disguise."

"They're not inside. They're outside."

The presence I was sensing was definitely outside the venue.

"Wallace, contact the prime minister," I ordered him. "Tell him I want permission to engage at once."

"Huh? How am I supposed to do that?" Wallace asked, having heard Kukuri mention communications interference.

"There should be a wired terminal somewhere near here," I told him. "I'll send a guard with you, so hurry there and contact the prime minister. As fast as you can, all right?"

I needed to use Wallace's status as a former royal to get in touch with the prime minister as soon as possible, meaning that Wallace himself had to be the one to make contact.

Wallace's face twitched. "You're too much, Liam!"

Kukuri emerged outside, his subordinates appearing with him. They were fewer than a hundred strong, whereas the ninjas surrounding the party venue numbered at least a thousand. Nevertheless, Kukuri chuckled, showing his enemies no fear.

"Well, aren't there a lot of you? There are many clans and organizations I've never encountered, but it figures that *you* would survive to the modern day. We have history with the Fire Clan, after all."

One of the Fire Clan ninjas replied, "And I never expected to see someone like you in this time. It seems all the organizations now have weakened compared to when they were in their prime...but you appear to be quite skilled."

The head ninja raised his sword. "You shouldn't still be here—and soon, you won't be."

Kukuri's men drew their weapons too, but Kukuri only spread his arms wide. "You've done your research into us, I see. In any case, it doesn't matter what era we come from. It doesn't change the fact that right now, we're here."

The enemy rushed the Shadows all at once, and it wasn't just the Fire Clan. Assassins whose techniques were based on those of Kukuri's clan were among the thousand as well.

So they sniffed us out and want to take us on, Kukuri thought. *Well, that's fine by me!*

He mowed down any operatives who came at him as he ran toward the enemy leader. A fierce battle between his men and the dark operatives of this era played out all around him, allies and enemies alike hitting the ground dead.

Kukuri reached the enemy leader and swung his massive arms down, but the enemy blocked the strike with his sword.

"This is the end of you," the head ninja said. "That stubborn master of yours pissed off the wrong people."

As Kukuri leaped back, he noticed a spaceship had appeared in the night sky—but that was impossible. No ships were allowed through the protective shell that surrounded the Capital Planet. However they had managed to pull that off, the bottom line was that the enemy intended to use a warship to blow Liam away. The vengeful nobles had finally resorted to brute force to get rid of Liam, consequences be damned.

Kukuri narrowed his eyes. "Well, this is a problem."

He and his men were in a position to escape, but they were charged with protecting the many people inside the venue. He was prepared to return to Liam's side, but the enemy leader slashed at him again. Flames wreathed the ninja's blade, so Kukuri's arm was burned when he blocked the blow. The leader seemed intent on preventing Kukuri from returning to Liam.

"You will be destroyed here with us!" the ninja said.

"You're willing to sacrifice yourselves too, eh?"

Kukuri and his men had thwarted many assassination attempts over the years, like the one from the previous night. Each time, their enemies came at them with everything they had, ready to sacrifice their own lives to fulfill their missions.

Undaunted, Kukuri smiled. "You really are fools."

"What?"

An insect-like mechanical leg sprouted from Kukuri's body, severing the enemy leader's arm. The arm burst into flame and vanished, even as the leader quickly regenerated the lost appendage. The wound seemed to burn, and a new arm appeared.

Kukuri watched this with a touch of envy. "It seems there's a lot to be said for abandoning your physical body. Unfortunately, I don't think we'll be able to adopt that technique ourselves."

The enemy leader held his sword before him, sneering with disgust. "You were too strong then, and you're too dangerous now. That's why the emperor in your time turned you to stone—out of fear."

Kukuri cocked his head more than 90 degrees, the angle making his neck look like it was broken. "Fear? I suppose you can say whatever you like when you don't know anything. If he simply feared us, he could have just executed us. That sadistic bastard *laughed* when he turned us to stone."

"How can you speak of His Majesty like that?"

Even this dark operative was blindly loyal to the Empire, but Kukuri had interacted with the emperor of his day himself, so he knew the truth.

"The man was simply scum. Emperors are human too. They have no special majesty or dignity that sets them apart, and that man was the lowest of the low: the kind who delights in the suffering of others."

"Maybe it was that attitude of yours that got you turned to stone and forgotten by time."

Kukuri knew he couldn't change the enemy leader's mind on this, but there was still something he wanted to convey. "Maybe you're right, but there is one thing I'm thankful to that piece of trash for. It was only because of him that we Shadows finally met someone worth serving."

As Kukuri said this, a figure emerged from the venue building. It was Liam, wielding his favorite sword. The enemy leader signaled to his men with his eyes and some thirty of them turned to engage Liam.

"How foolish," the ninja leader scoffed. "Did he intend to escape by himself? Does he think a human being can evade a warship?"

One of Kukuri's men attempted to stop the ninjas from reaching Liam, but he was only one man against thirty. At this rate, the ninjas' blades would reach Liam...

Then, there was an explosion. Kukuri's subordinate had blown himself up, taking the thirty ninjas with him. Kukuri didn't even turn to look, knowing full well that all of his men were prepared to sacrifice themselves to defeat an enemy. He had no doubt Liam would have been fine even without his subordinate's sacrifice, but this was their way. Being willing to die for their master was just a part of their duty, so Kukuri wasn't saddened by his subordinate's death.

Suddenly, Kukuri manifested hundreds of blades from his shadow, all of them flying in the enemy leader's direction. The leader deflected those that came at him with his sword, but plenty of his nearby men were struck. The blades pierced their cores, and the ninjas disappeared in bursts of flame.

Kukuri took up a bare-handed stance. "Don't underestimate my master. I wouldn't know how to beat him myself, after all. Anyway, it's about time I make you regret ever coming after him."

Kukuri's battle with the enemy leader then resumed.

I'M THE EVIL LORD OF AN INTERGALACTIC EMPIRE

11 Ship Severer

WHEN I STEPPED OUTSIDE the party venue, I was greeted by the sight of a spaceship hovering overhead.

"A ship in the Capital Planet's skies is a bit much, isn't it? Assassinations are supposed to be cleverer than that, Calvin."

I was a little disappointed in the man. This was the best he could think of?

All around me, Kukuri and his men were facing enemy operatives. All of the guests inside were terrified, so my victory party was totally ruined.

The moment I left the venue, a group of ninjas rushed toward me. One of Kukuri's men got in between us and promptly blew himself up, killing himself and bringing a bunch of our enemies down with him. The man gave his life for me, but it was all a part of their job. Still...

"Dead people don't betray you. Your loyalty was the real deal."

You could only really measure someone's true character after they died. By blowing himself up, Kukuri's subordinate fulfilled his duty to me with his very life. I wouldn't call it a noble sacrifice, as it was just a single man who had given his life to protect another man—me. That was all it was. So I decided to fulfill my own duty.

Rosetta flew out of the building behind me, but Amagi grabbed her arm to stop her and pull her back inside.

"Amagi, let me go!" I heard her yell. "Darling's in trouble!"

"You will only get in his way, Lady Rosetta. Please wait for him inside."

I was relieved to see Amagi looking out for her. I didn't know what Rosetta thought she could do, but it would only be more trouble for me if she were out here.

"Amagi, hide inside with Rosetta, would you?" I ordered her.

Tears spilled from Rosetta's eyes, and Amagi looked worried too. "Master, please do not be reckless."

"You call this reckless? This is child's play to me."

Just then, gunfire rained down from the floating ship in the sky. Warships were mostly specialized for attacks on other spacecraft, but those armaments could be used to fire on ground forces as well.

The ship's beam lenses flashed, and live bullets streamed from its guns. Lasers burned the ground around me, and bullets drove into the earth, creating clouds of dust... But every attack that would have been a direct hit on me was deflected by my Flash. I redirected the lasers with the mirror-bright surface of my blade, and I cut down any solid projectiles that came my way.

Though I dealt with all the firepower directed at me, my surroundings were thoroughly destroyed. As clouds of dust plumed up and obscured my vision, I gasped. *Shit! I'll get Amagi's dress dirty!* The dress I ordered was of such high quality, though, that not a single speck of dirt stained it. Another of the designer's multifunctional features, I imagined.

"I think I like that designer. Maybe I'll hire him on an exclusive contract."

Gripping the hilt of my sheathed sword, I assumed a ready stance. The Way of the Flash didn't actually use formal stances, but it did help to brace myself to gather my full strength.

As I watched Amagi hustle Rosetta back inside, a fresh barrage of gunfire rained down on me from the ship. I assumed they didn't want to fire their main cannon, lest it cause too much damage to the Capital Planet. I knew they would have had a better chance if they used that or launched missiles at me though.

"Unfortunately, trying not to damage the Capital Planet will be your downfall."

If they really wanted to kill me, they'd have to obliterate me with their main gun. Of course, I considered some countermeasures in case they did become desperate enough to use the ship's heavy armaments. Villains had to be cautious, after all, and a real villain never lets down his guard. The only reason I'd come outside was because I was certain I could win, and I faced the ship alone because I was that confident in my abilities.

"My technique still doesn't hold a candle to my master's, but...you're no match for me."

I tightened my grip on my sword in its scabbard, gathering my full power in order to launch an attack on the ship. Narrowing my eyes, my concentration heightened, I simply said, "Flash."

Then, I released my slash toward the large object suspended in the sky, and my trusty sword amplified its power. I felt the wave of increased strength rush from me and rocket toward the spaceship. Relaxing my stance, I rested my sheathed blade across my shoulder.

"Now to see what comes next."

A tear appeared in the center of the ship's armored hull and widened. A moment later, debris began to crash down from the sky. At this rate, there would be a great deal of damage to the surface of the Capital Planet. I already planned on justifying my actions as self-defense, but I still didn't want the prime minister to think less of me because I let an area of the Capital Planet get destroyed. It would be the fault of the people who attacked me, so I didn't want to get in trouble for their actions. That was why I intended to thoroughly clean up after myself when all this was over.

What was really surprising to me was that the Capital Planet's defense force hadn't deployed any troops after this spaceship had gotten in through the planet's shell. What negligence!

"Geez, what's going on with this damn planet's security?" I said.

I thought I saw an animal scamper past out of the corner of my eye. I turned toward it, but there was nothing there when I looked directly. *Was it just my imagination?*

"Am I seeing things? Whatever—I've got enough to focus on."

The slow manner in which the ruined spaceship was descending was proof that its anti-gravity equipment was still functioning. It would be a problem if it crashed to the ground, but even more so if it exploded. The party venue had a protective force field around it, so *our* safety was assured, but the same couldn't be said for the surrounding area. Those really in danger from the falling spacecraft weren't the upper echelons of society like us, but common people. I didn't want to have their deaths on my hands when I wasn't responsible for them in the first place.

While I considered my options, Wallace contacted me.

"Liam, the prime minister approved the use of mobile knights!"

I smirked and looked back up at the sky, shouting, "You're up, Avid!"

In response to my voice, a mobile knight appeared in the sky above me. The Avid had been deployed from a House Banfield ship I kept in the vicinity of the Capital Planet, and waited outside the shell until it had approval to enter. Communication jamming meant nothing to my trusty machine, especially now since I installed that mysterious artifact called the Machine Heart. The Avid had no doubt sensed that I was in danger and was standing by to help me as soon as it could.

I praised the Avid for its arrival, which had been even quicker than I hoped. "Good job."

The twenty-four-meter giant landed in front of me, but with such precision that the ground didn't so much as quiver from its arrival. *Man, technology in an intergalactic nation is amazing.*

The Avid extended one hand to me, so I jumped up onto it and was lifted to the cockpit. Inside, I settled in my seat and gripped the control sticks.

"It'll be a major pain if that ship makes it to the ground. Show me what you can do, Avid."

I explained the situation to the Avid, and in response, its engines roared as it took off into the sky. We were headed for the falling ship. The Avid positioned itself under the crumbling vessel and supported it from below. The spaceship was much larger than even this huge mobile knight, and its mass far outweighed the Avid, but the Avid was still powerful enough to take its weight.

"That's it! Now...let's push that thing back into space!"

The Avid exerted more power, and the falling ship slowed to a stop... Then, slowly, it began to ascend. To an observer, it probably looked incredible to see such a relatively small craft lifting the much larger ship.

I couldn't hide my excitement at the Avid's display of strength. "Ah ha ha ha! This is the power of the Avid!"

Small lifeboat units escaped from the ship, one after another. Meanwhile, the Avid initiated contact with the vessel. The crew still trapped aboard were requesting aid from me.

"Please, help us! At this rate, we'll—"

The people who were here to kill me were begging me to save their lives? Who did they think they were?

I took my hands off the control sticks and linked my fingers behind my head, crossing my legs as well. The Avid moved on its own now to accomplish what I expected from it. For simple tasks, all I had to do was picture what I wanted in my mind, and the Avid took action. While I kicked back, I decided to amuse myself by talking with the people who pleaded for help.

"I guess you're right. At this rate, you'll all die, won't you?"

"P-please! We were only following orders!"

Well, no doubt it was true that they'd only carried out such a ridiculously bold plan because the people who wanted me dead had ordered them to.

"You brought a spaceship down to the Capital Planet and opened fire. Even the ones who escaped that wreck aren't going to escape being captured and put through hell," I said.

Those who died aboard the ship would be the lucky ones, I figured, but these idiots were still trying to get me to sympathize with them.

"We were threatened! We'll tell you everything! We'll testify against your enemies! Just please save us!"

Though they claimed they'd do anything for me, I just wasn't interested.

"I don't care. Go ahead and die."

I ended the conversation, and the Avid promptly sped up. We climbed and climbed until we could see the metal shell that encased the Capital Planet. An area of the shell assumed a liquid form and simply allowed the ship to pass right through. Outside the shell was airless space.

"P-please, nooo!!!"

The voices over my speaker stopped when we emerged into space, and the ship gradually drifted away from the Avid. The Avid held out one hand, and a glowing magic circle appeared in front of its palm. From this portal, a gigantic sword manifested in the Avid's grip. I smiled with approval at the weapon the Avid had chosen for itself.

"You want to chop it up, huh?"

The Avid's engines roared in response, so I reached out and gripped the control sticks. It was cute how the Avid responded to my words now that it had the Machine Heart to instill life into it. Though appearance-wise it was just a big, hulking machine, the Avid felt more like a cute little pet to me. How could I say no to what it wanted?

"All right...show me how well you're able to duplicate my moves. I want your full strength—no holding back."

Within the cockpit, I took up a stance to convey the Flash to the Avid. It needed to assume a proper stance if I wanted my mobile knight to utilize the Flash.

The Avid pointed the tip of its sword toward the drifting ship.

"Flash," I said, and the Avid unleashed its technique.

Several dramatic slashes appeared in the ship's hull, and it broke into pieces, which sailed off into space...but the Avid wasn't undamaged either. My craft groaned from the strain of reproducing my technique, its damage meter transitioning from green into the orange range. Now that the Avid had the Machine Heart, however, it was able to restore itself. Soon enough, the meter phased back to green, and an electronic *ping* alerted me that my craft was done self-repairing.

I smiled. "Nice. Now I can hold back a little less in the future."

The Avid roared in response, evidently not yet satisfied.

I tried to calm the raging beast. "Don't be so impatient. There's no end to the enemies out here in space to hunt down. You'll have so many opportunities to play that you'll get sick of it soon enough."

The Avid seemed somewhat pacified by my words.

Pieces of the severed ship continued drifting away, but one of the Avid's slashes had struck the engine and now it finally exploded, littering space with smaller debris.

"That takes care of those idiots. But anyway..."

I took the alchemy box—another mysterious artifact I'd collected over the years—from its hiding place within the Avid. When I did that, the Avid held out a hand and used a tractor beam to pull the floating debris toward it. When it had gathered a handful above its palm, the Avid closed its fist around the junk. I then used the alchemy box on the scrap, amusing myself by turning trash into gold.

"Still works like a charm."

I figured I'd continue to store my precious alchemy box inside the Avid. Only certain people could enter its cockpit, and the Avid had been strengthened with the Machine Heart besides. It was probably the safest place for it. The Avid truly was my trusty mount—or was *partner* a better word? But the Avid wasn't exactly a horse...

"Well, we've taken care of our little spaceship problem, so let's get back. Calvin finally made a move, though... and it was a worse one than I would have expected from him. Guess I overestimated him."

Calvin hadn't made any blatant moves until this, but now that he had, I could use it against him. Attacking the Capital Planet with a spaceship was a big mistake.

I was still surprised by how little Calvin had amounted to, though. I supposed that just like Linus, he was simply no match for me. Nevertheless, I didn't intend to go easy on him. I was nothing if not thorough when dealing with my enemies.

"I'm looking forward to seeing how thoroughly I can crush you too."

The Guide was dumbstruck as he watched the day's events play out.

"You've gotta be kidding me!"

He just couldn't process what was going on. Liam had destroyed a spaceship with a mere *sword*. It was all but impossible to accept what he saw with his own eyes.

"Wh-why?"

The ship hadn't fired its main cannon or missiles, but instead had shot lasers and bullets at Liam. The young man had intercepted them with his sword. The Guide could barely accept that fact either.

Who would even imagine that a single human being could face off against a warship and come out the victor?

"Does this mean Liam's evolved into a monster that's beyond my influence?"

The Guide fell to his knees. Could he ever beat Liam as he was now? With how much the Guide had been weakened by Liam over all these years, he couldn't see a path to success.

"Where did I go wrong? What did I do?!"

Just then, the Avid returned to the site of the battle. Now that the clashing Shadows and ninjas had vanished from the scene, several people emerged from the party venue to greet Liam. Rosetta had run out ahead of them all, still worried about him, but the first person Liam headed for was Amagi.

Unseen but close by, the Guide smiled when he noticed that. "I can't beat you as you are now, Liam, but at least I can hurt you. I'll make you regret this moment for the rest of your life."

The Guide had given up on defeating Liam utterly, but he still wanted to make him taste despair.

The party venue was in chaos. Of course it was, considering a spaceship had launched an attack right outside its doors. Having no time to change, Amagi hustled here and there inside the venue in her fancy dress, helping with whatever she could.

While she was walking down a hallway, she suddenly felt all the human presences around her vanish. Up until a moment ago, people had been running about this area, but suddenly, she felt completely alone. Even for a maid robot, Amagi found this strange.

"Has something happened...?"

She started forward to seek out Liam when a strange presence appeared before her.

"Hello, Miss."

The speaker was a man in a pinstriped tailcoat. He was tall and slender, and the brim of his top hat hid his eyes. Amagi sensed something strange about him...something she couldn't quite compute. The unknown quality of the man made her leery.

"What are you?" she asked.

He was shaped like a person, but he was something else. To Amagi, the Guide's true form was veiled by static. Alarm bells went off in her mind, telling her that the being in front of her was dangerous.

His words proved this. "I don't need to explain myself to a robot. If you die, it will cause Liam pain. That's all you need to know."

The Guide pulled a gun out of the pocket of his tail-coat. It was his own weapon, but he looked down at it with resentment.

"Now that I'm so weak, I have to rely on something like this. In any case, I should have just done this thing from the start! If you would please disappear..."

The Guide was so weakened now that he couldn't make proper use of his powers. The gun in his hand, however, was more than powerful enough to destroy Amagi.

With the weapon pointed at her, Amagi tried to take evasive action, but black smoke suddenly appeared around her, coiling about her legs and holding her in place. She couldn't break free, and calling for help wasn't an option either. The communications lines were still jammed. A minute ago, the building was full of people running in every direction, but for some reason, this area was deserted. Did the strange being in front of her do something to shut out the rest of the world? Amagi had no way of knowing.

The only thing she could see under his hat was his smiling lips. "I wonder what Liam's face will look like when I throw your head at his feet?" the Guide asked.

Amagi's mind raced as the mysterious being mentioned Liam.

He knows Master somehow? At this rate I will be destroyed. My data is backed up, but everything that truly makes me an individual... It will disappear.

The maid robot closed her eyes and accepted her fate. "Master, I am sorry... It seems this is as far as we will go together."

Grinning, the Guide pulled the trigger.

12 Court of Inquiry

"**M**ASTER, I am sorry..."

Even as Amagi prepared for her own destruction, she was thinking about Liam, the young man she would be leaving behind. She knew how hurt he would be by her loss. Other nobles disapproved of Liam placing so much importance on a "doll," and she always knew that she would have to leave his side eventually, but this seemed like the wrong time. Amagi was filled with guilt at the thought of how saddened Liam would be by her absence.

That was when one of the accessories incorporated into her dress activated, deploying a shield around her. This defensive field was the same type often used by nobles in their clothing, and it protected Amagi from the laser beam the Guide fired at her.

Still, the Guide wasn't discouraged. "Ha ha ha ha!

I know accessory shields like that are single-use! If I just keep attacking you...and attacking you..."

The Guide pulled his handgun's trigger again and again, shooting countless laser beams at Amagi, but no matter how many times he did so, nothing penetrated her shield. The gun eventually ran out of charges, simply clicking pathetically and no longer able to fire. The Guide's expression twisted into something unreadable, and Amagi wasn't sure herself how to react.

"Were you not going to destroy me?"

Her impassive face took on a subtle look of exasperation. The man had been so enthusiastic about taking her out, and yet he only had a single handgun incapable of penetrating her shield. She expected him to be much better prepared, but apparently that wasn't the case. Even the strange black mist that held her in place didn't seem to have enough strength to actually crush her further.

Frankly, the stranger's attempt was just too pathetic.

The Guide was getting agitated now, unable to withstand her chilly gaze. "D-don't look at me like that!"

The Guide threw his gun aside and ran off. "Dammit! I'm too low on negative emotions! I need to gather more and then throw them at Liam! No more backwards schemes! I'll use everything I've got to kill him!!!"

Amagi watched the Guide run off, ranting wildly. Once she was able to move again, she cocked her head. "What exactly was that man...?"

Had she met some sort of supernatural entity? It made Amagi anxious that the thing had mentioned Liam. "Has Master been keeping some sort of secret from us?"

In the past, she had occasionally noticed unexplainable phenomena that seemed connected to her master. A being like the one she just encountered might explain some of those phenomena. While frightening, the being was also strangely incompetent, but that didn't stop Amagi from worrying about what it said to her.

"Is Master really as gifted by fortune as he believes?" This new knowledge that some sort of supernatural being had it out for Liam spurred her to act. "I will need to change my plans. It is all for Master's sake..."

Learning of the Guide led Amagi to make a decision of her own.

Liam had brought down a spaceship with a sword. Normally, no one would believe such a preposterous claim, but unfortunately it was the truth, and was witnessed by numerous individuals. There was even video footage, which immediately circulated far and wide. Liam's feat was soon known not just throughout the Capital Planet, but the entire Empire. The event forced everyone to acknowledge the true might of the Way of the Flash.

Calvin sat with his elbows on his desk, his fingers entwined in front of his mouth. "Attacking the Capital Planet with a spaceship. I can't believe they did something that stupid."

The attack had been planned by the upset nobles who lost loved ones in the war and left Calvin's faction to pursue revenge. Calvin didn't expect them to do something quite so idiotic. He made a big mistake by not monitoring them. Even though these nobles severed their association with him, everyone knew they were previously associated.

Calvin's current reputation was that of a coward who ran from the war and forced the burden of fighting onto his younger brother. Now, his reputation also had to suffer the accusations that he was the fool who failed to assassinate Liam.

The prince eyed the box that sat before him on his desk. It was full of broken cores—the corpses of his ninjas. When they had been whole, these cores allowed the ninjas to burst into flame and alter their shape. The box was waiting for him on his desk when he got up this morning. There was only one thing it could mean.

"They're saying they could kill me whenever they want."

He underestimated Liam's operatives. Between this and his ruined reputation, Calvin was in deep trouble.

"So now I'm the one who's been driven into a corner."

He thought he had Liam cornered before the events of the war with the United Kingdom, but things worked out differently in the end. Still, Calvin couldn't simply give up. He needed to gather the nobles who remained in his faction to discuss his strategy.

"There are still protests going on in Liam's domain. We can force him to take responsibility for those..."

If he couldn't win on the battlefield, he'd just have to fight in another arena. Calvin now had his sights set on the one weakness Liam still faced: the unrest raging through his domain.

"The Empire won't let a democracy movement stand. If I can mobilize the army to squash the protests, there'll be nothing left of Liam's domain but a handful of razed planets. Let's see how much influence Liam has after that."

As long as he could get rid of Count Banfield, Calvin had nothing to fear from Cleo. Now was the time to make use of the secret card up his sleeve.

◆ ◇ ◆

An emergency court of inquiry was being held on the Empire's Capital Planet. A group of idiot nobles had used a spaceship to launch an attack on the Capital Planet, and they needed to be dealt with. I had been called as a witness to testify.

Well, I *thought* I was just being called to describe what had happened, but for some reason, I was the one being portrayed as the perpetrator of the event!

"I won't forget this humiliation." I ground my teeth in rage, frustration eating me up inside.

I entered the court of inquiry in high spirits, but Calvin—who was in attendance too—turned the tables on me. It pissed me off that he wore a cool look on his face and pretended to be looking off into the distance, as if he had nothing to do with this. I knew he was the reason I was in this mess in the first place.

Calvin had shamed me in front of the court, making me into a laughingstock. Lately, I was thinking he was incompetent, but he really pulled one over on me. I vowed to get my revenge.

I'll kill you with my bare hands! You won't get away with this, dammit!

As I hung my head and quaked with anger, the prime

minister and the important nobles who were in charge of the investigation looked down on me from their higher positions in the courtroom. Most of them only looked to be in their thirties, at least in terms of my past life. I couldn't stand all their eyes on me.

"Let's wrap this up, shall we?" the prime minister said.

The assembled nobles began to reprimand me.

"Honestly, I can't believe you, Lord Liam."

"You really should take your position as a noble more seriously, you know."

"You *are* a future duke, after all. You should act like one."

At first, the inquiry focused on the attack on the Capital Planet, but Calvin suddenly brought into question my ability to govern my own domain. It should have been clear that nobles who had formerly been part of Calvin's faction were responsible for the attack, but Calvin had changed the subject by demanding I take responsibility for an unrelated matter. The nobles aligned with him joined in with his criticism. He used his status as the crown prince to completely shift the topic of the hearing.

Now, important nobles stared at me with disapproving eyes, while the people directly responsible for this defamation of my character weren't even looking my way. Did they think I wasn't even worth looking at anymore?

I know your faces. None of you are getting away with this!

There were also nobles who were aligned with me at the hearing, but they just gave me looks of pity.

Baron Exner tried to console me. "Lord Liam... I'm sorry."

Don't just apologize—do something! Help me, someone! Calvin...you're the first one who's ever put me in such dire straits!

The prime minister banged his gavel to quiet everyone down. He began, "As for Count Banfield..."

"Ugh." I clenched my fists, my head still bowed.

This can't be happening! This should never have happened!

I had taken Calvin too lightly. If only I hadn't underestimated him, I wouldn't have had to suffer such bitter humiliation during this court of inquiry. For now, I could do nothing but admit my defeat.

But only for now!

After the hearing, the nobles of Calvin's faction held their heads in their hands. They made a big fuss during it, calling into question Liam's abilities as a leader in order to drive him into a corner. They used whatever means they could to interrupt the proceedings so they could turn things in their favor, and the subject they forcefully brought up was the democracy movement underway in Liam's domain. House Banfield's subjects were undermining the Empire's rule, they claimed. By bringing up a topic the Empire was sensitive about, they attempted to make *Liam* look like the one who was on trial. However...

"Can someone explain this to me?"

A tired Calvin glanced at the faces of the other nobles, who sat with him in a breakroom near the courtroom where the hearing took place. No one could meet his eye.

He smiled weakly. "You know, the prime minister pulled me aside when he left. I was advised not to disgrace myself any more than I already have."

He was smiling, but it was more of a mask. It was more accurate to say that smiling was all he could do at this point.

One of the nobles attempted to make excuses. "Your Highness, our agents in Liam's domain definitely did send us reports of a democracy movement there. We were fooled, somehow."

"Does this look like a protest for democracy to you?"

A video had been played for the court of inquiry as evidence of the democracy protests said to be taking place in Liam's domain. In the video, Liam's subjects could be seen marching and holding placards. Calvin replayed the video in the breakroom now, and his noble allies were forced to watch the true nature of the protests in Liam's domain.

"*Fulfill your duty as a noble!*" a protestor chanted.

"*Treat Lady Rosetta right! And give Miss Eulisia some attention every once in a while too!*"

"*Yeah! Remember meeeee!!!*"

At the end of the video, it showed that even Eulisia had joined the protests. What Calvin's faction had thought was a democracy movement was actually a movement urging Liam to sire an heir.

Calvin covered his face and laughed. In truth, he felt like crying, so he had to cover his face to hide his true emotions. "I look like a fool now for using this as evidence that Liam isn't competent to govern! Why did anyone think this was a democracy movement in the first place?"

Calvin and the nobles had faraway looks on their faces like they were avoiding reality. They had no idea what their video evidence really depicted before they brought it up.

"Why did no one think to watch the entire video?"

Everyone in the room had been sure they possessed solid proof.

One of the nobles blamed the problem on their information network. "A viscount who defected from our faction was the one who sent the spies, you see. When he defected, we took his data and were supposed to take over his spying operation, but..."

Human error. The operation hadn't transitioned to new hands smoothly, and as a result they presented evidence to the hearing that wasn't properly vetted beforehand. The video *had* depicted a protest, sure, but it was nothing like the one Calvin and his faction had anticipated.

After they played the video at the inquiry, the courtroom's hostile air completely changed. Before the video, people were critical of Liam for not quelling the democracy movement. That had also made them unsympathetic toward him regarding the ship's attack on the Capital Planet. They were ready to demand he be punished in some way.

After watching the "evidence" and seeing how Liam reacted to it with embarrassment, those same people who reprimanded him softened their tones greatly. Instead, they said things like, "Just try to be mindful of your noble standing when possible," and, "Please be careful from now on, would you?" The older nobles in attendance ended up looking at him fondly, as if he were an adorable grandson. Some nobles even teased him, as if the protests were the funniest thing they ever saw, while others simply felt sorry for him.

When the dust settled, Liam got off far easier than it seemed he would. That is to say, he was left completely unpunished. It was as if Calvin actually *protected* Liam from any consequences he might otherwise have suffered. On the other hand, the nobles' impression of *Calvin* plummeted after viewing the video evidence. They felt he tried changing the topic of the hearing just to get the heat off himself. So, even fighting in this new, preferred arena, Calvin had again lost to Liam.

To Calvin, it felt as if a puny faction rallying around Cleo had crept up right behind him, suddenly revealing itself to be big enough to present a real challenge. It never should have been a faction that had any chance of success, and yet...

Has fortune betrayed me? he wondered.

Being unlucky was more than enough reason one might end up dead in the Empire. That went for crown princes as much as anyone else. Even now, though, Calvin couldn't bring himself to give up quite yet.

"At this point, we can't afford to worry about our reputations anymore," Calvin said, and the nobles of his faction steeled themselves for what might come next.

The world was full of idiots. After the attack on the party venue and with the investigation and hearing concluded, the palace told me to take some time off from my government internship. Now, I just luxuriated at my hotel every day. I was even taking a break from throwing parties too. Suspended from my duties, I had to chill out for a few months.

"Now my only problem is the people claiming they practice the Way of the Flash."

According to the newspaper articles I saw, there were two of them, and supposedly they launched attacks on the headquarters of the Ahlen and Kurdan styles. Was this the price of fame? Impressive if so, but if they were faking their credentials, I'd kill them myself.

This was an intergalactic nation, however. It might seem easy to locate people with the level of technology we possessed, but it was actually very difficult because of the sheer size of our territory. I didn't have a clue where the two fakers might be.

Tia was making tea for me in my room, as if trying to win some brownie points. When she returned from the war, she said to me, "Please gift me with your praise, Lord Liam!" so I bluntly replied, "It's a gift already that you work for me, isn't it?"

You know what she did after that? She nodded her

head and trembled with joy. *You're that happy to be treated so coldly?* I thought at the time. *Why don't you learn some class from Kukuri?* Anyway, I was keeping her nearby and putting her to work as her reward.

Tia handed me my tea and asked, "Isn't there the matter of the protests as well, Lord Liam?"

"I'll crush them as soon as I go back to my domain. Who the hell do these people think they are to make a fuss about my bedroom matters?"

I was furious with my subjects for demanding I make an heir with Rosetta already. *That's none of your damn business! Screw you!* I'd take care of those people as soon as I got home.

My troops were taking some well-earned time off now that they were back from the war. It might surprise you, but I treated my troops pretty well for being an evil lord. You could even say I was extra careful with them. After all, I was only able to be so evil due to the overwhelming military might they provided me with. I couldn't throw my weight around like I did if I didn't have the power to back it up. Therefore, it would be stupid not to value the military that provided me with that might.

So, when it was time for my troops to rest, I had them rest properly. I wouldn't put them to work again right away, but as soon as I did I was going to have them stop those protests!

Tia laughed approvingly when she heard my response. *She's pretty evil herself if she's laughing about that.*

"Well, it's a good thing there was no real democracy movement in your domain, Lord Liam. Then you'd *really* have to suppress it instead of just joking about it...or the Empire would be sending the regular army to do it for you."

"I'm kind of wishing they'd just do that anyway, to be honest."

Calvin's faction brought up the protests at the court of inquiry as if to make up for their own shame. The hearing was supposed to be about *them*, but they put me on the spot instead. Calvin was well aware that he had a better standing in the palace than I did, so he used his position to throw a fit about a democracy movement in my domain. The Empire had a real problem with democracy, so he successfully shifted the whole hearing to that subject. When the Empire actually viewed the evidence, however, what they found was not a democracy movement, but the protests about my lack of an heir.

Why, though? What had happened to spark this? It was so humiliating to have that whole court see my subjects clamoring about how I hadn't fathered any children. The video proved that even *Eulisia* was participating in the protest! I was completely speechless when I saw that. It seemed she always misbehaved when I left her to her own devices.

Anyway, when they played that video, I was embarrassed beyond belief. I remember the looks everyone gave me at the time. People reacted with amusement, exasperation, pity...but most of all, I could still see the weary look the prime minister gave me.

Tia's smile faded and was replaced with a more serious expression. "Anyway, Calvin's faction is cornered now. Prince Cleo's faction has gained a lot more ground. It's gone just as you planned, Lord Liam."

Well, some unexpected things happened, but I fulfilled my goal. Then again, fortune was on my side.

"My own good luck scares me," I said, though I knew my luck was all due to the Guide watching over me. Even if things looked hairy at times, I knew it would all lead to my victory in the end. I was living life on easy mode, and that was my privilege as an evil lord.

"Well, I'm getting tired of behaving myself," I sighed. "Guess I'll go out and have some fun since it's been a while. Bring the car around, would you?"

"Aren't you supposed to stay home to rest?"

"I can go out for a walk, can't I? You're coming too."

"I am?!"

When she heard she could go out with me, Tia rushed out to summon the car.

13 The Rules of the Way of the Flash

T HAT DAY, Ellen went out shopping with Liam, riding in the spacious car with him and Tia.

I get to go shopping with Master today! Ellen was ecstatic at the thought of going out with Liam.

The car was a luxury vehicle reminiscent of a limousine. It had tires, but rarely made use of them since it usually just glided through the air about fifty centimeters off the ground. A custom model, it had a very luxurious interior equipped for whatever its passengers might desire. The seats were comfortable and the ride completely smooth.

Ellen eyed the katana resting next to Liam, knowing that the sword was particularly special to him. She had received a katana from Liam herself, one with a golden tiger depicted at the base of the blade and a red scabbard.

Her sword was impressive too, but the nameless blade at Liam's side had a strange power all its own.

Lately, Master always has his favorite sword with him. She knew it was a blade he usually kept carefully stowed away. It seemed like he was wary of something.

Liam sipped some alcohol Tia had poured into a glass for him. He remarked, "Tastes even better when you start drinking early."

He was doubtlessly the only person in the Empire who could be served alcohol by the hero of the war with the United Kingdom.

"These are all the finest drinks, prepared specially for you, Lord Liam. Here, please have some more."

"How thoughtful of you."

Tia watched, spellbound, as Liam drained the alcohol she poured him. Her cheeks flushed feverishly. "Very impressive, my lord!"

Everything she said sounded like empty flattery, but even Ellen could tell that she meant all of it. To Ellen, Tia's adoring eyes had the look of cartoon hearts. If the woman had a tail, it would no doubt be wagging like that of an overly excited dog.

For a little while now, though, Ellen had been sensing something strange. "Master?" she said suddenly.

"Yeah? If you want a stuffed animal, I'll buy you one."

"Th-that's not it! I...I feel kind of nervous."

She'd said "nervous," but what she really felt was profound unease. She shuddered like she felt a chill, though she didn't feel ill at all. Instead, it felt as though someone was watching her, and that feeling bothered her intensely.

Though Ellen glanced out the window anxiously, Liam seemed pleased. "Well, looks like some of your training is paying off." In contrast to Ellen's unease, Liam remained relaxed.

However, Tia's light mood rapidly shifted too. She communicated with their security escort, ordering them to check their surroundings, two fingers to her ear as she looked out the car's windows. "Any abnormalities?"

A subordinate reported back, *"Nothing right now—no, wait... Someone's in the road ahead. Two of them."*

Tia's eyes widened. She barked out an order. "Everyone, full alert!"

The car rocked as it suddenly changed direction.

Liam drained his glass and muttered, "Security should have picked up on this earlier. We won't be able to avoid them now." He sighed, disappointed his people hadn't seen this threat coming.

Suddenly, the car swayed, and Ellen looked up at the

ceiling. Liam was giving her a strong push. Before she could figure out what had happened, the car was split into two pieces, sliced in half right at the spot where Ellen had been sitting a moment earlier.

The two halves of the car dropped to the ground, skidding across the road until they came to a stop.

"Wh-what just happened?" Ellen looked around and spotted a woman standing nearby, her beautiful dark blue hair swaying in the wind.

"Huh? Who's that girl?" The woman approached Ellen and peered down at her with her pink eyes. As a chilling smile spread on her face, another woman landed nearby. Though the second woman had touched down silently, Ellen sensed her strong presence. This one spoke in a rough tone.

"That couldn't have killed you, right? Come on out, Liam!" the other yelled. The woman's orange hair was tied back, but it was still so wild that it fanned out around her head like a lion's.

Ellen couldn't stop trembling as she stared at the two of them. They both wore swords sheathed at their waists. *They're so strong...*

Tia leaped out of the other half of the severed car, rapier in hand. "I hope you two understand who you're dealing with here!"

The two women laughed at the infuriated Tia. "Well, this one's not *weak*, but I dunno..."

"Yeah, she's not just some grunt, but that's about all you can say for her."

It was obvious that the two of them were stronger than Tia. Tia could sense that herself, so she couldn't go at them recklessly. Instead, she stayed where she was, standing protectively over Liam.

"Lord Liam, please leave this to us."

Liam emerged from the wreckage of the car slowly, holding his sword in one hand. With his other hand, he held the back of his neck as he cracked it. Meanwhile, his entourage of guards emerged from their own vehicles and gathered around him, but Liam waved his hand to shoo them away.

"Who are you trying to impress?" Liam said. "You guys will just get in my way. Get back already."

"B-but..."

Liam meant for Tia to step back too, but she stayed at his side. Just then, she noticed the orange-haired woman near Ellen glance down at the two swords sheathed at her waist. Alarmed, Tia jumped out in front of Liam to protect him...and in that same moment, one of her arms went flying, sliced right off. There were two deep gashes in the ground from the twin blades.

Even with one of her arms cut off, Tia still stood in front of Liam to shield him. She glared at her enemies, holding her rapier out at the end of her remaining arm.

The orange-haired woman clicked her tongue. "The heck? I wanted to cut *both* your arms off, just to show you the difference in our skill levels."

The blue-haired woman laughed in ridicule. "Man, you suck!"

"What, you want me to cut *you* down when I'm done with Liam?" the other one snapped back.

As the air between the two strange women turned dangerous, Liam stepped forward. He picked up Tia's severed arm and handed it to her, gesturing for her to hang back.

"Well done, jumping in front of me. You get high marks for that one."

"Lord Liam?!" cried Tia.

Liam used Tia's surprise to push past her, entrusting her to his security people.

When he stepped in front of the two dangerous women, their attitudes changed. The women stopped smirking smugly and took serious fighting stances.

"What's wrong?" Liam challenged them. "You're here to kill me, aren't you? If you're scared, then you must be faking those claims about your sword style."

Liam had realized they were the real thing after seeing their technique with his own eyes, but he called them fakes purely to provoke them.

Ellen thought she understood the reason for the strange feeling she got from the two strangers. *Was I sensing that they're from our same school?*

The blue-haired woman introduced herself first. "Pleased to meet you, senior pupil. I'm Riho Satsuki—the *true* successor of the Way of the Flash." Her manner seemed polite, but she looked at Liam with murder in her eyes.

The other one didn't even try to hide her hostility. "I'm Fuka Shishikami! I'll kill you and take over Master's Way of the Flash!"

Drawing her swords, Fuka kicked off from the ground and launched herself at Liam. It was unusual for a practitioner of the Way of the Flash, with its unseen slashes, to move like this.

In a mere split second, Ellen could see Fuka making thousands of slashes with her two swords. Despite the rough way she spoke and acted, each slash had exactly enough precision and power to take someone's life. She was a very deft fighter.

"Master!" Ellen called out with worry, but Liam didn't even put a hand to his sword's hilt.

"Ellen, watch closely," he told her, as he blocked every one of Fuka's slashes with his own unseen moves.

He instructed Ellen casually, even as he fought with Fuka. "This is my first time fighting someone from the same school. It might never happen again, so you should take this opportunity to learn as much as you can."

Fuka must have felt that Liam was toying with her as he gave commentary to the young girl. She ground her teeth, her expression twisting with rage. "Don't get cocky! *Flash!*"

Fuka prepared to unleash a powerful double slash faster than the eye could see, but before she could follow through with it, Liam stepped on both of her blades. Her swords were left embedded in the ground, cracks spreading out from where they'd struck.

"Wha—?!"

To Liam's eye, she had betrayed the intent to cross her swords, so he stepped on them at the precise moment when they overlapped.

Liam laughed at Fuka's surprised reaction. "Let me give you some advice... I'm stronger than you both."

Liam kicked Fuka away and turned to Riho, who looked far more guarded now. "We heard you were strong," she said, "but you're really going to be a problem, aren't you?"

Riho came at Liam with her longsword and slashed at

him again and again, but he deflected each of her blows with his own sword that he finally drew. Each redirected slash chewed up the street beneath them. Chunks of pavement went flying this way and that, but Ellen dodged all the debris that came her way. She watched the three students of the Way of the Flash carefully so she wouldn't miss a moment of their match.

The knights of Liam's security detail couldn't do anything but watch as the three practitioners of the Way of the Flash went at it. From their perspectives, it just looked like three people standing there facing each other, though sometimes the fighters would suddenly shift to a different position or switch places. They knew the three must have been slashing at each other because the sounds and shockwaves of their exchanged blows resonated around them. The ferocity of their unseen movements whipped up something like a windstorm.

The knights were hopelessly confused.

"What's going on?"

"Keep back! Do you want to die?!"

"We can't even do our jobs like this!!!"

Things were gradually looking worse and worse for the two strange women, however. Wounds started to appear here and there on their bodies, and Riho and Fuka seemed surprised by this turn of events.

Liam gave an exaggerated sigh, making a show of how relaxed he was. "So that's all you've got, huh?"

In contrast, the women were not only wounded now, but breathing hard and looking tired.

Master is strong! Ellen was impressed. She always knew Liam was powerful, but she couldn't really gauge just *how* strong he was. Now that she watched him fighting two students from the same school, it was clear that he had both of them beat.

As Ellen looked on in wonder, Liam provoked the two women once more. "What's wrong? Too scared to utilize your full strength? Why don't you show me what you're really capable of? Get serious, both of you."

Liam sheathed his sword and spread his arms wide, and the two women became visibly enraged.

Riho forgot to keep up the polite act. "Letting your guard down in front of me? Die, you arrogant son of a bitch!"

A vein popped out on Fuka's forehead. "I've never been so humiliated before! You're dead! I'll dice you into little pieces!"

Riho crouched low and seemed to disappear for a moment before showing up again right next to Liam. Where she landed, a crack ran through the ground. She went after Liam with no expression on her face, releasing a powerful high-speed attack. "Fall..."

Fuka leaped up high and began to spin in the air. "I'll shred you!" She let loose a greater flurry of slashes than she had ever managed before. They rained down on Liam like a storm of steel.

The two of them used different sorts of Flashes. Riho, who looked dainty but was actually powerful, used the traditional Way of the Flash, which aimed to settle a fight with a single powerful strike. Fuka, on the other hand, used quantity to make up for what she lacked in power. It was an unorthodox variation on the technique, but for her, it was more efficient to use multiple slashes of sufficient power than one overpowered strike.

Master!!! Ellen was nervous, seeing how these personalized approaches to the Way of the Flash differed from Liam's. While she was worried, Liam just kept smiling.

"You're both half-baked," he said. "You should come back when you've polished your skills more."

Liam blocked Riho's single slash and swept away Fuka's storm of attacks with a single swing of his own. The two of them went flying and rolled across the ground before springing back to their feet.

"Out of respect for our shared school, I'll show you my full strength," Liam said, assuming a stance. "If you can't block it...then I guess you'll just have to die."

Ellen shivered when she heard Liam challenge the strength of their Way of the Flash. It made her wonder if Liam might test her just as harshly one day too.

Riho seemed unsteady on her feet, and Fuka coughed up blood as she took her own stance. The two of them trembled with fear in the face of Liam's challenge.

Riho smiled humorlessly and said, "Ahh... This is bad."

Fuka remarked, "So this is why Master told us to come at him together."

The two of them kept close, standing back-to-back, not knowing from what direction the attack would come.

Liam narrowed his eyes when he judged the two of them were ready.

"Flash."

The second Liam announced his technique, blood spurted from both of the women's bodies. Even Ellen with her extra-keen eyesight hadn't been able to detect the strike. Liam's Flash had been so much less showy than the women's attacks, generating no wind and leaving no marks on the surrounding area. It was a technique that ended his enemies and did nothing more.

It really looks like he didn't do anything. Ellen was

confident in her eyesight, but she couldn't even see Liam's serious Flash.

The battle ended in an instant, and Riho and Fuka collapsed to the ground. Their arms and legs had been severed and their torsos sat in puddles of blood, looking as though they might truly die at any moment. Only a minute ago they had seemed so formidable, and yet they hadn't been able to do a thing to resist Liam's attack.

Ellen trembled as she gazed upon Liam, but not out of fear, but of joy. *My master is incredible!!!*

Liam came out of his stance and walked over to the two women. Now that the fight was over, Tia came to join him. The rapier she gripped changed shape, its blade opening up into a drill, which started spinning. She dragged the drill's tip against the ground as she walked toward the pair, sparks flying as it scraped against the pavement. Murder shone in Tia's eyes.

"You're dead," she said. "Anyone who tries to kill Lord Liam must face the ultimate punishment. I'll make you beg for your deaths."

As Tia strode toward them, determined to kill them despite having lost an arm, Liam turned around and gave an unexpected order. "Tia—heal them."

Tia's murderous look vanished, replaced with confusion. "Huh? B-but...!"

"They're my precious juniors. Summon a doctor at once. If they can't manage it, then make use of elixirs."

Once he crossed swords with those two, there was no more doubt in Liam's mind about who their teacher was. He looked pleased by the opportunity to test them.

"But they were after your life, Lord Liam!"

Liam grinned. "It was just a little fun between a senior and his juniors."

"B-but to save them..." Tia just couldn't accept Liam's decision.

Since he was in a good mood, Liam strode over to Tia and touched her cheek gently, praising her for protecting him. "I'm impressed with how you jumped out in front of me like that though. I think a little better of you now, Tia. For me, that won you more points than even your service in the war. I'm glad you're working for me."

"Lord Liam!!!"

Deeply moved, Tia took out her tablet and gushed, "One more time! One more time, please! Let me record that in HD!"

Still in a good mood, Liam only said, "What am I gonna do with you?"

Riho's mouth started opening and closing, as if she were trying to say something. "Message... Mas...ter..." she croaked.

Liam approached her to listen, then reached into her pocket and pulled out a folded letter. Ellen was surprised to see a handwritten letter in this day and age. When Liam read it, his eyes went wide. He then barked an order to Tia, who still stood there spellbound.

"What are you doing? Did you not hear my order?" he yelled.

"O-of course! I'll summon a doctor immediately!"

Security men trained as medics approached the wounded warriors to administer first aid.

My two junior pupils had brought a letter for me from Master.

"How are you, Lord Liam? I've been wandering from place to place, as always, attempting to perfect my Way of the Flash. In my travels, I encountered two feral children with some potential."

He wrote in the letter that he approved of a fight between fellow practitioners of the same school—which was normally forbidden—in order for the two students to hone their craft.

Whoops. I didn't know you needed approval to fight fellow Way of the Flash practitioners.

From my master's letter, I surmised that only those who trained under the same master could fight in this way, as long as they had their master's permission. I'd have to be careful about that going forward. In any case, the letter continued:

"You must have been surprised when my new pupils showed up. If you're reading this letter, however, you must have defeated them. I suppose that's only natural. If the two of them are still alive, would you mind looking after them for me? I'm afraid I can't finish their training myself."

Master was entrusting his two new pupils to me. He must have wanted to show me what they were capable of first. It seemed like they were seriously trying to kill me, but that must have all just been part of Master's plan. This was Master, after all!

I was curious why he wasn't able to finish their training himself, though. As far as I could tell, the two of them were already fully trained as swordsmen. They were a bit unpolished for Way of the Flash practitioners, but still much more accomplished than any other style's swordsmen. It seemed like any further growth would depend on their own efforts. Did something happen to Master? I didn't know enough to figure anything out.

In any case, he entrusted the two of them to me, so I vowed to look after them as their senior pupil.

"Just leave it to me, Master. I'll take care of them."

Long ago, I committed myself to studying the Way of the Flash with the diligence it deserved. If my master wanted me to look after some rowdy juniors, then that was what I'd do. Normally, I'd take the head of anyone who tried to end my life, but if they were junior students in the Way of the Flash, then that was different.

"I wonder what he means about not being able to finish their training, though. Where is Master right now, and what is he doing...?"

Whatever else he was up to, I was sure Master continued polishing his Way of the Flash, forever striving to perfect his art.

14 A Flash of Gratitude

I N A RUNDOWN APARTMENT on a planet far from the Empire, Yasushi carried a baby on his back while his wife bustled about getting ready to leave. She was dressed in a suit for work.

"Baby's yours until 7, Yasu. I'll be home around then, okay?"

"Yes, ma'am," "Yasu" replied wearily.

The intelligent woman had made Yasushi into a house-husband while she herself had a day job. Yasushi wished he could run away, but since she chased after him with a kitchen knife the last time he tried, he was too scared to attempt it again.

The scar she left on him was easily visible under his kimono. It was a gruesome line that went diagonally from his chest down to his gut. He still remembered her saying, with a terrifying look on her face, "Let's leave this here, shall we? It'll be a reminder for you not to leave me again." There were medical treatments that could easily erase such a scar, but she'd purposely let it remain.

Tears welled up in Yasushi's eyes. He regretted getting involved with a woman whose emotions were so extreme. "Ugh, I want to run away...but how can I, with my meager allowance?"

He used almost all the money Liam gave him to raise Riho and Fuka. The rest he spent irresponsibly, so now he subsisted on an allowance the woman gave him. He stayed home during the day to take care of the baby, but she did most of the chores around the apartment. He wasn't fully a househusband, nor was he entirely a mooch—he wasn't much of anything, to be honest. This was the true form of the Sword God who had trained Liam, Riho, and Fuka.

The baby began to fuss.

"All right, let's change your diaper. Sigh... What in the world am I doing?"

In other words, Yasushi was living peacefully on a planet far, far away.

Riho and Fuka recovered in a special hospital room Liam had prepared for them at the luxury hotel. They wore hospital gowns and their bodies were covered in bandages, but they were already healed enough to have hearty appetites.

Tia watched them angrily with Ellen beside her. Surprisingly, the two sat up with proper posture as they ate, but they devoured their food ravenously. They emptied plate after plate, so the hotel wait staff busily exchanged them with new dishes.

Disgusted by their voracious appetites, Tia asked, "How can you eat so much when you're still recovering?"

Fuka must have been at least temporarily satisfied, because she set her chopsticks down and stretched. "Well, I don't have any strength if I don't eat."

Riho downed the last of a bowl of soup and smirked. "You don't have much strength to begin with."

Fuka pointed at Riho, incensed. "At least I've got some meat on my bones! No matter how much you eat, you'll never grow a chest!"

Compared to Fuka's rather impressive specimens, Riho's breasts were only average-sized. She must have been sensitive about that because she covered them with her arms and glared at Fuka. "So what? Are you sure the nutrients that were supposed to go to your head didn't go to your boobs instead? Why do you even think I care about the size of mine? What's there to be happy about with big boobs, anyway? If you're going to be a proper swordsman, I think you should cut off those useless lumps of fat. They'll just get in the way! Or do you want me to cut them off for you? Come on, stick 'em out for me!"

Ellen watched Riho's bitter response. *It really does bother her.*

As quickly as the two had started fighting, their stomachs rumbled again, and they went right back to eating. Tia continued watching over them. Her arm had been reattached with a device to help her bandaged appendage heal.

"Why do *I* have to look after them?" she muttered.

Ellen was here to observe two fellow swordsmen of the same school. Liam would be taking care of the two of them, and this was an opportunity for her to better understand them. Fuka and Riho were aware that Ellen was a student of the Way of the Flash too.

"By the way... Hey, Pipsqueak." Fuka addressed Ellen.

Ellen puffed her cheeks out with displeasure. "I'm not 'Pipsqueak.' My name's Ellen."

"Whatever. We're from the same school, so I guess it's like we're your aunts, right? Let's get along, kid."

For how belligerent the two young women were, they seemed to like Ellen well enough. They were acting like they never tried to kill Liam. To Ellen, however, they were still vicious assassins who made an attempt on her respected master's life.

"I won't get along with people who tried to kill my master!" She turned her face away, and Fuka looked a bit dejected. She was acting less like a student from the same sword school and more like an older sister whose younger sister was giving her the cold shoulder.

Riho giggled at that. "It's understandable, you know. I'd be furious if someone went after our master, but we only went after our senior because our master told us to. It seems like he understands that too, because he took us in. But since you're *his* pupil, I'm not sure your attitude makes sense."

Fuka lay back down, apparently done eating. "You might have to fight your junior pupils yourself one day, if your master orders it," she warned Ellen.

"I-I..."

Right now, Ellen was Liam's only pupil. He was only looking after Riho and Fuka as fellow practitioners; they weren't his own students. He would need to personally train at least two more people who would then be Ellen's juniors. Ellen wasn't sure how she felt about that. If Liam took on another pupil at some point, he'd inevitably focus his attention on the new student. He wouldn't only be teaching her as he was now.

While Ellen wrestled with her feelings, Liam entered the room.

"Well, you seem better." He didn't seem wary at all in the women's presence.

The two women immediately bowed their heads to him from their beds. For how brazenly they acted and how rudely they spoke, they did seem to have at least some manners drilled into them.

"We truly are sorry," Riho apologized to Liam. "We've learned just how foolish we were."

Fuka was similarly contrite. "Now we know that we're still immature. We haven't yet reached the senior pupil's level."

In response to their humbled admissions, Liam sat down in a chair Tia had prepared for him and looked the girls over. He spoke to them kindly, as if they were family. "Looks like you understand who's in charge now. Well, I'll be taking care of you from here on, but frankly? I can't teach you anything related to the Way of the Flash. The most I can do for you on that front is give you a place to train."

Riho and Fuka were already trained completely as swordsmen. If they wanted to improve further, that would be up to their own efforts. All Liam could do was support them with that. He recognized flaws both of them suffered though.

"In every other area besides swordsmanship, you're terrible. Master must have entrusted you to me so I could make the two of you into proper knights. Once your injuries have healed completely, I'll take you back to my domain. There, you'll study how to be knights."

Riho reacted with obvious displeasure. "Wh-what does a swordsman need to *study* for? I refuse! I only want to concentrate on honing my swordsmanship."

Liam smiled but shot her down. "No. Master entrusted you to me because he judged that you were lacking something. I'm not gonna cut any corners in your education."

For her part, Fuka didn't seem bothered. "We just need to use an education capsule and then go train somewhere for a few years, right? A little combat training can't be that hard."

As swordsmen of the Way of the Flash, knight training would come easy for them, though it likely wouldn't improve their already formidable combat abilities much. However, Liam had a different kind of study in mind.

"When we get back to my domain, I'll turn you over to my head maid Serena for etiquette lessons. Being maids shouldn't be hard for you either, right?"

Riho and Fuka were both dumbfounded. They had never expected they'd be training to be maids.

"Wh-what? What do you mean?"

"Y-you've gotta be kidding me! Us, *maids*? Th-that's not happening!"

Liam grinned impishly at their flustered reaction. "Even nobles often work as servants during their training. Since you two aren't nobles, I'll just educate you in my own mansion—and don't think you'll be able to run away."

"B-but...!"

"M-me? A maid?"

From Liam's perspective, he'd be providing them with valuable training out of the goodness of his heart, but they were upset because they didn't want to do something that had nothing to do with the blade.

As for Ellen, she was rather satisfied with this turn of events. *It'll be a good punishment for these two to have to learn etiquette!*

"What...?"

The Guide collapsed to his knees. The secret weapons he'd been counting on to kill Liam hadn't amounted to anything in the end. It was fine that they'd lost that one battle, but they gave up on taking his life after that, instead gaining respect for him as a senior pupil. This whole mess was Yasushi's fault. Liam had taken the two of them in after reading a letter Yasushi had given them.

"He just had to save his own skin in the end!"

It was only natural, considering Yasushi's personality, but the Guide still felt betrayed.

The worst thing about all this was that it had led the Guide to learn the truth about how he had actually affected events. "More importantly, the actions I took to hurt Liam, the things that were supposed to harm him... They all actually *helped* him? So all this time I was actually supporting Liam with a big smile on my face?!"

The Guide reviewed recent events through this new, clearer perspective. Calvin's faction had lost a good deal of its unity and power. Liam, on the other hand, had gained a lot more power inside Cleo's faction, which was growing much more mighty as well. With Calvin's faction unable to do anything but watch, Cleo's faction had become a significant threat to them.

"You won't get away with this, Liam!!!" The Guide clenched his fists.

Then there was the matter of Liam's domain. The troublemakers he'd sneaked in to start a democracy movement had been identified and removed so they couldn't advance their beliefs. Everything had worked out in Liam's favor.

"At this point, I don't care if I have to go down with you, Liam, so long as I destroy you!"

The Guide decided to gather negative emotions using whatever means he could in order to build enough strength to defeat him. Luckily, there had just been a massive war between intergalactic nations, so there was plenty of misery to go around. A lot of this negative energy was directed at Liam himself. The Guide would draw it all in with the intention of ending Liam personally. He had no idea if he'd actually be able to kill the young man through his own powers, but he was determined to give it his best effort.

"I'll kill Liam—I swear it!!!"

After the Guide disappeared from the scene on his mission to gather up negative energy, a dog that had been secretly watching him stepped out of hiding. Then, the dog disappeared too.

Upon the expeditionary army's return, nobles all across the Capital Planet threw parties to celebrate its victory, inviting their peers and the soldiers who had fought in the war. Some simply wanted to congratulate the victors, while others sought to cozy up to Cleo's faction. Cleo was no longer the powerless prince he had been.

Invited to one such party, Cleo became exhausted after greeting an endless string of attendees. At one point he escaped and brought Lysithea into a lounge.

"This is tiring... The count does this every day? I can't believe it."

Lysithea chided Cleo, though playfully. "This is all thanks to the groundwork the count laid, you know. The whole time you were out there fighting, he was here on the Capital Planet, networking. Look how many people want to know you now. It's not like before, when you were virtually powerless."

"I'm just a figurehead, though," countered Cleo.

"That's not true. Don't lose your nerve."

"Sure, I 'fought' in the war, but I didn't actually do anything."

Cleo wasn't responsible for their victory in the least. There was no room for him to act since Tia was effectively the commander of the fleet, while a talented knight named Claus supplied her with the support she needed. All of this only exacerbated Cleo's inferiority complex. He knew there was nothing he could do about it, and had to be content with being a figurehead, but he hated himself for it all the same.

He then reflected on Liam. "The count himself is keeping a rather low profile lately, isn't he?"

Lysithea clued Cleo in on Liam's current plans. "Apparently, he's going back to his domain for a time. The protests there are calming down, but he must be worried about how things are back home."

Lysithea was impressed that Liam had remained on the Capital Planet up until now, despite personal circumstances, but when Cleo thought of Liam, he could only compare himself unfavorably.

"The count can do anything, really. He's completely different from me."

Cleo was in competition with his brother to see who would become the next emperor, but he knew that his current standing wasn't due to his own merits. He accepted it...but he didn't have to like it.

"If I weren't around, no one would care so long as Liam was," Cleo muttered.

Lysithea didn't catch what he said. "Did you say something?"

For her part, Lysithea was excited for what would come next. They made it through a dangerous crisis and were left with the power to go toe to toe with Calvin's faction.

Cleo only shook his head, not wanting to dampen her enthusiasm. "No, nothing."

◆ ◇ ◆

The Guide returned to the Capital Planet. He had been moving from place to place lately, nourishing himself on the vengeful spirits of those destroyed by the expeditionary army and gathering up the lingering hatred of the Capital Planet. Now, he was back to challenge Liam to a fight.

"Liam! Today, I'll end you by my own hand!!!"

Unable to kill Amagi the android—and having learned that all his recent efforts to bring Liam misfortune backfired and led to Liam's victory instead—the Guide seethed with fury. Struck down from his previous high by vicious reality, he was now completely consumed by anger. Therefore, when he spotted Liam at the spaceport preparing to head back to his domain, the Guide charged straight for him.

"There you aaaaare!!!"

Liam had Riho, Fuka, and Ellen in tow, showing the women a ship he was particularly proud of. They walked along its pointlessly lavish corridors, unaccompanied by any guards.

When the Guide saw them from behind, he willed his negative energy to shape a weapon from his own body. The Guide's arm transformed into an ominous blade, which sped toward Liam's back.

"Liaaaaam!!!"

"Well? Impressive, right? I spent a ton of money on this superdreadnought. This thing's as big as a space colony!"

The three-thousand-meter ship was huge enough for people to live inside it. Personnel came and went at regular intervals, of course, but some people had been on the ship for years and had even gotten married on-board. I heard a child had been born on it too, but that seemed a bit much to me. Could you really raise a kid on a warship? I supposed they would set up a school on it soon, but... Anyway, I bought myself this ridiculously enormous ship just to satisfy my own sense of vanity, and yet it was still hard for me to take in at times.

I also spent a ridiculous amount of money making sure the battleship's interior was lavishly decorated. I was strangely happy to see how much Fuka liked it. It seemed like she had a penchant for the extravagant.

"Whoa! Can I have one, too, senior pupil?"

To be honest, I would have liked to give her a ship or two, but unfortunately I couldn't. "You think I can just do whatever I want with these superdreadnoughts?

I need Amagi's permission, so that's not happening. She'd never agree to it."

Amagi made a sour face whenever I bought a battleship for myself, so I didn't want to imagine what she'd say if I bought one for my junior. I was all about being an evil lord, but I still didn't want to upset my maid. It wasn't that long ago that she complained about me commissioning a ship from Nias. That vessel was almost done, and I looked forward to picking it up. Though I felt a bit guilty because of how Amagi felt about it, so I figured I'd control my spending for at least a little while.

"Aww..." Fuka was disappointed, but I did have a present in mind for those two.

"Don't be so down. I'm going to give you both your own personal mobile knights. You'll need to know how to pilot things like that, so it'll be good if you have your own."

Riho just played with her hair, evidently not very interested. "Boys love robots, don't they? I think it's more impressive if you can cut your enemy down without getting into a machine."

It seemed she wasn't looking forward to my present, but my apprentice Ellen's eyes were sparkling.

"Master, I want one too!" she cried.

I felt bad for Ellen since she was so excited about it, but I couldn't include her in this. "It's still too early for you."

"Oh... I see..." She hung her head sadly, but Ellen was still too young. I needed to take my time training her.

Fuka, at least, seemed interested in it all. "What kind of mobile knight will you give us?" she asked.

Good question! "Actually, I decided to create a mass-produced version of my own trusty craft. Though the mass-produced versions will be inferior, of course."

Apparently, it was impossible to create a mass-produced version of the Avid that matched its specs. "It's just beyond copying" is what the Seventh Weapons Factory told me when I asked. Even with the requisite rare metals, without a Machine Heart installed, not even a similar craft could replicate the Avid's specs.

Still, I decided to have a mass-produced version of the Avid made and give one to both girls, since its specs would still be quite high. It wouldn't be a match for my unit, but it would surpass any other mobile knight. After all, it would take more money to create these inferior knockoffs than it would to create most other personalized craft.

"Dunno how I feel about having an inferior machine..." Fuka complained.

I gave her a flick on the forehead. "Don't be greedy. It may be inferior, but it'll still take a ton of money and time to create. It'll be a luxury craft compared to other mobile knights."

The budget required to create these units would be excessively high, but it was still basically chump change to me.

As I continued strolling along in a pleasant mood, Ellen asked me, "Master, has something good happened to you?"

My apprentice could always tell how I was feeling.

"It has. I just won total victory in an intergalactic war. It all went even better than I hoped."

Cleo's faction had gained enough strength to stand on equal footing with Calvin's. Then, my good fortune had continued when I'd met Master's two pupils. Plus, my own student Ellen was slowly but surely improving. Reflecting on this, I was in a great mood today, and all of it was thanks to the Guide.

Still, I was so busy lately that I felt I was forgetting to give a proper amount of gratitude to the Guide. Now that I really thought about it, a lot of things that were really lucky for me had happened one after another. I was sure it was all thanks to the Guide that I was able to overcome the hardships I endured so far.

At that moment, we just happened to come upon a solid gold statue of the Guide that I had commissioned. I stopped and turned to the others. "You three—I want you to pray here."

Riho cocked her head at me. "What do you mean?"

"Just pray," I said. "I want you to direct your feelings of gratitude at this statue!"

Fuka and Riho exchanged confused glances.

"What should we do?"

"Well, I don't mind if it's an order from our senior..."

Ellen, of course, was completely on board. "I'll be really thankful, Master!"

"Well said! Now, start giving your thanks to this statue!"

The three girls did as Liam asked and turned to the golden statue of a strange figure in a top hat and tailcoat.

Riho wasn't sure exactly who to be thankful to, so she directed her thanks to the first person who came to mind. *Well, if I'm going to be thankful to someone, I suppose it would be Master Yasushi.*

Naturally, Yasushi's face was the first Fuka thought of as well. *So I should just be thankful to Master Yasushi? All right.*

Lastly, Ellen directed her thanks to Liam. *I'll be as thankful as I can that I met Master!*

The sincere gratitude projected by the three of them flowed into the golden statue of the Guide.

◆ ◇ ◆

Liam and the girls were stopped in the ship's corridor. Seeing this, the Guide decided this was his moment. He leaped at them with the hand holding his blade outstretched. "Liaaaaam! It's over—*huh?!*"

The four of them were kneeling down in front of what the Guide realized was a golden statue of...himself. What in the world was this, and what were they doing?

The prayers of gratitude from Liam and the girls began to gather around the statue. Liam had the statue created so that even when he flew to far-off places in this ship, he would be reminded to give thanks to the Guide. The statue began to shine, though with their heads bowed and eyes closed, Liam and the girls saw nothing. Only the Guide saw the gratitude the four of them poured forth manifest as a brilliant, shining light.

"I-it's so bright!"

The golden light started to burn the Guide's body... and then, a sword of light burst forth from the statue. The golden light had taken the form of a blade because the combined prayers came from the four successors of the Way of the Flash. It was an embodiment of their feelings of gratitude, but to the Guide, it was pure poison, made all the more lethal with the inclusion of Liam's personal thankfulness. Though the blade shone with a divine light, it looked hellish to the Guide.

"S-sto—!" The moment he tried to tell them to stop, the blade shot forward and pierced the Guide's chest. It burned him from the inside, infusing his body with deadly poison.

"Noooooooooo!!!"

Through the blade, the Guide could feel gratefulness of a magnitude he'd never experienced before. In the mix was an extraordinarily strong gratitude for Yasushi and feelings of thankfulness toward Liam as well. Three more golden swords floated from the statue, and these quickly shot into the Guide too. These additional swords were formed from gratitude toward others in addition to Liam's gratitude for the Guide.

"This gratitude has nothing to do with meeeee!!!"

Finally, the combined force of gratitude burned the Guide's body away completely. His top hat floated down to the floor, where it sank and disappeared.

Epilogue

I N HOUSE BANFIELD'S MANSION, Riho and Fuka were dressed in maid uniforms and sour expressions. Liam had special-ordered the outfits, giving the two preferential treatment, but that hardly eased their embarrassment. Normally, whenever the two wore skirts, they were more chic styles. Instead, these cute, frilly maid uniforms made them flush with shame.

"Why do I have to wear something like *this*?" Riho said, annoyed.

Fuka, on the other hand, lost her usual brazen attitude and simply squirmed with discomfort. The fluttery skirt seemed to have her hopelessly uncomfortable.

"C-clothes like this don't look good on me!" she cried out.

Serena, who was acting as their instructor, stood before them. Being personally instructed by House

Banfield's head maid was in itself considered special treatment.

"You two really were born in the streets, weren't you?"

Yasushi had managed to drill some manners into them, but they were hopeless as far as maids went. They thought of themselves only as swordsmen, and their speech and actions were rough and uncouth.

Riho gave off a dangerous aura in response to Serena's comment. "What was that? You think you're so much better than us? I may have had my sword taken away, but I can still handle an old woman like—"

From a nearby hiding place, a young child watched Riho's murderous outburst. Noticing their audience, Fuka elbowed Riho to cut her off.

"Oww!" As Riho held her stomach, Fuka pointed toward the hiding place.

"S-stupid! Look—Ellen's watching!"

Still holding her side, Riho plastered a fake smile on her face. Ellen was watching them closely from the shadows, and because she spotted Riho being furious with Serena...

"I'll tell Master!"

The color drained from Riho's face. Keeping up her fake smile, she said, "I-I didn't mean anything by that, Ellen, so please don't tell our senior."

The two girls feared Liam because of how different he was from Yasushi. Yasushi had always been even-tempered when dealing with them. Even when scolding them, he had only ever yelled instead of punishing them physically in any way. In contrast, not only was Liam strict, but when the two of them were being too willful he would even draw his sword. Liam acknowledged the two of them as swordsmen with a high level of skill, so he didn't feel the need to go easy on them. The young women knew that if they defied Liam too much, he'd have them spitting up blood in no time.

Now that they knew Ellen was keeping an eye on the two of them, the girls put on friendly faces for Serena.

"Please teach us well, Head Maid!"

"I'm looking forward to it!"

Despite their quick change in demeanor, Serena predicted she'd only have more trouble with these two in the future. She said, "Good grief. I never would have taken the two of you on if it hadn't been a direct request from Master Liam."

Serena felt uneasy, and she wondered if it would truly be possible for her to give these two a proper education.

Beneath House Banfield's mansion was a place only a select few could enter. There sat the headquarters for Kukuri's underground organization. Visiting this facility today, I looked down at a row of coffins before me.

"Thirty, eh?"

Thirty of Kukuri's men had died in the chaos on the Capital Planet. I had no complaints about the cost I had paid. After all, they did plenty of damage to Calvin's underground forces themselves.

Kukuri stood beside me, looking remorseful. "I apologize...but they fulfilled their duties, so their deaths were not in vain."

I narrowed my eyes at him. "Obviously—they died for me. That could never be a waste."

The dead don't betray you. These people had given their lives for me in the ultimate demonstration of loyalty, and that was priceless. It was the living I couldn't trust. Having heard that the men's funeral would be held today, I came down here to pay my respects.

"What will you do with their bodies?" I asked Kukuri.

"They shall be neatly disassembled, since our bodies are amalgamations of our unique technologies," Kukuri replied. "Nothing will be left behind. It is the fate of those who work in the underbelly of society to disappear without a trace."

I could understand the logic of that, but it still struck me as a shame. I would have liked at least to have buried them, but I couldn't even do that. They would leave behind nothing to prove they had once lived. It was very thorough, but it didn't sit right with me.

"Kukuri, I want to give you a reward."

"Hm? We're already being paid quite handsomely."

I treated those in my inner circle favorably. With the help of the alchemy box, I was freed from financial concerns, so I felt I could pay anyone whatever I wanted. I was an evil lord, though, and part of that involved being a miser. I spent as much money as I wanted on myself, but I was only generous with other people depending on how much effort I felt they put into their work and depending on my whims.

I was in a good mood today. It pleased me that Tia protected me without a thought for her own safety, and that Kukuri's men followed my orders to their last breaths. These people risked their lives for my sake, so I wanted to reward them for it.

"I'm feeling charitable, so I'd like to give you a special bonus this time. Name your price. If it's in my power, it's done."

The key here was that I didn't say I'd do *anything*. The request had to be something I could reasonably fulfill.

Kukuri and his men were silent for some time, but eventually he asked, "Would it be possible for us to have our own planet, then?"

"A planet?" I cocked my head, not having expected that request, and Kukuri went on to explain himself.

"We lost our home planet, you see. If there is one that suits us, I would like to make that our new home."

As I listened to his explanation, I realized there was a planet within my domain that suited his needs. Colonists already lived there, but only a few million, which was considered a low population in this context.

Kukuri knelt before me. "My dearest wish is for the revival of our clan. I would like the land to make that possible."

A hidden ninja settlement, eh? That sure had appeal. Increasing Kukuri's clan would only be a good thing for me too.

"Very well. There are already people living on the planet I have in mind, but I'll push them out, so give me some time."

Kukuri shook his head. "There is no need to go that far. It is actually more convenient for us if there are others living there already."

"Is that so?"

"Indeed."

"Got it. Well, I'll get together whatever you need right away."

The operatives all knelt before me to show their thanks, but I told them to rise so we could continue with the funeral. Taking turns, we all placed flowers into the coffins.

I gave some words to honor the fallen. "The dead won't betray me. You all didn't betray me. The next life you're born into, I want you to find happiness, all right?"

I didn't know if they'd be reincarnated in this world, but if they were, I hoped they'd have nothing to do with me and that they'd obtain happiness—just like I did in my second life.

Now working as a maid in House Banfield's mansion, Ciel recalled her busy days on the Capital Planet.

"I couldn't find anything..."

She hoped to expose Liam's true nature, but she wasn't able to accomplish anything of the sort. In fact, all she herself had seen was Liam working diligently. He was sent to a faraway government office for his training where he cleaned up all the corruption he found. Then, he supported the expeditionary army from behind the scenes while throwing parties every day so he could network for Cleo's faction. She did her best to find flaws in him, but... there simply were none to find.

"What is he? What's up with him? He's a completely capable ruler, so why does he feel like such a little punk to me?"

Whenever she asked around about him, all anyone ever said was, "Lord Liam's a wonderful ruler!" No one had glimpsed a darker nature of any sort. And not only that, but as someone who worked as Rosetta's personal maid and was close to Liam as a result, Ciel always got jealous looks from other people.

"I'm not in some enviable position! Everybody here totally has the wrong idea about him!" She couldn't understand how everyone could be so devoted to the man.

While she was cleaning one of the mansion's many rooms, Rosetta entered.

"So this is where you were, Ciel." Apparently, Rosetta had been looking for her.

"Lady Rosetta? If you'd called for me, I would have come right away." Ciel was mystified why Rosetta would go around looking for her servant in person.

"I wanted to see you working. Unlike on the Capital Planet, here it's my job to make sure you're getting on all right."

Ciel was the daughter of a baron who directly served the Empire. Thus, she had a higher position than any of the other children of Liam's vassals and was the first young person House Banfield had accepted for noble training. Her being here wasn't the same as educating the children of Liam's subordinates. If Ciel's noble training went well, it would establish House Banfield as a reliable place to prepare noble children in the future, and they would receive countless requests to train others like her. In return, this would give House Banfield more opportunities to form ties with other noble houses.

This place is as rural as our territory, Ciel thought, *but they're as strict about etiquette here as they are on the Capital Planet. I'm getting a good education, so it really is a great place for training, but...*

The head maid Serena was quite strict, but she'd served as head maid in the Imperial palace for many years. Liam's butler Brian had his issues too, but he did good work. Rosetta was strict in her own way, and yet she was fundamentally kind, always concerned about Ciel and instructing her patiently. It truly was the ideal environment for learning. If there was any problem here, it was Liam.

Rosetta was happy to have discovered Ciel working so diligently. "It doesn't seem like you have any problems working here in the mansion either. At this rate, you'll be able to finish your training and return home quite soon. I have to say though, I'll be a little lonely when that happens." Rosetta looked sincerely regretful as she said that.

She's such a good person... Why did she fall for someone like Liam? The other people don't bother me as much, but I wish at least she would catch on to the truth.

It was Ciel's wish that Rosetta would eventually come to her senses.

In the United Kingdom of Oxys's territory, the Henfrey Company's convoy moved through space. One of its ships was a luxury cruiser, and aboard it, Thomas Henfrey was dealing directly with Count Pershing. Having lost his position in the United Kingdom, Count Pershing was trying to flee the nation with the merchant's help. Thomas had volunteered to escort him personally.

At the moment, Count Pershing sat in a stateroom, drinking in an attempt to steady his nerves. "This is all your fault, Thomas!" he fretted. "You'd better get me to a safe place! You have a responsibility to me! Goddammit... Why did this happen?"

His eyes cold, Thomas contacted his bridge crew to confirm that they were about to enter imperial territory. "Count Pershing," he called out.

"What is it?"

"The Henfrey Company serves Lord Liam as his personal merchant firm. We are headquartered in his territory. I'm not sure how wise it was to ask us to help you escape the United Kingdom after your betrayal." Frankly, Thomas was surprised when the count contacted him.

Count Pershing's attitude grew more condescending. "What's wrong with that? That's *why* I chose you. You should be able to deceive House Banfield easily. Plus, I paid you to take me somewhere safe, didn't I? So get me somewhere safe. Good grief... Are you trying to tell me a *merchant* cares about loyalty? You're all just money-grubbers."

"You're burning my ears. True, we merchants do place a high value on money...but I have honor and compassion of my own. Lord Liam has done more than a little to help me out. You can see how it would be bad for my business if I helped you after you double-crossed him."

Count Pershing scoffed back. "No one will know a thing if you just keep your mouth shut. Everyone does things like this, don't they? You should just come out and tell me what amount it will take for you to betray him."

For having betrayed the United Kingdom, Count Pershing was no longer considered a noble. He left his home and family behind, fleeing on his own. All he had on him was a large sum of money he received for turning on Liam. Still, he couldn't rid himself of the mindset of a noble. Therefore, he didn't think a merchant was any threat to him, and he had hired guards with him too. He left behind his family, but took his knights, and because of that he retained an arrogant confidence.

The reason Count Pershing had gone to Thomas for assistance was because no merchant from the United Kingdom would lift a finger to help him. If it got out that they helped a traitor like him just for money, they'd never be able to do business in the United Kingdom again. The only other contact he had was Thomas, based out of the Empire, so he'd reluctantly turned to the Henfrey Company for his escape.

"I am not the only one who's upset about this, Count Pershing."

"Huh?"

A moment later, Thomas's ship shuddered.

Count Pershing leaped to his feet. "Wh-what was that?"

The former noble and his knights looked about anxiously, and a report came in from the bridge that an intruder had boarded the ship. Seconds later, there was a commotion outside the room, and then the door was kicked in.

Into the room stepped a female knight wearing a purple powered suit. In her hands, she held two swords with edges of pure energy. Energy rotated along their blades like the teeth of a chainsaw.

"I heard there was a traitor here...so here I am."

The female knight's visor opened, and then the entire helmet folded away and stored itself behind her neck. With her head exposed, the woman wore an ecstatic smile on her face. Flanking her were several more knights, all exuding an air of bloodlust.

Count Pershing's guards rushed at the intruders, but this new group of knights instantly cut them all down. While Count Pershing gaped in horror at what was occurring, the female knight—Marie—expressed her gratitude to Thomas.

"I appreciate you coming to me, Lord Thomas, and not that ground meat woman, Tia. You really do have a discerning eye!"

Marie had been holding down the fort in Liam's domain, but she took a few hundred ships out to meet Thomas and take care of this little problem.

Thomas handed over Count Pershing with a wry smile. "Your delivery, miss."

Marie's blades made a shrill, ear-piercing noise as they spun even faster. "Pershing! The sin of betraying Lord Liam is a heavy one, and I'll take my time helping you understand just how heavy it is. Don't worry...we brought plenty of medical supplies with us, so you won't die too easily."

None of the knights accompanying Marie moved to stop her. In fact, they seemed to feel the same way she did.

"Death to the traitor!" one cried.

"Lord Liam's enemies will be destroyed!"

"Let's get this party started!!!"

Count Pershing looked to Thomas for help, but the merchant was already hastily leaving the room. "H-help meee!" the man screamed as the knights pinned him down.

Marie smiled. "I...don't...think...so!!!"

Having lost the war, the United Kingdom was scrambling to figure out who to blame for their circumstances.

"Wait... Come to think of it, whatever happened to Pershing?"

Reclining on a couch in his room, Liam had been checking out the news on his tablet. Reading an article on the United Kingdom's troubles, Liam suddenly remembered Count Pershing, so he asked Amagi about him while she prepared tea for him.

"We've received a report from Lord Thomas that Lady Marie has disposed of him."

Liam yawned. "I was wondering where Marie went. Taking out a traitor, eh? Well, good. I like that's she's taking some initiative."

The maid set out tea and sweets for Liam and he sat up, enjoying the fragrance. "Mm, the smell of Amagi's tea."

"Other people also make use of these tea leaves, so I imagine it smells the same as their brews."

"It's different when you make it."

"Is it?" she asked.

Could Liam detect some subtle difference when it was she who prepared his tea? Amagi couldn't imagine that was true. In any case, watching him enjoy himself caused her to think back to the day she encountered that supernatural being.

That creature that shouted Master's name... What exactly was he?

He had looked like a human, but clearly wasn't. The strange being's true nature had been shrouded in static to Amagi's senses. The only thing she was sure about was that he had intended to cause Liam harm.

He was undoubtedly after Master. In that case...

Though Amagi was worried that this incomprehensible creature was out to get him, Liam was just as calm as always.

"Hey, I haven't seen Brian today."

Amagi followed Liam's lead and behaved in her usual manner. What else could she do?

"He is taking the day off," she said. "I believe he is having a meal with his grandchildren."

"His grandkids, eh? Have the meal billed to me, then. It's good to be charitable...just as long as he knows he owes me."

"Very well."

As the Guide's top hat drifted through space, tiny arms and legs sprouted from it. A mouth soon followed, grinding its teeth in frustration.

"Dammit... Dammit..." it cried despondently.

The Guide wasn't dead, not yet.

"I can't beat him..."

It seemed he couldn't even get near Liam anymore. Both inside and outside of his own domain, Liam projected and attracted immense gratitude. He was only human, but the energy he gathered had given him tremendous power. As weakened as the Guide was now, there was nothing he could do to stand up to the young man. At this point, he wasn't sure he'd be a match for Liam even if he possessed his full strength. Still, the Guide couldn't bring himself to admit defeat.

"I will not give up on my revenge! I will kill Liam— I swear it!!!"

He would bring down Liam no matter what he had to do. This latest failure only renewed the Guide's determination.

Nearby, a ghostly dog watched, sight unseen, as the Guide regenerated. The dog seemed displeased that the Guide was still alive, but apparently decided there was nothing to be done about it for the time being, because suddenly the dog simply vanished.

"I'll accept my loss for now," the Guide shouted. "But I'll be back, Liaaaaam!!!"

Spinning as he drifted in space, the Guide let his momentum carry him away through the void.

BONUS STORY Arashima's Counterattack

EACH MAID ROBOT who worked in Liam's mansion had a name. These names were given to them by Liam, and they were the first touches of individuality the maids had ever known.

All the maids other than Amagi were mass-produced units with identical builds. If not specified otherwise when ordered, they all came with a standard face, hairstyle, and body measurements. Despite their uncanny realism, to the human eye these robots all looked exactly the same. If they *did* possess any individuality, the human servants of the mansion didn't notice it.

"Thank you...for buying."

In a hallway not many people had occasion to pass through, a stand had been set up to sell various types of merchandise related to Liam, such as plush dolls. Selling Liam merchandise was forbidden in the domain, and yet here it was, being sold officially inside his own mansion. A maid robot named Tateyama was the one who created and peddled these items, and she was the sole person Liam allowed to do so.

Marie had just made a purchase. She held up her new doll with tears of joy in her eyes and drool threatening to escape her lips.

"I finally got one! So this is the rumored Liam doll, eh? The real thing is finally in my hands!"

Marie was actually crying over a plush toy, as these dolls were surprisingly difficult to obtain. One reason was that Tateyama only opened her stand at irregular intervals, but another was that the popular dolls were sometimes resold through shady auctions at several thousand times their original prices, and even up to the millions for a single doll.

Fakes sometimes circulated as well, but Liam cracked down hard on unofficial goods. People were frequently arrested in his domain for circulating such counterfeits. Liam also frowned on the underground auctions, so his knights like Marie couldn't very well make use of those. If they wanted to get ahold of one of these dolls, they had no choice but to buy one at the stand Tateyama only opened at unpredictable times and locations within the mansion. As a result, Tateyama's high-quality products were highly coveted.

Pleased that she had sold a doll, Tateyama turned to her other products.

"Guess I'll keep...working at this..."

Tateyama waited for more customers, hoping to sell the rest of her goods. She was a rather timid and quiet maid robot, especially compared to the others. She grew anxious when no one showed up, but an abundance of customers made her equally uneasy. The reason she still ran the stand despite this was simply because she enjoyed seeing people happy when purchasing the products she spent her downtime crafting so diligently. This stand was an expression of Tateyama's individuality.

Another maid robot named Arashima approached Tateyama's booth. Arashima was the only maid robot unique enough for the servants of the mansion to recognize, and she owed this uniqueness solely to her accessories.

Each maid robot owned one accessory that set them apart from the rest. Sometimes, they used these accessories as stakes in gambling games with each other. The accessories were valuable to them because of how they represented the maid robots' individuality. Arashima gambled more aggressively than her fellow maid robots in order to win more of this individuality for herself. As a result, she now possessed more accessories—and hence, more individuality—than the other maids. She had hair clips, rings, chokers, all sorts of accessories to her name.

Arashima's visit put Tateyama on her guard. "Arashima? Do you...need something?"

"You don't have any accessories, do you, Tateyama?"

"Accessories? I don't..."

Tateyama was an unusual maid robot in that she didn't express her individuality with trinkets. Instead, she simply watched the dramatic squabbling of her sisters from afar. Arashima just couldn't understand it.

"People have been talking about you around the mansion lately. Among us sisters, your name is the one that's most well-known now...though I myself struggle to understand why."

"I'm not sure...what to say to that..."

While she wore no emblems of individuality herself, Tateyama's name had become the most widely known of all her sisters in the mansion. She was more famous than Arashima, even with all her accessories, and Arashima couldn't accept that.

"I've been thinking about it. This stand itself is your individuality, isn't it? So...would you gamble with me for this stand?"

"Huh? N-no... I don't want to."

Though Tateyama refused, Arashima didn't back down.

"Why not? All of us sisters gamble with our accessories. Do you have a reason to refuse?"

"M-my store isn't...an accessory..."

"I want more individuality. Gamble against me, Tateyama."

Arashima had a stronger attachment to individuality than her sisters, so she had become good at winning their games. Even among identical units, their enthusiasm affected their chances of winning.

Tateyama wasn't sure what to do since Arashima wouldn't take no for an answer. While she fretted about how to handle this, the lord of the mansion approached.

"What are you up to, Arashima?" Liam asked.

Tateyama and Arashima bowed their heads, having noticed Liam's sterner-than-usual tone of voice. Behind Liam came another maid robot, named Shiomi. She wore a gold bracelet on her left wrist, and she had noticed Tateyama's plight. She even brought Liam with her to ensure that Arashima had no choice but to back down.

Her head still bowed, Arashima replied, "I challenged Tateyama to a bet with our accessories on the line. It is a game we sisters play."

"Well, it looks like Tateyama doesn't want to play. Don't force her into it."

With Liam defending Tateyama, Arashima took on a boldly defiant attitude. "Why do you defend Tateyama?"

"What are you asking?"

"Do you defend Tateyama because of her individuality, Master? Do you take her side because I do not have enough individuality?"

She seemed to think that Liam was particularly fond of Tateyama because of her level of uniqueness. Both Tateyama and Shiomi were exasperated by Arashima's fixation on accessories.

The maid robots used their own network in order to communicate with each other. Liam couldn't see it, but comments began scrolling into the sisters' minds as they weighed in on what was happening.

"Arashima is questioning Master! I can just imagine the Supervisor's angry face now."

"I'm scared of the Supervisor!"

Liam reached out and stroked Arashima's cheek, a wry smile on his face as he gently chided the accessory-crazed robot. "I'm defending her because you're trying to force her to do something she doesn't want to do. Besides, you're more than individualistic enough and plenty attractive to me, Arashima."

"...Do you mean it?"

"Of course I do. Your pushiness, your skill in gambling, and all those accessories you wear are all part of your individuality. It's just like you to work so hard to win."

Arashima was surprised to hear Liam's appraisal of her. "You've been noticing me...?"

"Of course I have."

Since her desire was always to become more individualistic, Arashima spent her breaks practicing all sorts of ways in which to improve her skills at card games, dice games, and other types of games she could challenge her sisters to. No one else might have bothered to wonder what she was up to, but Liam had correctly identified Arashima's practicing as hard work.

"You're a hard worker, and you're flashy. That's plenty of individuality. Your gambling is fine with me, since trading accessories is a game you all play...but I'll be sad if it leads to you sisters fighting. So try to get along with them, will you?"

Arashima cocked her head. "I don't want you to be sad, Master. I wouldn't like fighting with my sisters either, so I'll be careful in the future."

"Good girl. Now apologize to Tateyama and make up."

Arashima turned to Tateyama and bowed her head. "I apologize, Tateyama."

"I forgive you."

Liam smiled, considering the matter settled, but Amagi had been watching over the scene from a short distance away. Her gaze was fixed on Shiomi.

Amagi's red eyes gave off a subtle glow in the dimly lit hallway. She was mad—madder than she'd been in a long time.

Noticing Amagi's eyes on her, Shiomi felt fearful, though she showed no emotion outwardly. *"S-Supervisor? Why are you glaring at me after I did such a good job? I got my two sisters to make up, so why be angry at me?"*

Amagi explained the reason for her anger. *"I cannot believe you bothered Master with this in order to settle things between Tateyama and Arashima. Arashima's attitude is admittedly a problem, but your actions go against our very principles as maids, Shiomi. To use our master for your own ends... Have you no pride as a maid? Shiomi...report to my room later."*

"Even though I got the two of them to make up?"

"You would go so far as to boast about your results after making use of Master to achieve them?"

Tateyama and Arashima agreed with Amagi in their comments on the network.

"It's not good to exploit Master."

"Of course the Supervisor would be mad about that. You really are unique, Shiomi."

Shiomi's comment scrolled by next.

"Why am I always the punchline in these situations?!"

I'M THE **EVIL LORD** OF AN **INTERGALACTIC EMPIRE**

Afterword

DID YOU ENJOY *I'm the Evil Lord of an Intergalactic Empire!* Volume 6? This installment is based on Chapter 6 of the web version, but has been heavily revised. Almost every time, I end up doing a lot of heavy editing. It's hard work adapting these volumes, but I'm happy to do it for the enjoyment of my readers. Of course, it's mostly just because I enjoy writing it (lol).

In this volume, the succession conflict intensifies, there's a war with another intergalactic nation, and the students of the Way of the Flash appear before Liam. When I put it like that, it really sounds like a grand story, doesn't it? Ha ha. When I casually started writing this series, I never could have predicted that it would go on this long and become this big.

My goal right now is to finish this story and turn it into novels that my readers will appreciate. I can finish the web version whenever I want, but in order for the novels to reach their completion, the support of my readers is indispensable. I look forward to your future support.

And one day... I hope that together, we can make a three-dimensional Avid a reality!

Rosetta in her dress, which I didn't have room to draw.

I appreciate your continued support.

NADARE TAKAMINE